CRAVEN

MW00962736

THE DEAD GIRL UNDER THE BLEACHERS

A CRAVEN FALLS MYSTERY

DONNA M. ZADUNAJSKY

Black Rose Writing | Texas

First printing

This novel is a work of fiction. Names, characters, places and incidents are either the product of the author's imagination or are used fictitiously. Any resemblance to actual persons, living or dead, events, or locales is entirely coincidental.

ISBN: 978-1-68433-469-8
PUBLISHED BY BLACK ROSE WRITING
www.blackrosewriting.com

Printed in the United States of America
Suggested Retail Price (SRP) $19.95

The Dead Girl Under the Bleachers is printed in Baskerville

*As a planet-friendly publisher, Black Rose Writing does its best to eliminate unnecessary waste to reduce paper usage and energy costs, while never compromising the reading experience. As a result, the final word count vs. page count may not meet common expectations.

To my baby bird

I would like to express my many thanks and appreciation to my readers out there who have given up their time to read my books and to take the journey inside my stories.

Thank you to Black Rose Publishing for taking an interest in my work and helping me to make it so much better and getting my books into the hands of my readers. The months of hard work and dedication making my stories stand out and thrive above the rest. Thank you all so much for your help at getting my novel into print.

I would like to thank Deborah Bowman Stevens for loving the storyline and helping with the editing process to make this book one of my finest achievements.

Last but never least, I give my love and thanks to my beautiful daughter, Tayla Lynn for the inspiration behind my books. Because of you I try harder. Because of you I keep reaching my goals. Because of you my dreams are coming true. I love you with all that I hold inside.

THE DEAD GIRL
UNDER THE BLEACHERS

ONE

I bent down, slipped off my high heel shoes that were sinking into the mud, and peered over my shoulder, scanning the football field. Darkness loomed like a haunted cemetery as if waiting for the dead to rise. I couldn't see a damn thing in front of me or behind me.

Water splattered behind me. I knew I had to get out of here fast.

I turned around too quickly and stumbled forward. My foot had caught the fabric of my homecoming dress, causing me to trip, but caught myself before falling completely to the ground. Once I righted myself, I took off running again.

The light posts that stood along the edges of the field cast a faint glow, but it wasn't enough for me to see where I was going. Suddenly, a lightning bolt shot across the sky, lighting my way. Up ahead I could see the bleachers. The same bleachers I had sat on since the beginning of high school at Craven Falls High. It was where we play football games in our small, quaint town. It was also the only place to hide from the person who was chasing me.

"I'm coming for you, bitch!" the voice closing in on me hollered.

I didn't stop; I just kept running until the connection of something hard hit my head, sending shock waves of pain through my skull and down my spine. My eyes squeezed shut, an instant reaction to the pain coursing through my cranium. The automatic reflex of my hand went to my head.

Feeling something warm and wet. I was sure it was blood and not the rain that had fallen from the sky. I didn't have time to think about how the person had caught up to me so fast.

I had to run.

I had to hide.

By the time I made it to the bleachers, hoping to find shelter, something hard struck me on the back of my leg. My high heel shoes and clutch purse flew out of my hand as I fell to the ground like a hundred and twelve-pound bag of potatoes.

I tried to scream, but the sound was knocked out of me when my body smacked the wet, hard ground. This was a nightmare. A bad dream. I couldn't be living this, but I was, and it was more real than anything I had ever experienced before in my life.

I grabbed my right leg as the pain shot through my body. Shattered in several places. I crawled, dragging my right leg across the wet, freshly cut grass, gritting my teeth. I slinked along, fighting the sharp, throbbing pain coursing up my leg and into my back. I would die if I didn't find safety, but the bleachers wouldn't save me, only camouflage me behind the monstrous metal seats, still, I moved toward them.

Once under the bleachers, I collapsed onto my side. My breath rushed out in quick gasps. I couldn't go any further; not only from the pain but because I was losing blood from the large gash I had on my head. Someone wasn't just trying to hurt me. They wanted me dead.

Water slid between the metal slats of the bleachers and fell onto my face. The rain changed from a light drizzle to pouring down in an instant, dropping onto my bloody split-open head. My vision was hazy as I looked out the corner of my eye, blinking away the water as it fell harder from the sky.

My head pulsated from the blow I'd received just minutes ago. A headache wasn't surfacing; it was already there, shouting out obscenities. My reflexes took over when a movement to my left appeared. I curled myself into a fetal position, which caused me more excoriating pain, but I needed to shield myself from what looked like a wooden bat about to slam into my body.

"Please, stop!" I screamed as the bat came down, shattering the bones of my ribs. A sharp pain surged through me. It became harder to breathe as I sucked in an agonizing breath and cried out again. "I'm begging you. Please stop!"

They didn't stop.

They would not stop until they ended what they had started. This person would finish the job, and I would die here. No one would ever know the truth of how I died. The school was closed on Monday. By Tuesday, who knew what I'd look like after lying in the wet, soaked grass for two days?

The blows came down hard one after another, hitting every part of my body. I could feel the anger in each hit. I believed my attacker hated me with everything they had inside of them. I would not leave here alive. They would make sure I didn't because I knew the truth about what they had done.

I whimpered.

They stopped.

I forced in another breath, holding it as I laid immobile on the ground.

Listening.

Waiting.

It was as if the world had stopped around me.

The rain dripped onto my head and ran down my face, mixing with my salty tears. I looked out the corner of my eye, not one, but two shadows were standing over me. Had there always been two people chasing me?

The second shadow knelt in front of me. I drew in a haggard breath, nearly choking. My lungs were screaming for me to exhale as a piercing pain sliced through my chest. I couldn't believe my own eyes who was kneeling in front of me.

"I'm sorry, but this needed to be done," the voice said.

"Yeah, you should've known better than to fuck with us, bitch!" another voice echoed.

Immediately I recognized the voice, and I knew who had beaten me to a pulp, leaving me broken and bleeding, unable to move. It was the one person I truly hated with every essence of my being.

I blinked several more times, unsure of what I was seeing. My vision distorted by the rain and the darkness surrounding me, but also from the blow to my head, making things blurry. I was hoping I had imagined it all, but I hadn't.

The person stood and walked away without a single goodbye as if I meant nothing to them. Another drop of rain fell from the black, thunderous sky above and landed on my body, soaking my already wet and ruined clothes. Pain surged through me, like a fury of fire.

I couldn't move.

I was afraid to move.

My body shattered.

Broken into pieces and left here to die under the bleachers.

No one would come looking for me, not on a night like tonight. Not in the pouring rain. I blinked and drew in one last and final breath, staring out at the football field.

Two

LAURA

One Month Earlier

I closed the door to my locker and turned just as Rachel Sawyer and Scarlet Fitzgerald, the Queen Bees of Craven Falls High, came strutting through the entrance doors of the school. They were both laughing as they paraded down the hall just like they did every day that school was in session.

They don't talk to me. In fact, they don't talk to any of the girls here unless they acknowledge them first. Not that I wanted to be in their circle. To be considered a slut or a stuck-up snob. I like who I am.

I like being the outcast.

A nobody.

If I stay who I am now, no one will bother me. I can be on the outside looking in and watching everything everyone else is doing. Besides, there are only eight months left before graduation. There was no reason to change my life now, right?

Who was I kidding? I'd be lying to myself if I said I wasn't jealous of them because I am. They get to do whatever they want, and everyone looks up to them. They get invited to the best parties and date the hottest guys, like Travis Evans. He's like the God of hotness. Is that even a thing?

I would give anything to go out with him. For him to be my boyfriend. I've pictured us together more times than I could count. He'd take me to the movies and the Homecoming Dance. We would be crowned King and Queen at our Prom.

Someone knocked me from my thoughts as my body pivoted forward and my books went flying out of my arms. I watched as they soared through the air in slow motion like in an action movie. The pages of my books turning and flapping then plummeted to the floor. They scattered around me as if the gravity was sucked out of the room. When I realized what was happening, I dropped to my knees—hard, knowing a bruise would appear later. But that wouldn't be anything new. It would only match the bruises I already have.

I gathered my books and papers before they'd get kicked down the hall. I've seen it done too many times and was glad it wasn't me until now. Now, I was the idiot everyone was staring and laughing at, and glad that they weren't me.

I glanced over my shoulder to see who had knocked into me. Kyle Tanner, a guy from the football team, swim team, and the baseball team, was standing behind me. He was also the biggest asshole in our senior class who got away with everything.

He looked down at me and shouted, "What the shit are you looking at? You better watch where you're going, *dweeb*," then joined in with his buddies as they all laughed.

I wanted to stand up, get in his face, and tell him he was an asshole who doesn't even know what the word *dweeb* means. I don't get in his face. I don't say nothing to him. Because that would be a death warrant and the end of staying invisible for the rest of my senior year. No, I needed to stay hidden until I could get the hell out of this town for good.

Kyle was also one of the popular kids. You don't talk to them unless you're one of them. Or unless spoken to and they want you to answer. Even if he talked to me, I'd ignore him, which would make him mad. I hope he wasn't expecting me to apologize to him. He was the one who rammed into me.

You get to know the surrounding people when your locker is next to theirs. Things other people here don't see or know. I wanted to laugh because he thinks he's God's gift to women because that's what he says to himself through the metal locker doors. "Yeah, she thinks you're hot," Kyle would say to himself. Answering his own questions. I wondered what Scarlet would do if she knew the secrets, he kept from her?

After collecting my books, I stand and make my way down the hall when I hear, "Excuse me, but what do you think you're doing?" I flinched, wrapping my arms tighter around my chest, squeezing my textbooks into me. God, I wished I had the power to become invisible.

I stopped in my tracks as I recognized the voice talking to me before I even turned around. Scarlet Fitzgerald spoke in her snobbish, annoying, high-pitched voice loud enough for everyone standing around to hear. She sounded like a pig squealing the way she talked sometimes.

She had always been the girl everyone noticed. She thrived on having everything her way. Though it was because of her dad, who was the Mayor here in Craven Falls. God, I hated her as much as I wanted to be her. To be her friend, but that would never happen, and it was probably best that I didn't become her friend. Eight months was all I had, and I was out of here forever. Out of this small, unpopulated town. Good riddance Craven Falls.

Turning my head, I looked over my shoulder and saw Rachel and Scarlet gawking at me. Without hesitation, I stepped aside and waited for them to pass. Scarlet tossed her red hair over her shoulder, lifted her head high as if she were trying to sniff the air as she went.

After they walked by, I headed to my first class, which was with Scarlet and Rachel. I wasn't sure what difference it made who got there first. Stay invisible, my head repeated.

⭍ ⭍ ⭍

Although it felt as if I had just sat down, the bell rang, and class was over. I gathered my things and stood, walking out of the classroom. I jumped back, ramming my back into the metal frame of the door. "Fuck," I murmured, squeezing my eyes shut to eliminate the abundance of pain shooting down my back. The pain I'm so used to since it's all I ever feel anymore.

When I opened my eyes, Rachel and Scarlet were standing in front of me as if they were waiting for me, but that couldn't be? Why would they be? I feared what they would do to me, but neither of them moved, which seemed to frighten me more.

"Hey, Laura. What are you doing after school tonight?" Scarlet asked.

My mouth dropped open and quickly closed it. My eyes moved from Rachel to Scarlet. "Um," I started to say and then began to stutter. "Wh… what do… do you mean, what am I doing tonight?" I sound beyond stupid right now.

"W… w… well," Scarlet stuttered back, laughing directly at me.

I hated her more now than ever.

"We were wondering if we could like, get together and study math tonight. At your house," she concluded, throwing one of her smiles onto her face as if it would win me over.

Did she think I was one of her guy toys and could persuade me to do whatever she wanted? "Math?" I questioned. My mind was racing faster than a roller coaster. Zipping up and down the hills and turning fast until the rush of the ride was over and I was climbing out of my seat wanting to do it all over again.

"Yes, math," Rachel repeated. "We have an exam coming up, and we really could use your help. You're so good at it and…" she stopped and spoke again. "I know it sounds strange, Scarlet and I are talking to you because we never have before…" Rachel paused and swallowed.

My mind scrambled with thoughts. Rachel swallowing when she was talking was something she did when she was nervous. But why would she be nervous talking to me? Or was it because she was doing something she really didn't want to do? How would I know if they were serious or not? Should I accept their invitation? Should I believe one word they're saying? Why are they even talking to me? Why do they want to hang out with me of all people? I'm a nobody. My mind was battling with too many questions I didn't know the answers to. Did Rachel forget that we drifted apart at the start of seventh grade?

"We'd like to get together. You know, hang out after school. Do some homework. Talk about boys," Scarlet said, taking over the conversation as she tossed her hair over her shoulder.

"Oh… Uh," I replied, trying to come up with an excuse why I couldn't hang out with them, but I couldn't and replied, "Sure, I guess so. That sounds great!" Sounds great, I scolded myself. It's a horrible idea. Your mom will kill you if they come to the house.

Three

Rachel

At the end of the school day, Scarlet and I met Laura at her locker, then drove to Laura's house. Scarlet pulled alongside the curb in front of Laura's house. I looked out the passenger side window. The paint was peeling off the wood siding, making the house look weathered and old. I couldn't believe how many years it had been since I'd been here.

When we all went inside, the rooms were dark. You couldn't see where you were walking. I was expecting something to jump out at me, like in a haunted house. That sounds mean, but you'd probably say the same thing if you were in my shoes. The place reminded me of the movie Don't Breathe. I was just waiting for a blind man to come chasing after us.

We talked until Laura's mom showed up and ruined the mood. She looked older than I remembered. Was she sick? Was she dying? I didn't know. And how would I know since Laura and I weren't friends anymore, but that was her choice, not mine. She could've remained friends with me, but I know she couldn't stand Scarlet.

I hadn't really thought much about Laura since we went our separate ways back then. I've seen her in the halls at school, but she always slinked away, keeping to herself, especially in the past year. Maybe we weren't meant to stay friends throughout the rest of high school. Besides, meeting Scarlet has been a lot of fun.

Scarlet has always been a good friend to me, even if sometimes I think she can be annoying with her rude and snobbish attitude. It was better to be Scarlet's friend than her enemy. She has ridiculed other girls for no reason. That's why I'm a little afraid of what she might have planned for Laura. It's not like I can stop it from happening. Can I?

It was Scarlet's idea to ask Laura if we could come over, but I also didn't object either. Sometimes, Scarlet liked to play games on people. Games that ended up hurting them and the other kids would laugh. I suggested for her not to go too far, but when she looked at me with her blue eyes, it was like looking into the eyes of something evil. She asked if I had a problem with the way she did things. Of course, I said no; I was smart to stay off of Scarlet's shit list.

After leaving Laura's, Scarlet dropped me off at my house, and I went straight to my bedroom. I dropped my book bag onto the floor and threw myself down on my bed, staring up at the ceiling. I tried to picture my room the way Laura had hers with the two different color walls and the string of lights draped around the room, unlike mine which was just too dull. I couldn't believe that Scarlet asked Laura who she used as the designer? What a bitch she was being to Laura. Scarlet knew Laura couldn't afford someone to do her room like she could.

"Rachel," my mom said as she popped her head in through the open door of my bedroom.

"Yes?" I questioned as I lay on my bed still staring up at the ceiling.

"Everything all right?"

"Yes," I lied.

"Can you come help me in the kitchen with dinner if you're not doing anything?"

I couldn't refuse; besides, I needed to clear my mind and not think about Laura. I needed to think of a way to get Scarlet to stop whatever she was about to do to poor Laura. I couldn't explain it, but there was something not right with Laura and her mom.

After we prepared our dinner, and it was in the oven, I drove to my brothers' school a mile away. I have two twin brothers who are eight years old. My parents weren't planning on having more kids, but she announced one day, "I'm having twins." Sure, I was excited that she was pregnant. I had always wanted a sibling, or should I say two, although I wished they were a little closer to my age, but as the song says, "You can't always get what you want."

Once I had my brothers in the car, we drove back toward home. I slowed to a crawl, peering out the windshield of my car. Was I seeing things or was that Laura walking down the sidewalk in my neck of the woods? Laura's arms were wrapped across her chest as if she were cold. I wondered where she was going. She was far from where she lived as her house was on the other side of town. Where the less than average income families lived. I had never seen her out this way before, not since we used to hang out.

I pulled over to the curb to see if she needed a ride. Pressing the button, I powered down the passenger window. "Hey, do you need a ride?" I hollered to Laura.

She turned toward the car to see who was calling her. A look of surprise appeared on her face.

She stopped moving and turned her body toward me. There was blood on the side of her head and scratches down her arms. I threw the car in park and flung open the door. "Stay put!" I yelled at my brothers. Then ran up to her and examined her. She'd been crying. Mascara was running down her face. I had never noticed that she wore makeup.

"What happened, Laura?"

It was strange; in that moment, black clouds rolled in, and the rain started pelting down on us. Large clumps of hail the size of marbles spit at us at all angles. I assisted Laura to the car and opened the passenger door, helping her inside. Then I ran around the car and jumped in behind the wheel. My face and arms hurt from the hail that shot down from the sky.

Once inside, I turned and looked at Laura, but she was looking down at the floor and not at me. "Do you want me to take you home?"

She shook her head and whispered, "No, I can't go home."

"Okay, is there somewhere else I can take you?"

"I don't have anywhere else to go," Laura said, sniffling.

I decided without delay to just take her to my house and hopefully then, she would tell me what the hell was going on and what had happened to her.

FOUR
SCARLET

I caught a glimpse of myself in the mirror beside me, smiled, and tossed my red hair over my shoulder. I tapped the end of my pencil on the notebook sitting in front of me while perched at my desk in my bedroom. This was something I did when I was thinking of a plan. A plan to humiliate poor Laura Stevenson in front of the whole school at Homecoming, which was in four weeks. All I needed to do was to get her to think I really liked her and that she was one of us.

Thinking back to earlier. I can't believe she thought I adored her bedroom. That it was amazing! Like her room was better than mine because she did it all herself instead of using a designer to decorate as I did. Who did she think she was, anyway? She wasn't anybody special.

But that's not my reason for wanting to humiliate her. No, she's had this coming since Jr. High when she tried to tell Rachel that I wasn't worth her time and wouldn't be a good friend to her. Didn't she know who she was messing with? That we can't both have her? It's her loss for losing her when high school started. Besides, Laura wasn't pretty enough to be our friend. She wasn't rich enough to hang out with us but I was interested in seeing how far I could string her along.

"Scarlet, are you in here?" my stepmother Lianne asked as she opened my bedroom door. She never knocked. Just opened the door like it was her room, her house. She knows I don't like her. I can't stand her as much as she can't stand being in this house with me.

She's such a bitch. "Yes, what do you want?" I snapped. "Can't you see that I'm working on homework, Lianne?" Didn't she know that I don't like being bothered when I'm in my room? I've told her many times since she married my father, which I know for a fact was just to get her grubby hands on his money, not to come into my room. God, she was so annoying!

My father is a powerful man who gets what he wants. Maybe that's where I get my confidence from. He preaches to me daily, "Appearance is everything, Scarlet. Don't let them see you fall. One mistake and you will be looked down upon. I won't have a daughter who isn't successful or popular." I will succeed and be first at everything. That's just who I am. I'm a Fitzgerald, the Mayor's daughter. And this bitch, Lianne, needed to go before she ruined everything!

"Scarlet Marie, you know I can have your car taken away from you for a week," Lianne said in a stern voice.

"What?" I yelled. "You can't do that! You're not my mom!" How dare she use my middle name. Only my father could say it.

"Watch me!" she hissed. "You will get nowhere in life with the way you talk to people. If it were up to me, I'd send you to a boarding school a thousand miles away, but lucky for me you're graduating soon. So, I don't have to wait much longer," Lianne said a smile spreading across her face. "It will be a blessing to have you out of my house."

"Your house?" I questioned. "You think just because you married my father you own this house? That you own me?" Over my dead body. I wanted to tear this bitch apart but knew if my daddy heard me talking to her this way, I would be in big trouble. He was the enforcer of punishments in this house, and if I back talked my stepmom, all hell would break loose. Besides, I can't lose my car! I refuse to take the bus to school. If I took the bus, my classmates would laugh at me, like all the other dorks that have to take the bus since they don't have a car. But I can't. I'm Scarlet Fitzgerald, the Queen of the school. I say who can and cannot do something!

"Lianne, I'm sorry," I replied in a soft tone, even though I wanted to stab my eyes out.

She smiled at me, knowing that I was probably full of shit and didn't mean what I was saying. "Your father is home and we're about to have dinner. Finish what you're doing and come downstairs, please," Lianne said, leaving the door open. "Annoying bitch," Lianne muttered before walking down the hall.

I stared at the now empty doorway, hoping she would catch on fire or fall down the marble staircase and break her neck, but that was wishful thinking on my part. Did she think I couldn't hear her? Or maybe she wanted me too, so I would get pissed off and start something when my father was home. Normally I would but I had things to do right now.

I went back to finish what I was writing. The first thing I needed to do was to make sure that Laura believed she was one of us, then I would slowly Pick. Her. Apart.

⁂

Later that night, I texted Rachel to see what she was doing. We always texted goodnight to one another. I don't think we've ever gone a whole day without talking or texting.

"Hey, what are you doing?"

No reply.

Two minutes later, she still didn't text me back. It's unlike her not to get back to me right away. I tapped my favorites list on my phone and speed-dialed her number. The phone rang three times, then four. She still didn't answer. By the sixth ring, it went to voicemail. I have never since we've known each other, had to leave her a voicemail, and I'm not about to start now.

I pressed "end" and sat back on my throw pillow resting against the headboard. Where was she? My mind was racing, thinking the worst. We had just seen each other hours ago. What could have possibly happened in that amount of time?

I opened her contact information in my phone to see if I had another phone number. I didn't because I have never called her house phone or had ever needed to call it since we have cell phones. Then, I'd have to speak to whoever answers the phone and pretend that I cared to talk to them when all I really cared about was talking to my best friend Rachel.

I send her one text after another.

"Please text or call me, ASAP!"

"Is everything okay?"

"What is going on?"

"Why aren't you texting me back?"

But I get no reply from her.

Rachel almost always has her cell phone plugged into the charger next to her bed. Then, it clicked in my head. Maybe she was in another room and left her phone charging. That had to be it. I was sure of it. Rachel wouldn't intentionally not answer my texts, right? No, I was certain that wasn't the case.

There had to be something going on in that house of hers. Maybe her parents wanted to spend quality time with her. Gross, I thought to myself.

Sometimes, I honestly think they don't like me. But what was there about me not to like? I was the best thing that ever came into Rachel's life. We are like sisters.

My phone beeped. I had a text.

It was from Rachel:

"Sorry, my phone died. Can't talk now. See you at school tomorrow."

My mouth dropped open. What the hell was that all about?

FIVE

LAURA

Rachel accompanied me into her bedroom without her mother knowing, but she'd have to tell her because I smelled dinner cooking. Once in Rachel's bedroom, I stood shivering from the wet clothes on my body, waiting for her to get me something dry to wear. We are practically the same size. Thin in the hips with a flat stomach, although my legs were a tad bit longer than hers. If I think back far enough, Rachel used to be chubby, now she was thin, maybe too thin.

She closed the dresser drawer and walked over to me. "Here, you can wear a pair of my leggings and a t-shirt," she said, holding them out to me.

When had she ever seen me in a pair of leggings before? Of course, all the girls at school wore them, but I didn't because I don't like the way they shape your legs and butt, giving the guys something else to stare at. But I had no other choice. I had no other clothes to wear.

"Thank you," I replied, taking the clothes. I left her bedroom and walked into the bathroom across the hall. Once inside, I turned and looked in the mirror. I wanted to scream in horror. Besides the mascara smeared and running down my face, there were some red marks above my left eye.

I'd have to use Rachel's makeup to cover these up or people would ask me questions I wasn't ready to answer.

I peeled off my semi-soaked jeans, leaving my underwear on. There was no way I would borrow Rachel's to wear. Besides, they weren't wet like the rest of my clothes. I slipped one leg in the leggings and then the other, pulling them up and over my butt. They felt comfortable and smooth against my skin. I liked them on me.

I grabbed the t-shirt Rachel lent me off the counter and put it on. There was a plastic box that contained makeup remover wipes sitting on the counter. I pulled one out, wiped away the black smudges, looking almost human again. When my face was clean, I opened the door and walked back into Rachel's room.

She was sitting on her bed cross-legged doing her homework. Something we were to do together but isn't that how I got into this predicament? All because Scarlet and Rachel wanted to come over to my house and study. My mom doesn't allow anyone in our house, especially when she isn't home. That's a lie. My mother didn't allow anyone over to our house because then they would see who she really was and how she treated me.

Rachel turned when she noticed me standing in the doorway. "Wow! You look good in those," she said.

My lips formed a smile, something it doesn't do often. I can't remember the last time I smiled and meant it. "Thanks." A warmness stirred inside me.

"So, do you want to tell me what happened to you?"

I made my way over to the bed and sat down. "No, not really."

"I know we aren't friends like we once were, but something happened to you and you need to talk to someone about it. If not me, then maybe my mom?"

I would not talk to anyone about this. About my life. I'm not ready to share what happened and how I got the bruises on my body, although she didn't know about them. She had only seen my face. My arms.

"Well, I'm here if you want to talk. I promise to listen. If you don't want me to tell my mom, I won't," Rachel concluded.

Rachel was the friend I remembered when we were younger, but I needed to keep my guard up because she was now friends with Scarlet. It wasn't because I didn't trust her. It was Scarlet who would initiate the plan of attack and who I didn't trust. I've watched from the sidelines many times when Scarlet Fitzgerald belittled and humiliated other unpopular girls. Rachel wasn't too far behind her. One of Scarlet's puppets she could string around and do what she wanted them to do.

"You can spend the night and we can stop by your house in the morning if you want to grab some of your clothes," Rachel said. "My mom won't care."

Did she know what happened to me had to do with my mom? Because otherwise, why would I be afraid to go home, but she didn't push the issue. She didn't ask if that was the reason I was like this. "Okay," I agreed.

Rachel slept in her bed as I slept on the floor, mostly because I would not be falling asleep anytime soon and didn't want to keep her up. When I fled the house after the fight with my mom, I wasn't planning on going back home tonight. I wasn't sure what I was thinking when I grabbed my backpack from my bedroom floor and slipped out the window without grabbing clean clothes. I had planned to walk to the school and find shelter in the shed by the football field behind the bleachers where I've stayed before when things were bad at home. But when I got to the intersection, I turned right instead of left, walking toward Rachel's house.

I guess maybe I hoped that she'd take me in. Even though we had just started talking today. Why had I assumed she'd let me in her house and spend the night on her floor? I didn't. It just happened that way.

✢ ✢ ✢

The following morning, the sun filtered in through the curtains, shining onto my face. I could feel the heat behind my eyelids and turned away before opening my eyes.

I stared up at the ceiling until I was ready to get up. My glasses were next to me on the floor. I grabbed them and sat up. Luckily, they didn't break. I seemed to know when to remove them before the impact, which gave me the disadvantage because then I couldn't see it coming.

Turning my head, I noticed Rachel wasn't in her bed. I jumped up, scooping the blankets off the floor. I folded them and placed them neatly on the bed. My clothes were on the chair next to the wall. Her mom must have washed them for me or maybe Rachel had done them?

I peeked out the opened bedroom door before heading toward the bathroom across the hall. Just as I approached, the door to the bathroom opened and Rachel walked out almost running into me.

"Oh, good morning, Laura," Rachel said, stepping back, a smile spreading across her face.

Was she always this happy? "Good morning," I replied. "Is it okay if I take a shower and change?"

Rachel looked at me in a strange way as if I had asked if I should jump off the Brooklyn Bridge. "Well, of course you can. I'll get you a clean towel and use whatever you want in the shower."

I nodded and hurried past her into the bathroom, closing the door behind me. She was still talking as I stood on the other side of the door. Panic rising in my chest. I wasn't sure why I was feeling like this. Was it because Rachel was being so kind to me?

"I'll get you that towel," she said through the closed door.

A few minutes later, I finished my shower, which was the fastest one I'd ever taken, dried off and got dressed. I walked back to Rachel's bedroom, but she wasn't there. I grabbed my backpack off the floor and headed toward the kitchen.

I stood in the doorway and looked around at her perfect family. My heart ached because I missed the family I once had. Missing my dad and brother sitting around the kitchen table joking around like they did every morning. I missed the way my mom used to be before she became who she is now.

I placed my bag down on the floor near the doorway when Rachel's mom saw me. "Good morning, Laura," Mrs. Sawyer sang. She hadn't changed one bit. Still as happy as can be and always so polite.

There was a pang of sadness and guilt deep in my gut, as I stood there wishing I had her as my mom. "Good morning," I replied with a smile.

"Come sit and I'll make you some eggs. Do you still like them scrambled?" Mrs. Sawyer asked. "With cheese sprinkled on the top?"

"Yes," I replied. She remembered. "But you don't have to make me anything."

She waved her hand in the air. "It's no problem. Is Scarlet picking you up this morning?" Mrs. Sawyer asked as she cracked two eggs into a bowl and began to beat them into a solid yellow, adding a little milk before pouring them into the skillet.

Rachel looked over at me before answering her mom. "Um, can you drop us off this morning since my car is in the shop?" Rachel asked.

Without looking up from the stove, Mrs. Sawyer replied, "I'll take you, but we need to leave right after breakfast."

We both looked at each other, smiled and giggled. It was like we'd never stopped being friends and I wished that were true.

SIX

RACHEL

As my mom drove us to school, my mind went back to last night and how great it was to have Laura over. It was as if we'd never stopped being friends, but once we got to school, I'd have to pretend that she didn't exist. Scarlet would have a shit fit if she knew that Laura spent the night at my house last night.

Yesterday when Scarlet said she wanted to play a game on Laura, I agreed, but now—now after last night—I don't know if I want to. Laura had done nothing wrong. I knew Scarlet wouldn't let this game of hers end because of something that happened to Laura after we left her house. She wouldn't care. In fact, she'd probably say that Laura deserved whatever happened to her.

When the school comes into view, I take in a deep breath holding it just long enough to feel the lightheadedness swim in my head, then exhaled. I hoped that today would go smoothly because I didn't want to feel the wrath of Scarlet after sending her that text. I wasn't sure why I was so afraid of her. Well, I know why. I've seen what she's capable of, and I don't want to be on the receiving end.

My mom pulled up to the curb, and Laura and I climbed out of the backseat of her Lexus. I didn't see Scarlet's car when we pulled into the school parking lot. A slow smile surfaced, and calmness settled inside me. Scarlet wasn't at school yet.

Laura walked ahead of me as if she didn't want anyone to see us together. Shouldn't that be the other way around? I was the popular one, but I wasn't with Scarlet, so I didn't care what Laura did.

Once inside the school, I went to my locker, exchanged my books for the ones I needed for the morning classes, and hurried down the hall to my math class. I let out a huge sigh of relief when I didn't see Scarlet sitting at her desk. I took my seat and waited for the teacher to begin the class, which wasn't soon enough.

The bell rang. I looked up and toward the door just as Scarlet entered. Our eyes connected. I couldn't tell by the look on her face if she knew that Laura had spent the night at my house. But how would she know? I was just being paranoid.

Scarlet walked in front of my desk, bent down, and whispered, "Where were you this morning? I waited for you."

"My mom dropped me off, and I came to class early to get some extra studying time in for our test today," I quickly replied. I couldn't tell if she believed me or not, but I had a feeling I would find out soon.

Scarlet smiled at me, but it was a fake. She knew the truth, but how? Out of the corner of my eye, I watched as she sat down, looked over her shoulder, and back at Laura, who was sitting two seats behind her. Did she know Laura, and I came to school together? I couldn't tell. If Scarlet knew, she wouldn't be able to let it go. She'd get even with me. Why had I been so stupid bringing Laura back to my house? I wasn't good at lying, especially to Scarlet. I would have to fix this before it was too late.

The teacher laid the test down on my desk, causing me to jump in my seat.

"What's up with you today?" Scarlet asked.

I looked over at her, pasting on a smile. She seemed to buy it. All I needed to do was to keep it together until the end of the school day.

Taking my time, I finished the test a few minutes before the bell was about to ring, making sure that all my answers were complete. That was one thing about Ms. Culver, she loved her job and took it seriously. She would mark each mistake you made. If you forgot to show your work she'd give you a point off.

The bell rang, and I waited for Scarlet to stand and followed her out of the class just like any other day, but not before looking over my shoulder at Laura, who was still sitting at her desk with her head down.

Out in the hall, Scarlet linked her arm in mine, and we walked to our next class, neither one of us saying a word. I wasn't sure if that was a good thing or bad. Still, the day was early, hopefully by lunch I'd know what she was thinking. I needed time to think about what she'd say to me and what my answer to her would be.

+ + +

After school, Scarlet drove us to her place and when we got to her bedroom, that was when she finally came unglued.

"What's the deal with you and Laura coming to school together?"

My throat tightened. I had been waiting for this question all day. I swallowed then answered, "Laura called me this morning because she had missed the bus and asked if she could get a ride," I replied as my heart raced, hoping that she didn't know that Laura always walked to school. If I sounded or acted afraid in front of Scarlet, she would know. Sometimes I wondered if she were a bloodhound and could smell the fear seeping out of people's pores.

"Oh, then why didn't you just call me to come pick you both up?"

"My mom had already said she'd give us a ride. Besides, I didn't want to bother you with picking up Laura." I kept my eyes on her, so she couldn't see that I was lying. Eye contact was always the first rule when you're lying; everyone knows that. I finally relaxed my shoulders and exhaled the breath in my lungs. God, it was as if I were being tortured. I was lying to my best friend, even though it was in my best interests.

I walked to the bed and sat down across from her. "So, anything you want to do before I have to go home?" I asked, hoping that she would let what happened today go.

Scarlet smiled and opened the drawer of the nightstand next to the bed. She pulled out a notebook and handed it to me.

"Start telling the truth or you'll be in this book too," Scarlet said.

SEVEN

SCARLET

After I received the text from Rachel, something wasn't right. She had never sent me a text so blunt before, and I wondered what she was hiding from me. So, I slipped out of bed and threw on a pair of jogging pants and a sweatshirt. My father and Lianne were probably in their master suite getting ready for bed, so I went the opposite way and snuck out through the kitchen.

Rachel lived only a few blocks away. Normally, I would drive, but I didn't want to draw any attention to myself. It wasn't like I hadn't done this before. I'd snuck out of the house more times than I could count.

Once I got to the sidewalk, I made my way toward Rachel's house. When I got to her backyard, I walked around the house to where her bedroom was located, which faced the street. She left the curtains open a little, enough for me to see inside her room. There on the floor at the end of Rachel's bed was Laura Stevenson.

My hands clenched and unclenched. I hadn't felt this much rage inside me since Lianne married my father. What the hell was going on? Why was Laura sleeping over at my best friend's house? And why hadn't she told me in her text?

Part of me wanted to tap on the window and wake them up, but that would be too easy. No, I would have to wait until we got to school tomorrow to see what Rachel did or didn't do. No matter how much this infuriated me, I had to wait and get Rachel to admit it to me. If she lied, then she'd have to pay the consequences. No friend of mine would betray my friendship and get away with it! Who does she think she is, anyway?

As much as I didn't want to leave, I couldn't stay here. I cut through the backyard of Rachel's house and walked in the shadows to the next street. The last thing I needed was for someone to see me and call the police, thinking I was a robber, scoping out the homes, but this was also Craven Falls: A small, unpopulated town where most everyone knew everyone, but mostly they knew my father. He wouldn't take it lightly that his precious jewel of a daughter was out walking around in the middle of the night when she should be at home in bed.

Fifteen minutes later, I arrived back at my house and opened the door to the kitchen. I froze in the doorway, my eyes searching the dim-lit room. Was there someone here, in this room with me? I didn't see anyone, but that didn't mean they weren't hiding in the shadows. I closed the door, locking it behind me.

My brain was on overdrive and knew I would not get any sleep. I still couldn't believe that my best friend in the entire world was sneaking behind my back and being friends with that loser, Laura. I had to come up with something to get rid of Laura once and for all. Or maybe, I'd just make her think she was one of us. Just like I had planned and then pull the rug out from under her. I would humiliate her in front of the whole school.

A plan formed inside my head, making me smile. Laura was too naïve and would be so easy to please. She'd believe anything to be as popular as me, but she'll wish that she never crossed my path yesterday once I'm done with her. I needed to find out what Laura's greatest wish was. Something she had been wanting for a long time. Maybe a boy she liked but knew she wasn't worthy enough to have him. There had to be something she wanted more than anything.

⁕ ⁕ ⁕

The next morning my alarm blared loudly, I reached over and shut it off. I threw the covers off me and walked to the bathroom. Once showered and dressed, I headed downstairs to the kitchen to find Lianne sitting at the kitchen table drinking her coffee. My father was nowhere in sight, which meant he'd already left for the office as usual.

Standing tall, I strutted into the room as if I were the Queen of England. Well, I am the Queen of Craven Falls High. I grabbed a coffee cup from the cabinet and poured myself a cup, adding a spoonful of sugar. Then I turned and leaned against the counter and sipped my coffee. The hot liquid made its way down my throat, which felt invigorating. My eyes closed as I took another sip from the cup before placing it on the counter and getting a bowl of cereal.

As I sat down at the small dinette table in the kitchen across from my evil stepmother, I pretended she didn't exist. She knew that it was best not to talk to me unless I acknowledged her first, but I guess she didn't get that memo.

"Where were you coming in from last night?" Lianne asked without looking up.

My hand stopped in midair as I was getting ready to shove cereal into my mouth. Had I been right about the presence in the kitchen last night? I had to think quickly and come up with a believable response, but I had nothing. Act cool, my mind whispered. Don't let her see you sweat.

"Is it that boy Kyle you've been seeing behind your father's back?"

I choked on the cereal I'd put in my mouth. How had she known about him? My father would kill me if he knew I was dating Kyle of all people. He mentioned several times that Kyle was nothing but trouble, and I should stay away from him. That he would ruin my future. Although I think he was more afraid that Kyle could ruin his future more than mine.

"There was a noise, so I went out into the hall to see what it was. You were running down the driveway, but I didn't see you get into a car. So, where did you go?"

"I had to talk to Rachel about something last night, and she wouldn't answer her phone. What the shit is it to you, anyway? Are you spying on me or something?" A smirk spread across my face, though irritated by her questions.

"Spying on you is something I'm not into. I honestly couldn't care less what you're doing, but your father well, he would probably like to know what his daughter is doing out in the middle of the night. So, I suggest you watch yourself before he finds out," Lianne warned, pointing a finger at me. "If you so much as fuck up his chances of being re-elected as Mayor, he will disown your ass. Actually, I hope you do, and he finally gets rid of you and ships you off to some other place far, far away from us. All you care about is yourself anyway, Scarlet."

"Screw you!" I slammed my fist down on the table, spilling coffee from my cup. "It figures you'd do anything, say anything, to get him to see things your way, you're a worthless money-hungry leech," I shouted. The legs of my chair screeched as I stood, walked over to the counter, and threw my bowl into the sink, letting cereal and ceramic pieces of the bowl fly everywhere. Great fucking morning to you too, Lianne.

I left the room, ran up the stairs, and grabbed my things from my bedroom before leaving the house. Lianne pissed me off, but I was upset with myself because she knew about Kyle, but how?

When I pulled into the parking lot of the school, I hid beside Travis Evans' Dodge pick-up, not in my usual spot. My view of the entrance of the school was just visible enough for me to see when Rachel arrived.

Still fuming from the accusations with Lianne that I almost missed Rachel's mom pulling up in the drop-offline and Rachel getting out of the vehicle with Laura right behind her. I couldn't believe my eyes; Laura was still with Rachel. Did she really think she could swindle her way into our group and be Rachel's best friend again? Take over what I've created since the seventh grade? But hadn't I wanted her to believe she was our friend? Yes, but only when I was around. Not go behind my back and become Rachel's friend. That's when I realized Laura was out to steal Rachel from me.

The palm of my hand slammed down on the steering wheel, furious that Rachel of all people would do something like this to me. I wanted to scream, but I couldn't. I didn't need my classmates to see me like this. I've always presented myself as a confident, successful, and independent woman who didn't take shit from no one. Don't let them see you fall, my father's words repeated in my head. I needed to go into the school and make-believe that I did not know that Laura was at her house last night. That I didn't see her sleeping on Rachel's bedroom floor.

"That bitch will pay for this!" I muttered.

I waited until they entered the school to get out of my car and go inside, acting like I hadn't seen them together. When I got to my locker, I didn't see Rachel anywhere. We always waited for each other, but she was nowhere in sight. My nostrils flared as I unlocked my locker and gathered the books I needed, then slammed the door, storming off down the hall.

I had sat out in my car longer than usual this morning, so I had only seconds to get to math class. The bell rang just as I walked through the doorway. My eyes were glued on Rachel, who was sitting at her desk reading over her notes for the test we were about to have. She must have felt my presence when I entered the room because she looked up and we locked eyes.

I made my way to the desk beside her. "Where were you this morning, Rachel?"

"I wanted to get some extra studying time in for the math test," she replied without looking up.

What a lame excuse that was. Couldn't she have come up with a better one? Or at least looked me in the eye and lie to me?

When class ended, we walked to our next class together with my arm linked with hers. I wanted Laura to see that she won't win this battle. By lunch I had her all to myself again and would do whatever I had to, to keep it that way.

On the drive back to my house, we listened to music, singing to all our favorite songs. It was as if nothing had ever happened last night or this morning, but I had already planned to get the truth from her once we were alone in my bedroom. There would be nowhere for her to hide. She'd have to tell me the truth. She wouldn't dare lie to me, would she?

I pulled into the driveway and we both climbed out of the car and went inside the house. We stopped and grabbed two sodas from the refrigerator, though Rachel never drinks hers and then went to my bedroom.

"How come Laura came with you to school this morning?" I asked.

"Oh, ah, she called and said she needed a ride. That she missed the bus," Rachel replied.

She was lying. Laura walked to school. She never took the bus, but I wanted Rachel to come clean and tell me the truth. I didn't want to be the one to get it out of her.

I walked over to my bed and sat down, waiting for Rachel to follow. She did. I opened the drawer to my nightstand and pulled out a notebook and handed it to her. By the look on her face, she knew exactly what it was before she opened the notepad and started reading.

"You really think we can get him to do this?" Rachel asked.

"I can get anyone to do whatever I want them to do, and that includes you too," I replied with a smile.

Rachel smiled back at me, but I could tell that it was fake. I would not stand by and lose her over some poor, ugly, and unworthy bitch like Laura!

EIGHT

LAURA

It was a horrible mistake to accept the ride that Rachel offered when she saw me walking down the sidewalk last night. I hadn't wanted her to see me like that. And why hadn't I cleaned myself up before I left the house. Then Rachel asked me to spend the night. I couldn't say no because I really didn't want to sleep in the shed behind the school like I'd done many times before when my mom and I got into a fight.

I said nothing to Rachel about Scarlet sitting in her car watching us when we arrived at the school. She parked beside Travis' truck, not in her usual spot five spaces down. Scarlet looked pissed at Rachel when she came to math class, but Rachel must not have seen it. I watched her reaction the whole time, hiding my face when she looked at me before sitting in her seat.

Had yesterday been a dream? Because today the tension was in the air. I was back to being invisible again just like it should be. Now, I just needed it to stay that way.

Later that day, Scarlet was practically hanging all over Rachel as if she was her lover. Was I that stupid to think Rachel was different last night? That she cared about me, wishing she hadn't driven by at that moment.

"You're so stupid, Laura," I scolded myself. "You shouldn't have let them into your house, knowing that you weren't allowed to have anyone over. People will know that your mom is a drunk." Something my mom doesn't want the town to know. Yet, I had given my mother another reason to drink. Another reason to hit me.

My mom blamed me for the accident that killed my dad and brother, but I wasn't anywhere near them when the semi-truck hit my dad's car head-on. There wasn't even a chance to say goodbye; the newspaper had said they had died seconds after the crash.

I had always wondered what their last thoughts were. Did they even have time to whisper our names and say goodbye, begging for a chance to see us again? According to the article, it happened so fast that there wouldn't have been any way for my dad to avoid the head-on collision. When I got to the hospital, hoping to see them and talk to them, they were already dead; something the nurse hadn't told me on the phone.

My mom hadn't gotten to the hospital yet when I arrived. The nurse let me in to see my dad and brother. To this day, I'm not sure that decision was the right one. Mostly because it's the last image I have of them, lying there in the emergency room on the hospital beds—not moving, not breathing, covered in blood. Tears poured out of me as the nurse tried to take me away from them.

When my mom finally showed up, she became hysterical when she saw them. The days and weeks that followed were unbearable. Numbing herself from the pain she endured deep inside her heart. She was the one who had loved my dad first, but I was his little girl and that infuriated her the most, especially after he was killed. From that day on, she couldn't function without a drink. She couldn't function without making sure she hit me, as if making me pay for their deaths I didn't even cause.

I stood in front of the bathroom mirror at home, relieved that my mom wasn't home yet. The bruises from the night before became visible as I wiped away the makeup on my face. The one thing I was glad of when I spent the night at Rachel's last night was that she helped me cover up the bruises that started to surface on my face and neck.

Thank God it was Friday, and that I didn't have to see anyone from school until Monday. This would give my body time to heal. It was like walking on eggshells around my mom. It upset her I had Rachel and Scarlet over—I can't call them friends because, in all honesty; they aren't my friends.

"You don't have the right to have friends over!" my mom had screamed in my face. "You're an unworthy little bitch! I don't know what your father saw in you."

I wanted to reply that they weren't my friends, but then she'd laugh in my face that I was such a loser. If I've learned anything it's that I'd be in worse shape if I talked back. Soon her arm would go flying in the air and her hand would make contact with my face, arms, back, chest, anything she could hit. It was rare that she only used her hands. She usually found something around the house to use on me. A bat, lamps, picture frames, whatever was in her reach at that moment. Though sometimes I could run to my bedroom and lock the door, keeping her away from me.

I opened the door and walked down the hall back to my bedroom. It's my sanctuary where I can be myself and close the world off outside—away from my mother. Although she rarely came into my room after what she'd done to it before I repainted it. She had been on one of her tantrums and destroyed the walls. I had hidden anything that my dad had given me because she'd break them. She had apologized the next day and had never stepped foot beyond the doorway again.

My cell phone chimed and wondered who it could be from because my mom never texted me. I grabbed my phone from the nightstand and pushed the side button. Only a number appeared on the home screen. If it was my neighbor Mrs. Tucker wanting me to babysit, then her name would appear. I swiped right, and the message opened for me to read.

"Hey, sorry about earlier. Want to get together later?"

It had to be Rachel because I really didn't think Scarlet would text me to hang out. I wasn't sure how to respond and if she was being serious. Was she with Scarlet and this was a set-up? Scarlet to me was the Wicked Witch of the West, like in Wizard of Oz. She has never done a nice thing to or for anyone. In my dictionary under the word bitch, would be Scarlet's name in bold letters. And possibly a picture of her to go with it.

My thumb hovered over the letters, waiting for me to come up with a reply. Nothing came to me. Maybe it's best that I don't respond to her and make her think I hadn't seen it yet, but then another text appeared.

Rachel: **I know that you read my text. Why won't you answer back?**

How does she know that I have read her text?

Laura: **Why should I?**

Rachel: **Because I want to be your friend.**

Laura: **A little late, don't you think?**

Rachel: **It's never too late.**

Was this some kind of joke to her or to them? Did Rachel believe she could walk back into my life after all these years as if nothing had changed? Like she had never turned her back on me at the start of Jr. High.

My back sank against the pillows on my bed and I looked up at the ceiling. Why couldn't Rachel leave things as they were? Why suddenly did she want to be my friend again?

The front door opened, then slammed shut. My mom was home, and it didn't sound like she was in a good mood. Like that should surprise me.

I jumped off the bed, stood, and walked to my bedroom door, waiting for her to burst into my room, but she didn't. My ear was against the door, listening for her footsteps to come hauling ass down the hall.

Nothing but silence.

I stepped back and turned toward my bed, thinking I was in the clear when my bedroom door flew open, smacking me in the back. "Son of a bitch!" I cried out in pain, reaching a hand to the spot on my back that was just struck by the door.

I turned around.

My mom stood in the doorway.

NINE

Rachel

After I left Scarlet's house, I walked the long way home. I needed to think about what she had planned for Laura. I didn't want to be a part of it, but how was I going to get out of it? It was either be Scarlet's friend or be her nemesis. Once school was over and we graduated, I wouldn't have to deal with Scarlet anymore, but that was eight months away. What was I going to do before that time arrived?

Two days ago, I hadn't even thought about not being Scarlet's friend. Hadn't thought about Laura either, but here I am pondering who to choose. What I should do?

Scarlet had some good traits about her; she wasn't all that bad of a person. Well, that would be a lie. She had done some things that would've gotten her expelled; like slashing people's tires and spray-painting girls' lockers with obscene words. Yeah, sure, she had always gotten her way, and I've gone along for the ride. Some things we did to other girls were funny, and I had even agreed to humiliating Laura, but now that someone was hurting her? I'm not sure I want to be a part of Scarlet's plan anymore. Sometimes enough is enough. It isn't fun anymore. Not when someone will get hurt.

As I walked down the sidewalk, my mind reflecting over the last four years of my friendship with Scarlet, I'd have to say I don't like myself very much. I'm not sure how Scarlet can even sleep at night with all the things she's done to people.

Once home, I went into the kitchen and started preparing tonight's dinner: eggplant parmesan. I finished the dish and placed it on the stove, covering it. It won't take long to cook; something I can do once my mom gets home from work. I headed into my bedroom to start on my homework. My mind kept thinking about Laura, and I realized that I missed her.

My phone was on the table. I grabbed it and texted Laura. When she finally replied, our conversation ended before it even started. Had I been too late to reach out to her? It probably seemed strange that I texted her after Scarlet initiated this stupid plan of deception.

An hour passed when my mom knocked on my bedroom door and opened it. "Should I place the dish you made in the oven?" my mom asked.

I nodded.

"Is everything all right?"

I shrugged my shoulders. "I enjoyed being with Laura last night, but she doesn't want to hang out with me." Wondering why this bothered me so much.

"Give her some time. She'll come around."

"I don't know. I treated her bad at school today."

"Oh?" my mom questioned. "Should I ask why?"

Shrugging my shoulders again, wishing I had said nothing at all. Then again, my mom is someone I can talk to and count on when I need her.

"Scarlet doesn't like Laura, so I can't hang out with her while I'm at school." My eyes moved from my mom down to the phone in my lap. "I just texted Laura to see if she wanted to hang out later, but she won't answer me back."

"Well, she seemed fine last night. I'm sure once she realizes that you want to be her friend again, she'll come around," my mom said and added,

"I can't say that I like Scarlet all that much. I allow you to have your own friends, but she can be quite the drama queen and blows things out of proportion."

She was right, and I nodded in agreement. My mom usually was, but as I said earlier, I can't just stop being friends with Scarlet. Not if I know what's good for me.

✦ ✦ ✦

Later that night, as I'm lying in my bed reading If I Stay by Gayle Forman, one of my favorite books, there's a tap on my window. I scramble out of bed and hurry over to the window to see what or who is out there. I move the curtains to the side. Laura is standing outside, and she is crying. I place my book down on the dresser next to where I'm standing and open the window.

"What are you doing out here?" The chilly night air wrapped around my body, making me shiver where I stood. I rubbed my hands up and down my arms, trying to get warm again.

"Can I come in?" Laura whispered.

"Go around back and I'll let you in through the kitchen door," I tell her as I'm closing the window.

We meet at the kitchen door at the same time. I unlock the deadbolt and open the door. A blast of cool air pushes me back, and I almost lost my grip on the door handle. I hadn't realized how windy it was outside, nor heard the wind hitting the house.

Laura comes through the doorway as I'm about to close the door but not before I see a glimpse of something, or should I say someone along the fence line in the backyard. I couldn't tell if it was an animal or maybe the shadow of a tree because my mind didn't want to believe it was Scarlet watching my house. Waiting to see if Laura would arrive?

I had no idea that Laura would be coming over, especially tonight after what happened at school today and me avoiding her like the plague. She hadn't answered my texts about hanging out. So, again, I was surprised that she was here.

After closing and locking the door, I peeled back the curtain and peered out into the darkness. I needed to reassure myself that I was just imagining there was someone or something out there. Scarlet wouldn't sink to the level of watching my every move when we're apart, would she? This, I wasn't so sure about, and wanted to believe she wouldn't do something so immature, but who was I kidding? This was Scarlet Fitzgerald I was talking about.

My eyes sketched over the backyard but saw nothing. I blew out a breath and relaxed my shoulders. When I turned back around, Laura was staring at me as if I was losing my mind.

I nudged my head and took the lead, heading back toward my bedroom. Once in my room, I closed the door and looked toward the window. The curtains were open, so I walked over and pulled them shut, closing off the world outside. I also checked to make sure I'd locked the window.

When I turned back around, Laura was sitting on the edge of my bed. I hadn't noticed before that she had welts on her face and purple bruises surfacing. Something she didn't have last night or at school. So, what has happened since the last time we saw one another?

I walked over to the bed and lifted her chin with my hand. My eyes traced over her face, which looked like she'd been in a boxing match, again.

"What happened?" I asked.

Tears began to stream from her swollen eyes. "I… I need to stay here tonight," Laura cried. "Can I stay here?"

I didn't hesitate. "Yes, of course, you can stay." I pulled her to me and hugged her. She yelped out in pain. I pulled away, looking her over. Laura lifted her shirt and turned around. She had a large cut on her back. The blood was dry around the cut, but it still needed medical attention.

"Oh, my God, Laura. What happened?"

Ten

Scarlet

When it became dark, I slipped outside, knowing that Lianne was probably watching my every move, again. What a freaking bitch! But I couldn't worry about her right now. I had other things to take care of. I had to see for myself that Rachel would betray me and try to see Laura behind my back.

Once I was finished with Laura, I would end this charade between Lianne and my father once and for all. She didn't deserve him. What was her problem anyway this morning, being all cocky and trying to tell me, of all people, what to do? Didn't she know that she wasn't my real mom, and that she had no right to tell me what I could and couldn't do? I don't give two shits that she married my father, which we both know was only for the money. What thirty-year-old woman would want to marry a fifty-five-year-old man?

I walked the back way to Rachel's house and this time I stood along the fence line of her property where no one could see me. I sat on the ground in the shadow of a huge maple tree, waiting for the bitch Laura to show up. Hoping I was wrong about my best friend Rachel and that she wouldn't go behind my back and be friends with that loser.

It was five minutes to eleven on my watch when my ears perked to the echo of a deadbolt and a door opening. Laura stood at the kitchen door.

A gust of cold night air hit my face, making me shiver. My back slinked up along the wooden fence until I was standing. Making sure that I stayed inside the shadow of the tree. Rachel stood at the door and Laura walked into the house, then the backdoor closed.

I needed to sneak to the front of the house to Rachel's bedroom window and see what they were up to. I scurried along the property but kept near the fence, staying at least fifteen feet from the motion sensor at the back of the house. I didn't need the light turning on and someone coming outside to see who was out here. Once in the front yard, I crouched down under Rachel's window just as she closed the curtain and locked the window, sealing off their voices.

"Damn it!" I hissed under my breath.

Now, what the hell was I going to do? I couldn't see them or hear them talking and needed to know what they were up to. I wanted to understand what was so great about Laura that Rachel would deceive our friendship. Just thinking about Laura in my best friend's bedroom was pissing me off!

I would not get anywhere by hanging outside her window, especially where someone might see me. I stepped away from the house, making my way to the sidewalk.

Raw adrenaline flowed through my body as the images replayed of Laura being in Rachel's bedroom. Why had she double-crossed me? I didn't know, but I'd make it my business to find out.

✯ ✯ ✯

The next morning after a restless sleep, I crawled out of bed and into the shower. I needed to drive over to Rachel's and catch her red-handed with Laura in her room.

By the time I finished showering and dried my hair, it was almost noon. I picked out a cozy yet glamorous outfit and headed downstairs. Lianne stood at the counter as I entered the kitchen pouring a cup of coffee. There was no way I'd be able to avoid her. God, she seemed to be everywhere I was. The heat rose up my legs through my stomach until it hit my face. I wanted nothing more than to get her out of this house.

Lianne didn't even turn around when she spoke. "So, where were you off to last night, again?" Lianne asked as she stood looking out the kitchen window.

How the hell did she know I was standing here?

"I know you're behind me," she said, turning around. "You know, you can't keep sneaking out like this at night. One day your father will catch you," she said, smiling her pearly white teeth. "And when he does, he will have no choice than to ship you off to boarding school."

"Why are you so eager to get rid of me? What have I done to make you hate me so much? Besides, I doubt you have the nerve to tell him." A heatwave shot through my body once more. If my dad found out, there was no way I'd be able to lie to him. Would he believe Lianne over me? It would seem unfair since I was his daughter. His flesh and blood. I don't know why I came second to her sometimes, or I should say third since his job came first.

"Because you're a worthless piece of shit, Scarlet. You're a bitch to all of your friends, which I'm surprised you have any at all. I know how you treat them at school and how you ridicule other girls. And who knows? Maybe your father will look out the window one night when you're supposed to be in bed," Lianne said with a devious smirk.

"And I wonder who would tell him to do that?"

My wicked stepmom sipped her coffee, her eyes peering over the top of the mug at me. I wished she'd get hit by a car and die. Then I'd be done with her, and it would be just my father and me like it should be. Wishful thinking, I know.

"You may be the Queen Bee at school, but in this house, there are rules, and rules are to be followed. No exceptions!" Lianne growled. "Do I make myself clear?"

I walked up to her, standing inches from her face. I wanted so much to hit her, but I couldn't so I stepped to the side and opened the cabinet door, reaching for a coffee cup. I hated standing this close to her. Though I pondered the idea why we just couldn't get along with one another. She had been married to my father for a little less than a year now, and you'd think we'd be a happy family, but there was just something about her I didn't like.

"Yes," I replied and grabbed a to-go cup instead. I would not stick around. Not while she was here, which seemed to be always.

Five minutes later, I was out the door and, in my car, heading to Rachel's house. I'd have to come up with a reason for my visit since we had nothing planned today. I had to catch Laura at her house.

I pulled alongside the curb across the street from Rachel's and sat there watching the house. There was movement behind the curtains in the family room and knew someone was home.

I opened the car door and stepped out onto the street. Why was I so nervous? I was Scarlet Fitzgerald; I could get whatever I wanted whenever I wanted. Then why did I feel afraid? I walked up the stone path to the front door and rang the doorbell.

Eleven

Laura

Rachel was acting strange when we got into her bedroom. Like someone was watching us, but I didn't see anyone outside when I came around back. Yes, granted, it was dark outside, but I've heard that you can sense things around you sometimes. Things that will make the hair on your body rise. I didn't feel this.

After Rachel closed the curtains in her room, we sat down on her bed. Her soft hand touched the side of my face where my latest bruise appeared. Should I tell her who did this because she would ask me, anyway? No one shows up at someone else's house looking like she was in a boxing match and expects no questions to be asked.

"Talk to me," Rachel whispered.

My eyes moved from her to my lap, thinking of the best way to tell her. Who was I kidding? There was no easy way to tell someone that your mother abuses you. Damn' it! Things were going well at home until I allowed Scarlet and Rachel into our house. My mom can't seem to let it go that I had people in my room. In our home. What was the big deal, anyway! I screamed inside my head, my demons battling one another.

"Laura, please," Rachel pressed as she dropped her hand from my face and grabbed my hand that was lying in my lap, squeezing it into hers.

Tears streamed down my face as I whispered, "My mom gets mad sometimes."

Rachel sucked in a breath, and at that moment I wished I could take what I just said back, but I couldn't. It was already out there. The words hovered in the air between us. I wish I could open my mouth and suck them back in where they will stay hidden from the world.

"You're kidding me, right?" Rachel questioned. Her gaze ping-ponged from me to the wall to the floor as if trying to avoid direct eye contact with me. Did she think I was lying to her? That I would make something like this up? Her mouth opened and closed. She looked up and locked eyes with me. "Tell me everything. When did this start? Why does she do this to you? She's your mother. She's not supposed to hurt you."

Rachel threw out too many questions all at once. I hadn't known she would react this way. I would too if I were in her shoes. Taking in a breath, I held it for several seconds before letting it out. "Before I tell you everything you have to swear. You must promise me you won't tell anyone, especially Scarlet. If she finds out, she'll use it against me, you know that. Please," I begged, holding onto Rachel's hand and squeezed hers this time. "Promise me you won't tell her. Promise me, Rachel." Tears spilling from my eyes.

Rachel didn't hesitate. "I promise you; I won't tell anyone." Rachel made an X across her heart with her pointer finger. "And hope to die," she said.

My mind flashed back to when we were kids and we would make the X cross on our chests when we were making a promise to one another. It was so long ago but almost felt like it was yesterday. "Do you remember when my brother and dad died?"

Rachel nodded.

"Well." My mouth went dry and my throat tightened, refusing to let the words escape. Once I said to them, I couldn't take them back. I had told no one what I was about to tell Rachel. "My mom didn't take it too well, and she started drinking. At first, it was just a few drinks to help her function and to sleep at night, but then it got worse and she started drinking every night, the moment she came home from work. Then, one day she got furious and took it out on me. The first couple of times, she just slapped me," I said as tears rolled down my face. The images flashed in my head, making my head jerk back as if she, my mother, were slapping me in that very moment. "Then out of nowhere, she started punching me and using whatever was in her grasp. Lamps, books, my brother's wooden bat, whatever came across her vision when she was angry. Furious." Snot slipped from my nose, and I wiped it away with the back of my hand.

Crying wasn't something that came easy to me. I have learned to be strong and hold them in, but tonight... Tonight, I can't seem to keep them inside me. Why was it so easy to let my guard down around Rachel? We haven't been friends for so long. She made her choice when she left me behind and made new friends. She stopped being my best friend and now... now it's like it used to be when we were younger, but will it stay this way or was she just using me to get information for Scarlet? If she was, then it was too late. I had already opened the can of worms and let them spill, squirming away with the information. I had tried so hard to keep my life locked away from the world.

"Laura, I'm so sorry. You need to tell someone about this. You should talk to my mom. She's an attorney. She can get you the help you need."

"And what?" I snapped without meaning to. "Go into foster care until I graduate in June? No way!" my voice rising. I didn't need to wake her parents. "I can't," I whispered. "I just can't." The tears stopped as anger began to surface but immediately disappeared. It wasn't like me to get mad and snap at people. That was my mother, and I never wanted to be like her.

Rachel pulled me into a hug, and I let go, crying harder than I ever had before. "I'll do whatever I can to help you, Laura, I promise," she said, seeming sincere.

Could I trust her? To let her take my burden and make things better, but it was wishful thinking. No one could fix this.

Rachel helped clean me up, or I should say, helped clean the blood off my back. Like last night, I slept over at her house, but this time we shared the bed together. Besides, I didn't want to be alone. I had spent too many nights in the shed behind the bleachers after my mom had hit me. This was something better. Something I longed for but had no way of finding until today.

⚘ ⚘ ⚘

The next morning, I woke to find the spot next to me empty. Rachel was gone. I rolled over, facing the door to Rachel's room when it opened.

"Good morning, sleepyhead," Rachel said, in her nothing's wrong-with-the-world voice. Wishing I could be that way. That happy.

"Good morning," I said back. "What time is it?"

"Almost noon."

"What?" I shrieked. "Shit, I have to go babysit Mrs. Appleton's two kids. Shit, shit, shit!" I said, swearing like a comedian on stage. I jumped out from under the blankets and to my feet. Still wearing my clothes, I came here with last night.

"Can't you just call her and tell her that something came up and you can't do it today?"

Sitting down on the edge of the bed, I put my face in my hands. My head was pounding. My back felt stiff and bruised.

"I can't. Besides, she'll either call my house or walk over there. If my mom answers and I'm not home." I shook my head. "My mom will do more than just beat me," I replied, shaking my head.

"Fine," Rachel said. "I'll drive you to Mrs. Appleton's, but you're not going home without me with you. I don't care what your mom says. I'll call the cops if she lays a hand on you or me."

My brain was spinning in circles, thinking about what to do. My mom wouldn't be stupid enough to do something with a witness around. No, she'd just take it out on me later when we're alone. Usually, after a night of drinking, my mom would sleep until late afternoon. And you didn't dare wake her.

"Let me get cleaned up and we'll go," I said, walking out of Rachel's bedroom toward the bathroom. I closed the door behind me and locked it before flicking on the light. I looked in the mirror. Dark purple bruises appeared on my neck, where my mom tried to choke me last night. Her fingers leaving lines for everyone to see. Choking wasn't something she usually did, which meant that she could kill me if she wanted to.

It took ten minutes to apply heavy layers of makeup to my face. I'd have to borrow some of Rachel's clothes, something with long sleeves and maybe a turtleneck, grateful that the weather had been cooler lately and could wear a sweater with no one asking questions.

I exited the bathroom and headed back to Rachel's bedroom. She'd already laid some clothes on the bed for me to wear, which told me she'd seen the marks on my neck before I did.

I quickly changed into the clothes and walked out of the bedroom to the kitchen down the hall where I found Rachel and her two brothers.

"Do you want anything to eat before we go?" Rachel asked.

I nodded. "Sure, what do you have?"

"We have cereal, or I can make you a sandwich since it's lunchtime."

"Sandwich sounds good, but you don't have to make it. I'm capable."

"Sure, help yourself," Rachel replied.

I walked to the refrigerator and opened the door, gathering the lunchmeat and mayo, and placed them on the counter before grabbing the bread from the breadbasket.

"So," Rachel started to say. "What time will you be done babysitting the Appleton kids?"

"You're going to Cody's house?" Rachel's brother, Shawn asked. "He's in my class at school. We're like best friends. Too bad I can't go with you," he sulked.

"Well, maybe some other time then," I replied, smiling.

"Really?" Shawn said, bouncing up and down in his chair.

"Sure, if your mom doesn't care."

Rachel smiled at her brother and then looked over at me. I finished making my sandwich and put everything back in the refrigerator, taking a seat next to Rachel and started eating.

After scarfing down the food, I took my plate to the sink. Being here at Rachel's felt more like home than my house. The atmosphere in this place was way calmer than mine. They were an actual family. I wanted to live here so bad but knew I couldn't.

"You ready to go?" Rachel asked.

"Yeah, whenever you are. Do you know where Appleton's live?"

"Don't be silly. They're your neighbors," Rachel replied.

Yes, of course she did, they're my neighbors. I smiled, feeling like a nincompoop.

Fifteen minutes later, I was standing on the sidewalk in front of Mrs. Appleton's house, but staring at my house next door, waiting to see if my mom would come flying out of the house demanding where I was last night, but she didn't. I walked up the path to Mrs. Appleton's door and knocked. Rachel honked, waved, and drove away.

The door opened, and I stepped inside. Mrs. Appleton was going on and on about something the boys did, but my mind was elsewhere. God, I wished this day were over. I wasn't feeling up to watching her rowdy, unmannered, spoiled kids, but I was never one to back out after making a promise.

"I'll be back by five this evening. Call me if there's anything you need, but I'm sure you'll be fine," Mrs. Appleton said as she placed her hand on my arm. "I can always count on you, Laura. You're such a good kid. I will sure miss you when you graduate next spring."

Smiling back at her. "I'll miss you too." But I couldn't wait to leave this town.

TWELVE

RACHEL

After I dropped Laura off at Mrs. Appleton's, I drove over to Scarlet's house. I needed to get her to trust me by convincing her I didn't know that Laura was coming over last night, which I didn't. She wouldn't believe me, but I had to try. She'd make me pay for being friends with Laura behind her back even though I hadn't planned any of it. I was just praying that she wasn't in a bad mood. No, I hoped that I hadn't really seen her in my backyard last night.

A few minutes later, I pulled into Fitzgerald's residence and parked the car. Part of me wanted to put the car in drive and race back home, not wanting to feel the wrath of Scarlet. But then again, I needed to do this and have her see things my way without telling her what was going on with Laura and her mother.

Scarlet would use Laura's secret against her and everyone at school would know. They'd insult her and make her feel like she deserved to be beaten by her own mother, but that wasn't true. No one deserved to be hit, especially by their own parents.

I got out of my car and walked up to the enormous mansion. I had thought little about Scarlet's house until today. How big and beautiful it was with all the rooms it held inside. I stepped onto the last step, leaving a foot of space from the door. My hand reached out to press the doorbell when the door was yanked open. Startled, I jumped back almost falling off the steps. When I looked up, Scarlet was standing in the archway.

"Well, well. What brings Rachel the traitor to my house?" Scarlet snarled.

I could feel my face flush as if I had been caught stealing candy from a jar. Then, I realized she'd just given herself away. Had she been watching me all along? Was it really her in the shadows near the fence line last night at my house? Then it hit me like a hammer on a nail. She had been insecure about our friendship since the very beginning of seventh grade, so why did I think she wouldn't follow me? Wouldn't be watching my every move?

"Really?" I questioned. "You'd stoop that low and follow me? Watch me?"

"You believe I wouldn't?" Scarlet shot back.

"Whatever? I'm so done with you." I mumbled as I turned and walked down the steps toward my car. I would not stand there and let her treat me like she does everyone else. I was better than her. She wouldn't take me down with her words. I won't let her! But in all reality, I was shaking as if I had just seen a ghost. I just hoped she couldn't see it.

"That's it, run to your new best friend, you traitor!" Scarlet yelled from the doorway.

There was a crack in her voice when she said the last word. Was she about to cry over our friendship? She didn't seem like the type, although she was good at whining and getting her way. Yet it was clear my actions hurt her. I would need to watch my back. Scarlet doesn't let down easy. She'll come up with a plot to get even with me.

I turned back around to face her. "I thought you were better than this Scarlet. A real friend I could count on, but you're just a phony. No one can trust you with anything." I opened the car door and got in, powered down the window, and raised my arm in the air, flipping her off. As far as I was concerned, our friendship was over!

⁜ ⁜ ⁜

Within a few minutes, I arrived back home and went straight to my room. I was fuming with anger and didn't want my mom or dad to see me and start asking me what was wrong. Why hadn't I seen this part of Scarlet and how she really is A TOTAL FREAKING BITCH?!

She only cared about herself and no one else. Had I been too blind to see beyond my popularity at school, which would end as soon as Scarlet told everyone that I'd been hanging out with Laura, but I didn't care anymore.

I don't need her to be popular in school. It's my senior year and only eight months left to go. I could survive until we graduated and went our separate ways, which I was planning to do anyway. So, what difference did it make if I chose now to leave her behind? Well, because of what she was capable of. I will need to be extra careful. Scarlet will seek revenge against me after today.

In all honesty, I don't care if I wasn't popular at all anymore. Hanging out with Scarlet made me a bitch to everyone else. This may benefit me. The people at CFH have only seen my rudeness when I was around Scarlet, so if I was nice to them and made them feel special, they'll like me even more. I can be myself at school. The person who likes to help others, not destroy them. I'm an amazing person without that bitch beside me.

I smiled because everything that I was thinking was true. The other girls at school will want to hang out with me when I'm nice to them, but I wasn't looking for popularity. I just wanted to help Laura. To get her out of that house and away from her mom.

I can't believe her mother would do that to her. The law could protect Laura from the abuse her mother was inflicting on her, couldn't they? I wished she'd let me talk to my mom about what was happening to her. My mom could help her.

Once my anger subsided, I walked into the kitchen to see what my family had planned for today. I usually hang out with Scarlet on the weekends, but that boat has sailed, and I feel relieved.

I looked around the kitchen and saw no one. Had they gone out for the day and forgotten to tell me? My eyes fell to the counter where a piece of paper sat and picked it up.

Rachel
The boys have a soccer game this afternoon. We'll see you later for dinner.
Love, Mom

I placed the note back on the counter and pulled my phone from my back pocket. I texted Laura, asking if she'd care if I came over and hung out with her. No reply. But that meant nothing. She could be busy with the Appleton kids and didn't have her phone near her.

My finger tapped the side of the phone waiting impatiently for Laura to text me back, but there was still no reply. I shoved my cell phone back into the pocket of my jeans and walked to my bedroom. I gathered my books from my backpack and sat down on the bed.

My mind went back to the other day as I opened my math book. The day Scarlet had come up with the plan to humiliate Laura. Something at the time I was willing to take part in, but after learning what Laura has been going through, I just couldn't do it. She was hurting enough and playing a game on her would only cause more harm.

We have assemblies on bullying and teen suicides, so why does Scarlet continue to hurt other people? Does she think her words don't affect people and make them want to end their lives? I hoped not, but I would not be a part of her games any longer.

I turned the page in my math book and found a note folded inside. I hadn't remembered placing one in my book. I unfolded the small piece of paper reading the words, "You'll get what you deserve," written in red ink. A chill ran down my spine as my eyes surveyed the room, looking for something or someone that wasn't there. Was I being watched in my own room, but that couldn't be true? Scarlet hadn't been in my room in a week.

I folded the note and placed it inside a book I had in a drawer next to my bed. Had Scarlet slipped the paper into my math book when I wasn't looking? Yes, of course, she had to have. My mind replayed yesterday when Scarlet could have had the chance; it was definitely possible. Besides Scarlet had my locker combination, so she could have done it during the day at school.

I shook my head as if to shuffle my thoughts away and go back to my homework, but I couldn't concentrate. The words still danced in my mind. Had she already known that Laura was over at my house?

I lay back against the throw pillows on my bed, closing my eyes, my mind reeling with questions. The house was too quiet as if it was nighttime. I shot up, my back stiff. My head tilted toward the door as the floorboard creaked outside my bedroom door.

Thirteen

Scarlet

Why would Rachel betray me this way? She had been my best friend until the moment Laura crossed our paths on Thursday. Rachel turned on me as if I didn't matter anymore. "Well, the hell with her!" I screamed into my bedroom.

I needed to come up with a different plan. A plan that would get Rachel back and leave Laura behind. She needed to see things my way or… or I could just forget them both and find new friends. No! Rachel was my best friend, not Laura's, and I'll be damned if she thinks she can have her without a fight! People can't see that I'm nothing without her.

I throw myself onto my bed, punching my fist into my pillow beside me. "This was not part of my plan," I screamed into my comforter. We were supposed to humiliate and takedown Laura together, but Rachel deceived me, and I would not let her get away with it!

I stand and open the drawer by my nightstand, pulling out the book that has all my secrets in it. I know I should hide the book better than I do. If Lianne ever came snooping in my room and found it, all hell would break loose. There would be no more BMW or cell phone privileges.

It was time that I set plan one in motion, with or without Rachel's help. I laughed. This would be a great humiliation for Laura, thinking she could walk right in and steal my best friend away from me. We'll just see who's worthy of Rachel.

Opening the book to a blank page, I write suggestions. Things that could ruin Laura. She'll drop out of school once I'm done with her or maybe—maybe she'd just do us all a favor and kill herself. She could jump off the bridge down by the river that ran through Craven Falls. The same river they had found the body of five-year-old Sierra Miller two years ago. But that was a different story. She didn't try killing herself. The sheriff said it was an accident.

If she climbed to the very top and jumped the rocks below would finish Laura off. I chuckled over this idea, but I've never killed someone, but Laura deserved everything she had coming to her for taking Rachel from me. Laura will know it's me before she's dead. She'll beg me for forgiveness, and I'll see it in her eyes, wanting me to help her, but I won't. I won't save her because she's not worth saving. I write all my ideas as fast as they come to me and I don't stop until I get a cramp in my hand.

"Scarlet."

"Shit," I muttered. What did the bitch want now?

There was a knock on my door, then it creaked open. I slid the book under my pillow. "Yes?" I said.

"Oh, there you are. I wasn't sure that you'd be home today. You're usually out with Rachel. Your dad and I are going out. Do you want to join us?"

I shake my head. "No, I got things to do. Homework to finish, but thanks for the offer," I replied even though I don't mean the last part. It's rare that they invite me to spend time with them, so I know it was my father who wanted me to come, but it doesn't matter. I needed to plan my attack and who I had to talk to first.

"Okay, then. We'll see you later," Lianne said as she closed the door behind her. "What a bitch," Lianne muttered as she walked away.

Anger surged through me as she said those words loud enough for me to hear. I wanted to go after her and make her eat the words she'd just spoken, but if my father were home, which he was, then it wouldn't be a good idea. I'd deal with her later.

I grabbed the notebook from under my pillow and placed it in my oversized purse. I'd wait until they left before heading over to Kyle's house. We had some things to discuss and if I know him and I think I do; he'll be all-in on this game.

Fourteen

Laura

The floorboard creaked under my weight as I made my way down the hall. Rachel had just dropped me off at Mrs. Appleton's two hours ago, but the plans had changed, and Mrs. Appleton came home early and said that she needed to reschedule her appointment. Instead of going home where my mom was probably either still in bed hungover or starting her daily dosage of alcohol, I started walking toward Rachel's house.

When I reached the bedroom door, I stopped, listening as I placed my hand on the knob. I turned it and slowly pushed it open. She wasn't in her room, but a car was out in the driveway.

"Rachel," I whispered. "Are you in here?"

"Laura, is that you?" Rachel said from the other side of the bed where she was hiding.

"Yes, it's me."

"You scared the living shit out of me," Rachel swore as she stood.

"I'm sorry, I didn't mean to," I replied and walked to her bed. I watched as Rachel regained her composure. She looked frightened, and I was sorry for scaring her as I did.

"Is everything okay?"

"Yes. I mean no. Scarlet and I had a fight, and I told her in not so many words to go screw herself."

I laughed out loud. Then Rachel began to laugh too. We both chuckled for a few seconds longer before we looked at each other and smiled. It didn't take long for us to get back into our groove of being friends again. It almost felt as if we were never apart all those years. I wished that were true, but there was no reason to remanence over the lost time together, and we should just start over.

"Scarlet can get mean, and if you've heard the phrase, Payback is a Bitch, that's what Scarlet does to people who stab her in the back. Actually, I think she invented the phrase."

Rachel sat down on the bed and stretched out, placing her back against the pillows. She stared up at the ceiling, then as if she got an idea, she quickly sat up and asked, "What are you doing here, anyway? Don't you have to babysit? Is everything okay? Did your mom do something?"

"Mrs. Appleton's appointment got moved, and I didn't want to go home, so here I am. Is it okay that I came here? I probably should have phoned you first."

Rachel laughed. "No, it's fine. Instead of doing homework, do you want to go to the mall? I just don't want to sit here in this house all day."

"Sure, sounds good," I replied.

✢ ✢ ✢

Forty-five minutes later, Rachel parked the car, and we both climbed out at the same time. We walked around for a while and then went to the food court to get something to eat. As we rounded the corner, Scarlet and Kyle were sitting together. Their heads only centimeters apart, and they looked like they were on the verge of making out right here where everyone could see them. I had no idea they'd be here. Damn' it, I couldn't get away from this bitch. I elbowed Rachel, who seemed distracted by some guys playing around on the other side of the food court.

She turned to me. "What was that for?"

I nudged my head in the direction where Scarlet and Kyle were sitting, Rachel stiffened. "Oh shit. What are they doing here?"

"Do you want to go somewhere else?"

Rachel shook her head. "No, this place is big enough for all of us. We can sit somewhere else."

I nodded and looked around the overcrowded room of people. Had everyone spent the day at the mall? The temperature in the room rose as we stood there searching for a seat. There were no other empty seats but a few by Scarlet.

"Let's just go somewhere else to eat. I don't want to sit by them. Scarlet will probably start shit, and we'll get thrown out of here," I said.

Rachel agreed, but before we could leave, Scarlet's annoying voice rang above everyone else's.

"Rachel. Laura. Come here," Scarlet called out as she waved us over.

We both looked at one another and decided without words we'd just see what she wanted and then leave. I followed Rachel as she led the way to their table.

"Hey," Scarlet sang. "It's weird seeing you guys here. You must have been thinking the same thing we were."

"Yeah," Rachel replied. "We must have."

"Sit down and join us," Scarlet said. "Kyle and I were just talking about the two of you and about wanting to get to know Laura better."

Rachel and I looked at each other, knowing Scarlet was up to something. I was sure she was telling the truth about talking about Rachel and me. But not in a good way. This wasn't a good idea at all. We should just leave, but I pulled out a chair and sat next to Kyle, which felt awkward as hell. Two days ago, Kyle had rammed into me and called me a *dweeb*. Now we were sitting next to each other, and he was smiling at me. Gross.

Something wasn't right about this picture, and I told myself not to get sucked into their little charades they had something up their sleeves. I just didn't know what it was.

"What do you want, Scarlet?" Rachel asked.

"Me?" Scarlet replied.

She was acting as if nothing had happened between them earlier, or did Rachel make the whole story up? Was Rachel really my friend or was she in cahoots with Scarlet? I wanted nothing more than to trust her, but could I?

"Look, I know I said some mean things earlier and considered you a back-stabbing traitor, but after talking with Kyle, he said I should give you another chance and to get to know Laura better. I forgive you," Scarlet said, smiling her pearly white teeth at us.

"You do?" Rachel questioned. "Just like that as if I had done nothing at all?"

Rachel's stare was unfocused and then her eyes narrowed in on Scarlet. Either she was a good actor and was playing along, or she really didn't know what Scarlet and Kyle were up to.

"Of course, I do. You're my best friend in the whole wide world. Just because we have a small fight doesn't mean we're not friends anymore, right?"

Scarlet reminded me of spider hatchlings consuming their mothers. She was waiting for the right moment and would devour her enemy.

As I sat, listening to the two of them talk, a hand touched my leg. I jumped, making the chair scrape against the floor as I flew back in my seat away from the table. People that were talking around us seemed to stop what they were doing and stared at me. I hated it when people gawked at me. I didn't like the attention. Rachel reached out and touched my arm.

"Are you okay, Laura?"

It took a while before her words sunk in. "What, yes. Everything's fine," I replied, looking over the table at Kyle, who was smiling in my direction again. Why would he touch me? We had never acknowledged one another before, at least not in this way. His smile gave me the creeps and part of me wondered if he was being sincere. But I doubted it. This had to be part of the game Scarlet was playing. Because there was no way Kyle was into me. I looked over at Scarlet, she seemed oblivious to everything around her, including what Kyle had just done?

FIFTEEN
RACHEL

I couldn't tell if Scarlet was being my friend or if she was out for revenge? She seemed to be okay with me and Laura together. She didn't blow a gasket seeing me with Laura after our fight earlier. She may be fine with us all being friends. This could be a good thing.

"Rachel," Scarlet said. "What do you guys have planned for today? You want to hang out with us and walk around?"

I looked over at Laura to see what she thought of this invitation. She looked at me; her face pale as if she were about to pass out. I touched her arm, and she pulled away. "You okay?" I mouthed.

"Yeah, fine," Laura whispered.

I didn't believe her. Something was wrong, and I needed to find out what it was. "Can you excuse us for a minute?" I said as I stood and led Laura away from the table. We walked toward the corner of the food court.

"Is everything okay?" I asked.

"Yeah, it's just that…" she paused. "We were sitting there, and Kyle touched my knee with his hand. Why would he do that?"

I pondered her question over in my head. Though I've known Kyle to flirt around, but not in front of Scarlet? I didn't think he'd have the balls to do such a thing.

"Maybe it was an accident? Maybe his hand slipped," I replied, hoping that I was right, but knew in the back of my mind that Laura wouldn't lie about something like this. "Okay, let's say he touched you on purpose. Why do you think he'd do something like that?" Right after I said the words, the answer came to me. Would Scarlet tell him to make a move on Laura to see what she'd do? If so, then her mind was more screwed up than I thought, having her boyfriend do that.

"You know, let's just forget what happened. I don't want to ruin our day. You're probably right and it was an accident," Laura said. "Kyle's hand just slipped."

She was just saying that, but what could we do about it? "Do you want to hang out with them or go our separate ways? I'll do whatever feels comfortable to you."

"It's fine. I can tell you want to hang with Scarlet. I mean, she's your best friend and all," Laura pointed out.

Whether she meant to her words stung, but I could tell she wanted it to be just us. "All right, we'll get some food and walk around with them for a little while. Since we drove separately, we have an excuse to leave whenever you want to. Does this sound good to you?"

Laura nodded. "Sounds great!" she said a little too cheerful.

I wanted to know Laura better. Not the way she used to be when we were kids, I wanted to know the older Laura. To help get her out of that house, but I didn't have any idea how to do that. Especially since Laura wouldn't let me help her. I understood that she didn't want to be in foster care. Who would? Her birthday was six months away. March was too far away to do anything now, but if her mother hit her again, I couldn't promise that I wouldn't say anything. That I wouldn't go to my mom for help.

We ordered some food and sat back down at the table with Scarlet and Kyle. I had never seen them so romantic with one another before, and it looked good on her. My mind repeated what Laura said about Kyle putting his hand on her knee and knew that he hadn't meant to touch her.

⊹ ⊹ ⊹

Two hours later, we were back in my car and driving home.

"Do you want me to drop you off at home?" I could tell she was debating whether to answer.

"I guess my house," she replied. "I'm sure my mom is wondering where I'm at and I don't want to cause her any more grief."

I nodded. "Okay, your house it is."

I waited until Laura was inside her house before I drove away. As if expecting something to happen, I waited for Laura to come running out of the house and back into my car. But she didn't, so I drove away and headed toward my house.

We all sat around the dinner table eating the pork chops that I had cooked after returning home. I looked around the table at my parents and my two brothers. We were, mostly a happy family. We did things together like board games and went to my brothers' soccer games. We were a family that stuck together and helped one another when we needed to, so why couldn't we help Laura? I couldn't answer that question. Not right now. What I needed and wanted to know was if Scarlet was up to something?

After I cleaned up the dinner plates, I went to my bedroom and finished the homework I didn't do earlier. My phone buzzed; it was Scarlet. Every night we made sure that we texted each other. But she wasn't texting; she was calling me. This was my chance to find out what her intentions were. I answered, putting her on speaker.

"Hey, what are you up to?" Scarlet asked.

"Just finishing up my homework. You?"

"Same. I wanted to let you know that I thought it was cool hanging out with Laura today. We should do it more often. Maybe even have a sleepover."

"Are you serious or up to something?"

"Why would I say it if I didn't mean it?"

She had a point. Scarlet always spoke her mind. If she were lying, I'd know; wouldn't I? She always bit the inside of her lip when she was lying, but I couldn't see her to know. I could only hear her.

"I'll ask Laura and see what she says. When do you want to do this?"

"Next Friday at Kyle's bonfire party. We should go together and then sleepover at my place," Scarlet said.

I replied, "Okay," before my brain had time to reject the idea. "I'll talk to Laura and see if she can sleepover."

"Awesome! This will be so much fun!" Scarlet squealed into the phone, her voice ricocheting off my walls. "I can't wait to tell Kyle. We will set her up with one of his friends from the football team."

My mouth dropped open. Was she being serious? Laura wasn't interested in dating someone. Though I didn't know if that was true. "Who do you have in mind?" I asked, needing to find out all the information that I could.

"JJ."

"James Larose?" Everyone called him JJ because his middle name was Jacob.

"Yeah, isn't he a hotty? I think those two will make a cute couple."

JJ didn't do relationships. He hated them with a passion. "I didn't think JJ did couples. Ya' know, he likes to play the field?" I stated. Or was it the fact he didn't do commitments?

"Well, he hasn't dated Laura yet, besides she'll be totally into him. He's a football player."

"And what makes you think she likes football players?"

"Who doesn't?" Scarlet replied. "I've seen JJ without his shirt on. He's got chiseled abs that will melt your heart."

I wasn't so sure that this was a good idea, but I would not let Laura be surprised by this. She needed to know what could happen at this party. Good or bad, I would not let Laura fall into a trap.

Sixteen

Scarlet

When Rachel and Laura showed up together at the mall. It was as if a knife had punctured my heart. It hurt my feelings she had traded me in so fast. My best friend Rachel was slipping away from me, and I had to get her back before that bitch Laura took her away for good.

I have worked hard to be who I am, and I would not let Laura take it all away from me. Rachel was my best friend, and I'll do whatever it takes to get her back.

Thanks to Kyle's help, we came up with a plan to get even with Laura. All he had to do was get JJ to play along, which shouldn't be hard. Kyle said he had things he could use against JJ. He could blackmail him if he had to, to get him to do this for us.

Once I got off the phone with Rachel about getting together next Friday with Laura, my plan was in motion. I just needed to make sure that Laura would be there for this to work. She will be so distraught and humiliated she won't want to come back to school ever again. That's just fine with me.

✢ ✢ ✢

Sunday flew by and Monday arrived with blue skies and a bright ray of a yellowish-orange sun set high in the sky. I loved the feel of vitamin D on my skin and was thankful that summer was trying to stay longer.

I had an idea and texted Rachel that I would pick her up and then we'd swing by and get Laura on our way to school. I told her to text Laura because I didn't have her number, but that would change by the end of the day.

The door opened, and Rachel came out, but she didn't stop to close the door behind her. That's when Laura walked out after her.

"What the hell?" I muttered. Laura had once again slept over at Rachel's house, and she didn't even tell me when I texted her this morning? What was going on between them? Why was Laura living here and not at her own house?

My eyes scanned over the outfit Laura was wearing. Something I had never seen her in, but I had recognized as Rachel's clothes. Laura dressed in a pair of torn jeans and a turtleneck sweater that was much too warm for this weather we were having today.

Now she was wearing my best friend's clothes and staying at her house every night? I needed to find out what the hell was going on between them. But what infuriated me the most was the fact that my so-called best friend in the world didn't have the decency to fill me in. I had to wait and talk to Rachel when Laura wasn't around.

When Laura opened the passenger side door, I blurted out, "What's with the turtleneck?"

"Leave her alone," Rachel hissed. "Why do you have to criticize everything?"

"Sorry, I didn't mean to offend you." Rachel mumbled something under her breath, but I wasn't sure if I had heard her right, but it sounded like, "whatever".

Laura climbed into the backseat and I drove off down the road.

"Good morning," I said over my shoulder to Laura.

"Good morning," Laura replied, looking out the window.

She wouldn't even look at me. Maybe it will be harder to get her to think she's my friend. Or she heard what I said to Rachel, and she's pissed at me?

I'll just have to splash on some Scarlet charm and persuade her to trust me. Thinking this would be easy? If it were, I would have had her eating out of the palm of my hand years ago.

I parked the car, and we all got out, making our way inside the school. Classmates were looking our way, and I raised my head higher, pasting a smile on my face. I needed everyone to believe Laura was one of us until I was ready to snap her into pieces.

"Hey, babe," Kyle said.

I stopped beside him and leaned against the locker. "Hey, handsome," I said, leaning in and kissing him.

"Did you talk to JJ?"

Kyle nodded. "He's in."

I smiled and replied, "Great! When do you want to do this? Today or wait until the party on Friday?"

"Let's wait until the party so everyone can see them making out. He'll have no problems getting her into bed and taking naked pictures of her."

I nodded, kissing him before I left. I headed to my locker before class. This would be the best hate plan I have ever pulled off. Laura wouldn't know what hit her until I'm done with her. That bitch will have to kill herself to get away from me.

At lunch, I had Rachel ask Laura to sit with us, so we could discuss the upcoming weekend.

"Will you be able to sleep at my house on Friday?" I asked Laura.

She looked at Rachel before she answered my question.

"I'll try. My mom doesn't like me staying at other people's houses."

I wanted to shout at her and say she was a liar because I had seen her at Rachel's house these past few days. She was full of shit. I had to give her some credit for lying straight to my face. I looked over at Rachel to confirm the lie, but she had her head down so I couldn't see her face.

"Well, let me know so I can plan and have my stepmother get some food and drinks for us. She loves doing those things for me," I lied. "We'll get ready at my place and head to the party, then come back and have our own party at my house."

"Who's all going to be there?" Laura asked.

"Everyone here most likely. Definitely all the popular kids from school." This was my queue to find out who she liked. "Is there anyone from school you have a crush on?" I smiled at her.

Laura turned three shades of red before she looked away from me. "Nope, no one," Laura replied.

"So, what time should we be at your place on Friday?" Rachel asked, changing the subject.

"We can go to my place right after we get out of school on Friday."

"I don't want to bring my things to school. Can we stop by my place and grab them?" Rachel asked.

"Yes. What about you, Laura? Should we stop by your place and get your things?"

She shook her head. "No, I'll bring mine to school with me."

"Okay, then. Sounds like we have a plan. I can't wait for Friday to get here," I announced. Laura was falling right into my trap.

Seventeen
Laura

I couldn't tell if Scarlet was genuine. Did she really want to be my friend? I hoped so, but again, I needed to be cautious around her. I wasn't sure if she meant the things she was saying, or I was just another one of her puppets she could experiment with and make me do anything she wanted.

There was no way I would tell her I crushed on Travis Evans. I was sure she would tell everyone, and they would all laugh at me. Travis was way too popular to like someone plain like me. He was just a private dream of mine; besides once school was over; I wouldn't be staying here in this crappy town, anyway. I plan on leaving and will never look back at the people here.

"Hey, you okay?" Rachel asked as we walked down the hall toward our next class together. A class we had without Scarlet.

"I'm fine," I replied. "Just nervous about sleeping over at Scarlet's and going to the party."

"There's nothing to fear."

"I didn't say it scared me. I said I was nervous. Big difference," I snapped without meaning to, but I couldn't take it back. I enjoyed hanging out with Rachel. I didn't need to ruin whatever friendship we were having because I was panicking and stressed with things going on in my life.

"Sorry to misinterpret the meaning you were trying to portray. Just trying to be your friend, geez Louise."

"Are you my friend?" I stopped where I was and looked into her eyes.

"Yes, of course, I'm your friend. Why wouldn't I be?"

I started to open my mouth to bring up the past but decided this wasn't the time or place to discuss the long-ago friendship that we had before Scarlet took it all away. Rachel must have been thinking the same thing.

"Look, about what happened at the start of high school."

"Jr. High," I corrected.

"Okay, Jr. High. I'm sorry for how I treated you back then. I want us to start over. I want to be your friend, Laura. But you need to let me in."

She seemed sincere, and I wanted so much to believe her and forget it had ever happened, but it was hard to let go of the pain she once caused me. The way she left me behind as if I had meant nothing to her back then. Like I was a nobody. A loser. Maybe I was just kidding myself that I belonged in their group.

"Look, can we talk about this after school? That's if you want to come over and hang with me and my family," Rachel said.

I wanted nothing more than to be a part of a family. I longed to feel like someone's daughter, but I wasn't part of the Sawyer family, but could I be? Would Rachel and her parents take me in and shower me with the love and affection that I so badly needed? What was I thinking? That would never happen. I blinked, hearing a snap.

"Hey, are you listening?" Rachel asked, snapping her fingers in front of my face. "We need to get to class. Let's talk about this later. I don't want to be late."

I nodded and started walking. We both entered the classroom just as the bell rang.

⁕ ⁕ ⁕

After school, Scarlet dropped me off across the street from my house. I told her my mom didn't like people parking in our driveway, but they weren't staying so it wouldn't have mattered, anyway. Before we left school and away from Scarlet's prying ears, Rachel said she'd pick me up when she went to get her brothers from their school, which would be around four.

I'm not surprised to see my mom's car in the driveway as she sometimes beat me home, but not always. I used the key I had tucked into my backpack, unlocked the front door, and went inside. I locked the deadbolt by habit and turned around. The room was pitch black, darker than it usually was, and there was a potent smell coming from somewhere in the house.

I strolled toward the kitchen and flicked on the light. My eyes needed to adjust before they viewed the room. Empty bottles of vodka sat on the table and counter. The garbage can overflowed with every empty bottle of liquor you could imagine. It looked like she had a party when I was away, but I've known my mother to drink this amount of booze herself over the weekend.

There was leftover food on the counter that looked hard and crusted over. Plates and cups filled the sink, something I hadn't gotten around to doing since I hadn't been home all weekend.

I hadn't been at home much since Rachel picked me up on the side of the road last week. When I did come home, my mom was in her room and I snuck in and out without her knowing, getting clothes for the next day as I stayed at Rachel's house. I had never ventured to the kitchen or scoped out the rest of the house when I came home. Because I didn't want her to know I was here.

I gathered all the bottles and took them out to the garbage can beside the house. Once I finished cleaning the kitchen, making sure that it looked pristine, I walked down the hall to my mom's bedroom.

The smell seemed to get stronger as I made my way down the hall and feared the worst. I'd taken biology and worked with dead animals, but I didn't want to believe such a thing could happen to my mom. She was all that I had left.

Since my dad and brother died, my mother became someone else. She went to work every day but once she was at home; she did nothing but drink herself to sleep.

I cooked and cleaned. I made sure she ate, but nothing I did was ever good enough in her eyes. She missed my father and brother as much as I did, but she didn't need to take her grief out on me. I didn't cause the accident. I didn't kill them. I was just her punching bag. A release from her broken heart, but I hurt too. I was broken too.

I stood in front of her closed bedroom door like I've done many times before. Afraid to see what was lingering inside. The game show I used to watch when I was younger popped in my head. Do you want door number one, two or three? This wasn't a game, but real life and I had to open the door and claim my prize.

I placed my hand on the doorknob, turned, and pushed the door open. I took several steps back as the powerful stench I had smelled the moment I arrived home hit me. I covered my mouth and ran to the bathroom down the hall. Even though I had nothing left inside me, I dry heaved for another few minutes. Every time I breathed in through my nose, I gagged because I had let the smell out of the room and now it was making its way through the house.

When I finished, I covered my nose and mouth with the sleeve of Rachel's sweater that I was wearing and went back to my mom's bedroom. I stood in the opening and flipped the light switch. The luminous light accented the room. There she was in front of me, on the bed, lying on her back. Vomit jutted from her mouth and covered her face and the sheets lying under her. Her eyes were wide open, staring up at the ceiling. I didn't have to check if she were alive; the smell of her corpse filled the entire house.

How long had she been dead? A day, maybe two? It had to be long enough for the body to start decomposing. Had she been dead when I came to get some clothes? Had I let her die? Could I have saved her?

No, of course not. I hadn't known she was in here passed out to the point she choked on her own vomit. I wasn't to blame for her death, but I needed to call the police. I couldn't stand here and not do anything. Could I?

My life hadn't been perfect by any means. I'm not sure I had a word for what my life was like, but I could guarantee you wouldn't want it, especially now. What was I thinking and why was I thinking of doing nothing? I was the victim. Her punching bag and now she was dead. Now, I was alone and had no family. I did the only thing I could do; I called Rachel.

EIGHTEEN

Rachel

I held Laura tight in my arms. I couldn't believe what had happened. The moment she called saying she needed for me to come to her house, that something terrible had happened to her mom, I ran out of the house and drove as fast as I could. When I pulled up along the curb, Laura was sitting outside on the steps in front of her house. I parked the car and ran to her. She was crying and shaking.

"What's wrong?"

"My mom, she's… she's dead," Laura sobbed.

"What? Are you sure?" It was just something everyone asked in circumstances like these. Like she'd lie about something like that. "How? What happened?"

"You guys dropped me off, and I went inside." Laura hiccupped, tears cascading down her face.

"And what? Did she hit you again?"

Laura shook her head. "She was…"

"Was what?" Laura wasn't talking fast enough. I wanted to know what had happened after we dropped her off and why she was so hysterical.

"She was already dead," Laura bawled as she buried her face in her hands.

"Dead," I whispered. This couldn't be true. I had to know for myself. I left Laura on the stoop and went into the house. The moment I opened the front door, the smell caught me off guard, making me lose my balance. I steadied myself with the wall and covered my mouth and nose. I walked through the house until I came to the room her mom slept in. There on the bed was Laura's mom. Dead was an understatement. I hurried back outside, gasping for fresh air and called the police. Part of me wondered why Laura hadn't done this after finding the body, but I didn't want to go asking questions when she was already distraught over finding her own mother like this. I couldn't imagine what I would do if I found my mother dead.

It didn't take long for the police, ambulance, and firefighters to appear at the scene. The moment they had arrived, I held Laura in my arms. A woman police officer by the name of Officer Crystal Rosmus was asking Laura questions. The same questions that I had asked except in more detail. Officer Rosmus wrote in her small notepad as Laura spoke.

I was looking Officer Rosmus up and down. Her arms were thick as if she worked out, but her body was on the doughy side. Her face was smooth and neatly covered with a layer of soft make-up. She was a pretty woman, not beautiful, but pretty.

I looked over at Laura and listened to her tell the officer she'd been staying at my house since Thursday and only came home to get some clothes. She said she hadn't looked in on her mom.

"If the bedroom door is closed, I'm not allowed in. My mom doesn't like being bothered when she's resting," Laura said. "I grabbed some things from my bedroom and left the house on Friday and Saturday, only to return today."

Then out of nowhere, the officer asked. "Where did you get that bruise on your neck?"

Laura's hand shot to her neck, pulling the fabric higher toward her face.

"Did someone hit you? Try to strangle you?"

Laura began to cry before hiding her face in the crevice of my neck. I wrapped my arms tighter around her as she let out all the tears she must have been holding onto. Probably since her dad and brother had died in that horrible car accident last year. I hadn't known she was suffering all this time. Had I been her friend, I would have known what she was feeling and going through. I could have stopped whatever was going on in her house.

"I will need you to come to the hospital. I want to have you looked at," the officer said.

Laura looked at the officer. "What difference does it make, she's dead now!? What would it matter if I have the doctors look me over? She can't hurt me anymore."

Although the words seemed to have shocked Officer Rosmus, she stood tall and only nodded. "Your mother did this to you? She abused you?" Officer Rosmus asked; then said, "You're right, but it wouldn't hurt to make sure you're okay. That you have no internal damage, but I'll leave it up to you. I can't force you to go."

"I don't want to go," Laura replied.

"Is there anything else you need from her?" I asked as my mom headed up the sidewalk toward us. I had called her after I called the police.

"No, she's free to go, but I need a phone number in case I have to reach her."

I rambled off Laura's cell number to the officer.

"We'll keep in touch," Officer Rosmus said before walking away.

"Oh, God, are you all right, Laura?" my mom asked as she came to the other side of Laura and wrapped her arm around her. "I'm so sorry for what has happened. You can stay with us until we figure out what to do."

Laura nodded. "Thank you. Thank you for caring," she said as more tears ran down her face.

"Let's go back to our house. If the police need you, they can find you there," my mom said as we all made our way down the walkway to my car.

"I'll meet you both at the house. I want to talk to whoever's in charge here."

I nodded and helped Laura into the passenger seat before getting behind the wheel. I didn't know how to help my friend get through this, except to be the friend I used to be. To hold her or talk to her when she needed me to. I hated myself in the process for ditching her all those years ago. Now, now I could make up for what I did and be here for her.

I looked over at Laura sitting beside me. She was staring out the window at her home. A house she'd no longer live in after today. I wanted to know what she was thinking and where we were going from here. Would she stay with us? She wasn't eighteen yet. Would they force her to live in a foster home, which wouldn't be here in Craven Falls? I would have to talk to my mom about these questions. She would have the answers.

"What about my things?" Laura asked.

I had parked outside her house. "I can see if they'll let me in to get what you need," I said, even though they would not let me inside. It was a crime scene filled with evidence. The evidence they needed to collect.

"Could you? I don't want to go back inside. It's too…"

Laura couldn't finish the sentence. She didn't have to. I wouldn't want to go back inside that house either, but I didn't think I had a choice.

"Let me ask the officer and see if they'll let me." I opened the car door and climbed out. I dreaded going back inside the house. The house that reeked of death.

I walked around an officer standing around on the sidewalk as I approached the front door that remained open for the world to see in. At that moment, I twirled around to get a look at all the neighbors standing outside watching as if it was a freak show. Everyone gossiping about what they thought was going on inside this house. Had they heard the officers talking near the street and put the pieces of the puzzle together? Because I was sure if anyone had known what was going on inside this house, someone would have called the police and gotten Laura the help she needed. No one, not even I had known what went on behind these closed doors.

My mind flashed back to last week when Scarlet and I came over. The house was dark from the blinds pulled down. There were no bottles of booze laying around the house last week or today. They or someone had cleaned the place. No odor in the air like I smelled today, but I had seen Laura's mom that day. She seemed older but fine. It's funny how some people can be someone else in front of others, but a monster when no one else was around. Once again, saddened by the situation at hand. Sad for Laura.

As I made my way toward the house, a man in uniform and pale skin reached his hand out and grabbed my arm. Not hastily, but to stop me from entering the house.

"Sorry, I can't let you go in there," the male officer said. "It's a crime scene, and we need to collect all the evidence before any civilians can go in."

I liked how he said the word civilians like I was some kind of alien. "I just need to get my friend who lives here some clothes and personal items." I looked at his name tag. "Officer Swig," I said.

"Sorry, you can't go inside. Your friend will have to wait until our investigation is over."

"And when will that be?" I asked.

"Excuse me, what is going on here?" my mom asked, looking down at the officer's hand on my arm.

He must have seen where her eyes went because he let go of my arm and stood tall.

"She wanted to go inside for some things for her friend. I told her she couldn't go inside. It's a crime scene," Officer Swig replied, rattled.

"Rachel, is this true?"

I nodded. "Laura asked if I could get some of her things."

"Oh, well, she must wait. If she needs anything, we'll buy it for her, or she can borrow your things. They'll be done here in a day or two, then she can come and get whatever she needs."

I nodded again and headed back toward my car. My mom was right. I had listened to too many of my parents' talks around the dinner table about crime scenes and laws. I wasn't sure what I was thinking but then again; I did. All I wanted to do was to help my friend who was mourning the loss of her mother.

NINETEEN

SCARLET

After I had dropped off Rachel, I circled back around and parked down the street from Laura's house. I wanted to see if I could find out anything to use against her. Something that I could hold on to until I needed it.

I wasn't there long before Laura came outside and sat down on the steps. It looked like she was crying. Had something happened inside the house with her mom? Maybe they had a fight because the same car was in the driveway from last week.

Minutes had ticked by. Laura hadn't moved from her spot on the steps nor had anyone come out of the house. A familiar car passed me and parked at the curb. Rachel swung the driver's side door open, slammed it, and hurried up the walk to where Laura was sitting. I was glad that I had parked further down the street and between two other cars. I just prayed they wouldn't spot my red BMW parked here. It hadn't crossed my mind until now that my car stuck out like a sore thumb in this neighborhood.

Rachel sat next to Laura, putting her arm around her. What was going on between them? How had they become so close in the past few days? They were friends long ago, but they had just started talking recently or at least I think they had. I would have known if they were friends behind my back before I initiated the plan of attack, wouldn't I?

Rachel wasn't that good at hiding things from me. From anyone. Something must have happened right after we dropped Laura off for Rachel to come over and comfort her.

Hiding behind my over-sized sunglasses, looking like a movie star, I watched from my car as Rachel stood and glanced around the yard. I slouched in my seat, hoping she hadn't seen me. I waited and then slowly peeked out the windshield and saw Rachel go inside the house. Seconds later, she came running back out gasping for air, then took out her cell phone.

Minutes later, sirens blared in the distance and then appeared louder as they arrived and stopped outside Laura's house.

"What the hell is going on?" I looked around and saw that they trapped me when the police cars, ambulance, and a fire truck showed up at the scene. I had nowhere to go. So, I sat and watched not that I could see the entire house from where I sat.

It was going on four when the EMTs wheeled out a body bag. I could only assume it was Laura's mom because her dad and brother were deceased. There was no one left living inside that house.

Part of me was sad for her. To have no family left. I, too, had lost my mom a year ago. My dad said it happened fast, and that she hadn't known what hit her when the aneurysm burst. I was on my way to school when it happened.

The ambulance drove away, leaving Rachel and Laura talking to a female police officer. Then Rachel's mom showed up and wrapped her arm around Laura too, hugging her in close. My face grew hot with rage. Rachel's mother had never embraced me in that way. In fact, I don't think she really liked me at all, which made me even more infuriated.

I looked around and saw that I could back out of my spot and head in the other direction, away from the scene, before they saw me. I could pretend that I was in the area and saw all the commotion and wanted to make sure that everything was okay, but there was no reason for me to be here. Not in this part of town.

When I arrived home, I went straight to the kitchen to get something to drink. Lianne was sitting outside on the patio, sipping a cup of coffee. Was that all she did during the day, sit around and drink coffee?

My mind flicked back to Rachel's mom hugging Laura, and I wondered if Lianne and I would ever have that kind of relationship. I didn't see how that could be possible since we're always putting each other down. I don't think we've ever said a kind word to one another since she's lived here.

I had never thought about this before, but now I was thinking about when my father met Lianne. It wasn't long after my mother had passed that my father had brought her around. Had he? No, he wouldn't have done that to my mother. He wouldn't have cheated on her, would he? Now that I think about it, he worked long hours, coming home late. Long after I went to bed. I don't recall them ever fighting unless they did it after I left for school.

I didn't feel like getting into an argument with Lianne, but I needed to know if it was true. Were they a couple before my mom's death? It plagued me. Enraged me to the point I stormed outside and confronted her. "Were you and my father sleeping together when my mom was still alive?"

"What? Why would you ask me such a thing?"

"Because you came into this house, not even a month after my mom died. No one finds someone that fast and moves them into the house."

"I'm afraid you have it all wrong, Scarlet. Your father and I met at a banquet that was being held in Cleveland. We started talking and one thing led to another. He asked me to move in because I had just lost my house to my ex-husband."

"You were married before you met my father?"

"Yes, for eight years, then my ex wanted a divorce and took the house. He ended up with over half of what we owned together. I didn't want any of them except for the gifts that my parents had given me. I let him keep it all," Lianne replied.

I sat in the chair across from her and looked into her eyes. I hadn't known this about her, but did it matter? It didn't open the door for us to become mother and daughter of the year. What if we did? What if I allowed her to know me and we became close? I shook my head. Who was I kidding? And how did I know she was telling the truth?

"I can tell you think I'm full of shit. That I made up the story of my ex, and that your father and I were lovers long before your mom passed away."

How did she know what I was thinking?

"Come on, Scarlet, let's not play this game of truth-or-dare with one another. Neither one of us likes each other nor do I ever plan on being a mother figure to you. Maybe your friends are blind, but what I see is a two-faced bullying bitch," Lianne said as she leaned forward in her chair and stared me in the face. She whispered, "You may have your father fooled by thinking you're sweet and innocent, but you don't fool me."

I sucked in a breath and stood. "Fuck you!" I yelled.

"Scarlet Marie!"

I whipped around and saw my father standing in the doorway. Shit!

"Don't you talk to Lianne that way. She is your stepmother and deserves respect. If I catch you saying anything mean and disrespectful again, I will ship you off to boarding school for the rest of the school year. Do I make myself clear?"

"Yes, Daddy. I'm sorry," I replied. My father would have never sent me away to boarding school if my mother was alive. He wouldn't have even spoken the words, which told me that Lianne was responsible. Well, two could play this game.

"Apologize to Lianne at once."

Over my dead body. Just because I say I'm sorry, doesn't mean I have to mean it. I was good at pretending and lying around other people, so what would it matter if I did it with her too? "I'm sorry, Lianne."

"Turn around and say it to her face, Scarlet Marie. I raised you better than that."

"You didn't raise me, Mom did," I muttered. My father's face crumbled, and wetness formed in his eyes. I hurt him. "Daddy, I didn't mean it," I replied, running to him.

"Go to your room, Scarlet Marie," my father hissed as he turned and stormed away from me, rejecting my apology.

"See what you did. I don't care if you talk to me that way, but he's your father, your flesh and blood," Lianne said as she pushed past me to comfort him.

I stood there outside alone. The sky grew dark, and the clouds opened, letting droplets of rain come pouring down on me. I didn't run for cover like I normally would. Afraid the rain would ruin my hair and clothes. I never meant to hurt my father like I did, and it tore at my heart.

I replayed the moment before I told Lianne to screw herself. Her eyes left my face and looked to the side of me. She knew that he was standing there. She knew she could get me to call her names so that my father would hear me. She set me up.

"That bitch," I mumbled. With Lianne in this house, I have no say. I won't win against her. She had to go. I had to get her out of this house before she got rid of me first.

TWENTY

LAURA

Although I loved that Rachel and her family were being kind and were comforting me for losing my mom, I just wanted to be alone. I wanted to go for a walk by myself and mourn alone. Even after everything she did to me when she got too drunk, she was still my mom. Would always be my mom. I've heard the saying "Always love your mother because you never get another."

She was all that I had left of my family. My father was the saint of all saints. It wasn't until recently that I realized my mom may have been suffering way before they died. The days and weeks she laid in bed not wanting to get up, my dad and I would leave her at home. He would take me fishing or to the store; anything to get us out of the house. Then she became pregnant with my brother, Teddy, and she wasn't sad anymore. At least not until after he was born.

I think deep down she hated me because I was my dad's favorite. Sometimes she wasn't sick, and we all did things together, but I don't have many memories of her laughing and having fun with us. They would fight about her depression, but she wouldn't get help or go see a doctor.

"Are you coming to dinner?" Rachel asked.

"No," I said, even though I was hungry. I shouldn't be able to eat after finding my mother dead. And the worst part was, she'd been dead for at least two, maybe three days. When I left my house in the middle of the night on Friday and came to Rachel's was the last time I had seen her alive. The last time she'd laid a hand on me.

If I had been there could I have saved her? Would I have heard her choking and run to her room and turned her onto her side? I couldn't answer those questions because I wasn't there. A part of me wondered if I would have saved her. This was someone who should love me and protect me, but she only hurt and abused me. Would I have let her die? I can't answer that either. Besides it doesn't matter anyway, she's gone now. She's dead and there's nothing I can do to bring her back. Nothing I can change. I think she's the lucky one. She's with Dad and Teddy now, and I'm stuck here in this shitty ass world.

✝ ✝ ✝

As I lay on the bed in the guest room, I wondered if this was what my mom felt like every single day. The loneliness of not having someone beside you to love, even though she had me. I would have loved her back.

Someone knocked on my door and then the squeak of the door opening. Rachel poked her head in. "Can I sleep with you?"

I was the one whose mother had died, and yet, she wanted to sleep in my bed and not the other way around?

"Sure, I guess."

"Are you okay, Laura? Do you need to talk about anything?"

I go to shake my head but stopped myself because I wanted to talk about what I was feeling inside. It was just that I wasn't used to people asking me if I was all right. No one ever talked to me or cared about how I was doing.

"I don't know how I'm supposed to feel about her death," I said.

She nodded and pulled me into her, comforting me. Consoling me.

"Thanks for being my friend." I hadn't realized how much I missed Rachel until now. I wished at that moment I could rewind the past and we had stayed friends.

She squeezed my arm under the blanket. "I'm sorry for everything. I'm sorry I stopped being your friend back then. Will you forgive me, Laura?"

I had forgiven her the moment she started talking to me last week.

"Yes." Was all I could say. Feeling safe with her beside me and was glad she was here.

Twenty-One

Rachel

I forgot that Scarlet was picking me up in the morning and knew she'd have a cow about Laura staying at my house, but I didn't care anymore what she thought. She'd have to get over it. Laura was my friend, and I would always be there for her.

"Hey," I said after I climbed into the front seat of Scarlet's BMW. "Good morning."

"Morning to the both of you, too," Scarlet replied cheerfully.

I could tell she wasn't happy with Laura being with me. Only pretending to like her around me. "So, last night something bad happened, and Laura will be staying at my house until my mom finds a relative that she can live with."

"What do you mean live with? What's wrong with her mom?"

I swallowed. "She, ah, died yesterday."

"Oh my God! What happened?" Scarlet shrieked, whipping her head toward me.

I would not tell her how she died because really it wasn't her or anyone else's business.

"They're not sure yet. I guess they need to do an autopsy or something like that to find out the cause of death."

Scarlet turned and looked at Laura, who was sitting in the backseat. "I'm so sorry, Laura," she said, which sounded genuine and sincere.

"Thank you," Laura replied.

"Are you sure you want to go back to school today? I mean your mom just, you know."

"Ya', but I don't want to sit at ho… at Rachel's house," Laura corrected.

"I get that, but won't it be hard to concentrate? Thinking of your dead mom and all."

"Scarlet! Why would you say that?" I yelled. "You honestly can't find one nice word to say to someone who has just lost their mother? Unbelievable! Do you ever stop and think about what other people are going through before you speak? How would you feel if it was your mom?"

"My mom did die, you bitch!" Scarlet screamed at me.

"Then you should know exactly what it feels like and show some compassion," I said and opened my door to get out. We hadn't driven away from my house since Laura and I got into the car. "Come on, Laura, we'll find another way to school."

I slammed the car door and walked toward the house. I was glad that my mother hadn't left for work yet. When I reached the front door, I looked over my shoulder and saw Laura still sitting in the backseat of Scarlet's car. She was saying something to her, but I couldn't hear what was being said with the doors and windows closed. I hoped that she was laying into her. Scarlet deserved punishment for what she said.

I hollered, "Laura, are you coming?"

The back door opened, and she climbed out, then Scarlet drove away. I waited until she was close enough before asking. "What did you say to her?"

"I told her she couldn't help being the person she is. That if she couldn't find it in her to say one nice thing to anyone that she would get what's coming to her."

"Good for you," I cheered. I opened the front door and called out to my mom. "Mom, we need a ride to school."

As my mom drove, she explained to Laura that she would file for non-parent custody. "Do you have any family in the area?"

Laura shrugged her shoulders. "I'm not sure. We never really went to see anyone."

"No Grandparents, Aunts or Uncles?" my mom asked.

Laura shook her head. "Not that I'm aware of."

"All right, I'll do some digging and see if I can find anyone. Are you sure you're ready to go to school today? You could stay at home. No one expects you to go after what happened yesterday."

"I know, but I don't want to stay at the house. It's better if I keep my mind busy."

"All right, then. If you need anything, just have the office call me and I can move some things around and come get you."

"Thanks, but I'm good," Laura replied.

⁜ ⁜ ⁜

I didn't have every class with Laura, but when I did, I asked how she was doing.

"I'm good."

"Okay," I replied, not wanting to force her into talking.

When lunchtime came, we met up and walked into the cafeteria together. Scarlet was sitting in our usual seats. "Do you want to sit with her? We don't have to. She was a bitch to you this morning."

"It's fine. Scarlet can't help who she is. Besides, isn't she always a bitch?"

I laughed at her words. "Yes, she is."

We made our way over to where Scarlet was sitting and sat down. Neither one of us said anything to her. We just started eating our lunch.

"So, do you still want to come to Kyle's party on Friday?" Scarlet asked.

I looked over at Laura. She seemed to ponder over the question Scarlet had asked.

"Sure, we'll be there," Laura said.

"You guys are staying at my place, right? Just like we planned?" Scarlet asked.

Laura and I looked at one another. I had forgotten to ask her after everything that had happened. Laura shrugged her shoulders, showing that she didn't care. "I guess we are," I replied.

"Great!" Scarlet squealed in excitement. "We will have a blast!"

Scarlet started rambling about what outfit she would wear. "You will look so hot in the dress I have picked out for you."

Laura smiled. "If it makes you happy, Scarlet. But I'd rather just wear jeans and a sweatshirt."

"Fine, if you don't want to wear the dress; then we'll find something else in my closet you might like."

"Okay," Laura agreed without looking at Scarlet.

Twenty-Two

Scarlet

I didn't like that Rachel was pulling away from me. Ever since I suggested playing a game on Laura, Rachel had become friends with her instead. She was telling me I was rude and should be kinder to people. Maybe Rachel will get what's coming to her too.

I met up with Kyle after school and we went over our plan of deception. "Do you think you can get JJ to do this?" I asked.

"I already talked to him and he's willing. Said he owed me a favor anyway," Kyle smiled. "I've done some things for that guy, so we're cool. Besides, he said he's been wanting to see how Laura was in bed, anyway. You know, another piece of ass to scratch off his list."

Oh, okay. That piece of information wasn't necessary. I leaned over and kissed him on the lips and then moved down to his neck. "This will be the best joke I have ever played," I whispered as I made my way down his chest.

"Hey, did you hear what happened to her mom?" Kyle asked. "They found her dead in her home yesterday."

"Yeah, I know." Not wanting to talk about Laura anymore.

"How did you find out? It wasn't in the papers or anything?" Kyle questioned.

I pulled away and looked at him. I loved Kyle, but it was hard for me to trust him with all my secrets. Leaving his question unanswered, I turned the question back at him. He may be a football player, but his brain was as dumb as a sloth on speed. "How did you find out?"

"My dad was talking on the phone about it to someone."

"Did he mention what happened?"

Kyle repeated everything that his father had said. "Can you imagine? My dad also said that she was there for a couple of days."

"So, she died like on Friday or Saturday?" I remember Laura coming over to Rachel's house late at night on Friday and then they were together on Saturday when they were at the mall.

"I guess so," Kyle replied, pulling me close to him and kissing my lips. "Let's forget about her right now and have some fun of our own."

"Okay," I whispered, pulling him on top of me in the backseat of his jeep. Although my mind was wondering if Laura had killed her own mother.

⁕ ⁕ ⁕

When I arrived home later that evening, I walked into the kitchen but froze. Lianne was standing outside on the patio again. I wasn't in the mood to get into it with her like the other day, so I turned and climbed the stairs to the second floor.

"Scarlet, is that you?" Lianne hollered.

Did she have a nose like a hound dog or something? I stopped in my tracks, wondering if I should respond or just go to my room. I continued to my room and closed the door behind me, locking it. This time I wasn't taking any chances of her coming into my room when I was in the shower. I wouldn't put it past her to snoop through my things. Though she had all day to do it if she wanted to.

I went into the bathroom and closed the door, turning on the shower. Steam instantly filled the room. Lianne knocked on my bedroom door, but I ignored her as if I was already in the shower.

Fifteen minutes later, I dried off and slipped into my silk PJs and climbed onto my bed with my phone. I missed talking and texting with Rachel like we had done all these years. Now that Laura was staying at her place, she probably was too busy to want to chat with me, but I sent her a text anyway.

Me: **What are you doing?**

Rachel: **Just working on my homework. You?**

Me: **Just sitting in my room**.

Rachel: **Cool.**

Cool, that's her reply? Should I ask how Laura's doing? Not that I cared, but I didn't want to get off the phone with her.

Me: **How's Laura?**

Seconds pass and there's no answer.

Rachel: **Fine.**

Me: **Okay, let her know that I'm sorry for earlier. I should've been nicer and more considerate of her feelings.**

Rachel: **Okay.**

I could tell that was the end of our conversation, which meant Rachel didn't forgive me for what I'd said to Laura this morning.

Twenty-Three

Laura

I had thought it was a good idea to go to school, hoping it would keep my mind occupied with homework and not the images that crowded in my head since I found my mom the way I did.

After Monday had passed, Wednesday arrived, and Rachel's parents were driving me to the cemetery for my mom's funeral. I had told them I didn't want a service for her because there wouldn't be anyone coming.

Rachel's mom had found out that my parents had already paid for their plots in Craven Falls Cemetery. We will bury her next to my dad. My brother was on the other side of him, and the spot next to Teddy would be for me when my time came, which couldn't be soon enough.

I borrowed a black dress from Rachel because they still wouldn't let me go into my house to get my things. Rachel said she'd go with me when the time came. Part of me never wanted to go back into that house, but technically, it was mine now. Apparently, my parents also had a Will drawn up, leaving me to be the sole executor of our tiny estate. It wasn't like Teddy would fight me for it.

They set the funeral for ten and with only the six of us going it was over within twenty minutes. That's if you counted the time it took us to walk to the casket propped above the hole in the ground, which they no longer do.

I cried for her. This was my mother who gave birth to me. She married my dad. She had my brother Teddy and to finish it off, she physically abused me. I shouldn't be crying. I should be setting her coffin on fire or spitting on it. But those were only my thoughts, hidden away inside my head. Not for the world to know.

Rachel's mom planned a Brunch after the small service. I was starving when I should feel too sick to eat. I should grieve her loss but was smiling and laughing. Something I didn't do often.

Rachel stood by me and sat by me, holding my hand when I needed it. It felt good to have her back as my friend; something I had longed for, for so long. Being with her family has made me realize what I have been missing. It felt good to be a part of something, even if it wouldn't last forever.

✷ ✷ ✷

Friday arrived, and I was excited to go to Kyle's party. Rachel and I had done nothing but talk about it nonstop since after my mom's funeral. Scarlet kept begging for us to sleepover at her place. Part of me didn't want to, but I needed to give her the benefit of the doubt. I mean, what could go wrong? It was a party. I would be careful and make sure I did nothing stupid. I wouldn't get too drunk if I drank at all. Funny thing was, I've never touched the stuff before. Why would I? I have seen what it does to people. What it did to my mom and how violent she became after a few drinks in her. It wasn't who I wanted to be.

"Okay, so after school," Scarlet shrieked in excitement, which she seemed to always do. "We'll drive to Rachel's house and get clothes for the weekend and head back to my place. This will be an epic weekend!"

"Epic?" Rachel questioned.

"Yesss…," Scarlet replied. "It's a party that Kyle is throwing. You know it will be grand!"

I sat there listening to the two of them because what could I say? This was my first party in high school. I've never kissed a boy, not that I was planning on doing that tonight. I've never had sex before. I definitely wasn't going that far tonight. I just wanted to have fun with my classmates. Kids, I rarely hang out with. I wanted to see what the fuss was all about.

"Laura, are you excited?" Scarlet asked.

I looked at her and smiled. "Yeah," was all I said. I didn't want her to think I was weird or something, but she probably already knew that.

When the last bell of the day rang, the halls filled with rambunctious teenagers. They were shouting and cheering as they ran out of the school, excited that it was Friday or because of the party tonight, I didn't know. Scarlet and Rachel joined in, hollering and hooting as they gathered things from their lockers. So, I did too.

"Woo-hoo," I shouted as loud as I could. It sounded foreign coming out of my mouth. Not sure if that was bad or good. I deserved to have fun and not be sad and alone. It also was to be the most memorable year a person has in high school, especially their senior year. Something to look back on.

"I take it you're finally coming out of your shell, Laura?" Kyle asked as he slammed his locker door beside me. He smiled and said, "I guess I'll see you guys at my party tonight?"

My mouth closed, and my throat tightened. It was as if I couldn't speak, so I just nodded at him.

"Great! See you later then." He walked away.

I watched as he strolled to his fellow teammates, slapping each other on the backs and then they all walked out of the school doors. Could I be one of them, now?

Twenty-Four

Rachel

I hadn't been this happy in a long time. Hanging with Scarlet had been fun and spontaneous, but it was even better with Laura by my side. I wished she would have stayed friends with me when we entered Jr. High. We could've had so much fun together all these years.

Scarlet pulled alongside the curb and we all clambered out of the vehicle at the exact same time, which was bizarre and cool all at the same time. It was as if we were one person.

All three of us were in my bedroom going through my closet of clothes. I was feeling bad that Laura couldn't go to her house and get her things. I'd have to ask my mom when that would be. I didn't care that she was borrowing my clothes, but I was sure she'd like to be wearing her own things.

"That would look sweet on you," Scarlet said as Laura placed a flowery dress against her body and looked in the mirror.

"Yeah, maybe," Laura replied.

I wondered if all her bruises were gone now. The dress was short and sleeveless, not a dress someone should wear if they're hiding something. I was sure Laura didn't want anyone to know what her mother had done to her. I pulled out a different outfit, one that would cover her marks. "How about this one?" I asked, holding it up toward Laura.

She smiled, "That's pretty."

"You should try it on," Scarlet suggested.

"Okay," Laura replied, taking the dress and leaving the room.

"You don't have to leave on my account," Scarlet said. "I don't mind if you change in front of me. Do you, Rachel?"

I swallowed, trying to hide the shock and nervousness in my face. "Do whatever makes you comfortable," I said, making eye contact with Laura.

"Thanks, but I'll change in the bathroom if you don't mind," Laura replied.

"She doesn't need to be shy around me," Scarlet chimed after Laura left the room. "I don't care what her body looks like."

"Well, maybe she does," I replied. "Some people just aren't comfortable being naked or even semi-naked in front of other people. I'm okay with that."

"Okay, sure," Scarlet muttered, sounding annoyed.

Laura returned a few minutes later wearing the dress. I loved that it had a high neckline and long sleeves to help hide her bruises. It looked gorgeous on her. "Wow, Laura, you look great!"

"Yeah, stunning," Scarlet said. "You are so going to get some action tonight looking that hot."

"Scarlet," I scolded. "I don't think Laura's going to the party to get into some guy's pants."

"No, but she can if she wants to," Scarlet smirked.

I prayed that Scarlet wasn't up to anything that would hurt Laura's feelings. She'd just lost her mom. She didn't deserve to be humiliated or ridiculed by some game Scarlet wanted to play.

"You don't think it's too much, do you? I'm fine with wearing a turtleneck and jeans."

"A turtleneck? Since when had those come back in style?" Scarlet questioned.

"What is wrong with turtleneck sweaters? I find that they are very comfy," I said.

"It doesn't matter, I'll find something to wear."

"That dress is what you're wearing and that's final," Scarlet demanded.

Laura nodded and left the room to change.

"Go easy on her, will you? Let her be herself and have fun tonight. Not everything needs to be your way."

"Yes, you're right. I'm just excited because it's her first party. I want her to have a great time and mingle with our crowd, that's all."

"Are you sure that's all it is? You're not going to do something to her are you?"

"Me? Of course not," Scarlet replied. "I just want her to have a good time."

After I picked out an outfit, we said goodbye to my parents and my two brothers and left for Scarlet's house.

"Be home by noon tomorrow," my mom shouted as we all strolled out the front door.

"Okay, we will," I replied before shutting the door.

"Party downer," Scarlet muttered, but not soft enough for me not to hear her.

"My mom just cares, that's all. Nothing wrong with wanting us home at a certain time."

I could tell that Scarlet was fuming with what I'd just said. She wasn't liking the whole Laura living with me situation, but I didn't care. I was ecstatic to have her staying at our house. At least she was safe.

As soon as we arrived at Scarlet's house, we went up to her bedroom. The look on Laura's face when we went into the house. Her eyes grew wide as she took in the massive mansion and all that it held inside. The marble staircase and expensive paintings that hung on the walls. Spacious rooms with papered walls and heavy curtains over the windows. It was a little too gigantic and fancy for my liking.

"Laura, can I do your hair tonight? I think you'd look gorgeous with your hair French-braided, especially with that dress you're going to wear," Scarlet suggested.

"Sure, I'd like that."

"Do you have any contacts to wear?"

Laura shook her head.

"Let's see if your eyes can tolerate wearing what I have," Scarlet proposed.

"Okay, sure," Laura replied. "Can I use your shower and then we can get ready?"

"Of course, whatever you want. I'll have my stepmom order us a pizza, and we'll eat and get ready to par tay," Scarlet sang as she slipped out of the bedroom door and went downstairs.

Laura seemed to agree to everything Scarlet suggested. I just hoped she did it for the right reasons. I laid down on the bed and looked up at the ceiling. I couldn't wait for tonight. For Laura to feel like a part of something. This could be the best year yet. I could feel it in my bones. Scarlet, Laura, and I friends. That was the way I had always wanted it. I missed being with Laura and I think she missed me too.

Laura got out of the shower before Scarlet returned to the room. Her hair was wrapped up in a towel and she put on a pair of sweats and a long sleeve t-shirt that I'd loaned her.

"Hey, feel better?" I asked.

"Yeah, I can't believe how nice her shower is. But don't tell her I said that," Laura replied.

"She does have a nice house, doesn't she?"

Laura nodded and sat down on the bed beside me. "Where did Scarlet go?"

"To order a pizza." I watched as Laura stood and unwrapped the towel from her head. "I think there's a blow dryer under the sink."

"Okay, thanks."

While Laura was blow-drying her hair, I went in search of Scarlet to find out what was taking her so long. I walked down the hall toward the marble staircase that led to the main living area below and stopped at the top before going downstairs. There were voices coming from the kitchen. It sounded like Scarlet and her stepmother were going at it like feral cats defending their territory.

"I just asked if you would order us a fucking pizza. God, you'd think I was asking you to jump off a bridge or something," Scarlet snapped.

"And what's wrong with you doing it yourself? I'm not one of those moms that walk around pleasing their kids every time they need something, especially when they have friends over."

"You sound like I ask you all the time to do something. Never mind, I'll call for a pizza myself. What's your problem anyway?" Scarlet yelled. "I don't know what my father sees in you. You don't do anything around this damn house, and you don't even have a job."

"Look who's calling the kettle black? You haven't lifted a finger in this house either. You spoiled little piece of shit!" Lianne hissed back. "I'm surprised you have any friends. I'm sure you treat them the same way you treat me. Who's this new girl you've tricked into becoming your friend?"

"Her name is Laura Stevenson and she's nice. That's more than I can say about you. You're such a bitch. You're nothing but a money-hungry leech. I can't wait to get out of this house and away from you."

"Well, I'm so glad that you feel that way because you're now going to boarding school," Lianne replied. "I got it all on my phone. You talking to me the way you do. Your father isn't going to put up with this."

"You recorded us?" Scarlet shouted.

"Yes, because I'd have to prove it to your father what a bitch you are to me."

"I will kill you for this!" Scarlet screamed.

"I'd like to see you try! Get your grubby manicured hands off me," Lianne demanded.

Were they clawing at one another? I couldn't tell as I heard nothing. I waited for Scarlet to say something back, but no more words were being exchanged between them. I had no idea that things were this bad in her house. She had never told me that her stepmother and she didn't get along. Maybe things in Scarlet's life weren't as fantastic as she portrayed them to be. She was no different than any other family in the world. She wasn't as perfect as she let people believe and neither was her family. It felt good to know she had issues too. Not to sound mean or anything.

I turned and hurried back down the hall to Scarlet's bedroom. I didn't want to get caught eavesdropping because I was sure she would be furious with me if I had heard them fighting. It wasn't like I planned to hear what they were saying and had no idea that they would be arguing with one another. I slipped back into the bedroom and sat on the bed just as Laura was finishing her hair.

Twenty-Five

Scarlet

I took the back stairwell to the second floor. Lianne was being a total bitch as usual, and I would not let her get away with it. She may have married my father, but I was his daughter and needed to figure out how to get him to see that she was a fake and only wanted him for his money.

I slipped inside one of the five bathrooms we had in the house to calm myself down. I couldn't go back into my bedroom looking pissed off at the world. Rachel doesn't know about Lianne and I not getting along, not that it really mattered. Daddy wanted people to think we were a big happy family.

I pulled my cell phone from my back pocket and looked up pizza places near us and ordered a pizza. I didn't need Lianne to do things for me; I could take care of myself, but she would pay for recording our fight. If that bitch convinced my dad to send me away to boarding school, I will kill her.

After ordering the pizza, I left the bathroom and walked down the hall and into my bedroom where Rachel was sitting on my bed and Laura was on the floor in front of her.

"Hey, what took you so long?" Rachel asked. "Did you order the pizza?"

"Yeah, should be here within an hour," I replied.

"Great!" Laura said. "I'm starving."

"Me too," Rachel concluded.

I went into the bathroom and grabbed my hairbrush and the other things I needed to do Laura's hair. I came out and sat down on the bed. "Turn around with your back toward me," I said.

Ten minutes later, I braided Laura's hair into a French braid with a few strands of hair hanging down around her face. "Go look into the mirror."

Laura rose and went into the bathroom. "I love it," she shrieked in excitement. "Thank you, Scarlet."

"You're welcome. Now, let's see what you look like without those glasses on." I stood and went into the bathroom where I carefully placed contacts in her eyes although Laura kept flinching and pulling back when my finger got too close and had to try again. Why was she being such a spaz? When I finally got the contacts in, Laura turned and looked into the mirror, blinking. "The lenses will take some time to get used to, but can you see? Are things blurry?"

She shook her head. "No, I can see just fine. We must have the same astigmatism. How ironic is that?"

"You look great!" Rachel said from the doorway. "I haven't seen you without glasses since I've known you."

The doorbell rang, and we all hurried out of the bedroom and down the stairs. We were laughing as we all ran for the door. Minutes later, we were sitting in the kitchen eating.

By 8:00 p.m. we were climbing into my car and driving to Kyle's party. When we pulled into the driveway, I looked into the rearview mirror and saw Laura's face. She looked nervous and yet excited all at the same time. "Ready?" I grinned.

Twenty-Six

Laura

Scarlet parked the car, but I couldn't move my eyes away from the house. The music was loud enough for all the neighbors to hear, and I was nervous that they would call the police.

"Ready?" Scarlet asked from the front seat.

I nodded even though I wasn't sure she could see me. Both Rachel and Scarlet got out of the car, leaving me alone.

"Are you coming?" Rachel asked.

I opened the car door and stood. The music enveloped my body and my heart thumped inside my chest; it felt majestic. I loved music and the way it made me want to dance. Lose control.

Rachel slipped her arm through mine as we walked toward the house. Scarlet joined us, slipping her arm with Rachel's. We all giggled, at what, I wasn't sure. I was happy, something I hadn't felt in a long while.

We hadn't even stepped onto the wooden steps of the deck that seemed to wrap around the right side of the house when the door opened. Kyle stood there with a red plastic party cup in his hand.

"What's up, my sexy ladies?" Kyle said as he greeted us at the door.

My face grew hot from his words. I needed to keep my composure and not get all weird.

"Hey, Kyle," Scarlet said as she unlinked herself from Rachel's arm and wrapped her arms around Kyle, kissing him.

"Get a room," Rachel laughed as she pushed past them into the doorway with me in tow. "Let's get some drinks and see who's all here."

I followed her through the house, looking at all the people who were already here. There were teenagers crowded on the couches in the family room and others jumping chaotically to the music. We made our way to the back porch where the keg sat. I couldn't believe how many people were already here. I didn't remember seeing that many cars as we drove up the driveway, but I also had my eyes fixated on the house.

Rachel was hugging all kinds of people and then introduced me to everyone whom I recognized from our school. Some of them seemed shocked that I was here or maybe it was the fact that I was with Rachel.

"Grab a cup and let's check out the party," Rachel said as she pointed to the cups on the table.

I was nervous to take one because, to be honest, I'd never had a drink before. Watching my mom get drunk and then her hitting me, I wasn't sure I wanted to go down that road, but I didn't think one drink would make me a drunk like her. I grabbed two cups, handing one to Rachel.

"Thanks," Rachel smiled.

I followed her through the crowd of teenagers hanging out by the pool and talking to other kids from our school. As we walked by, they all seemed to stop talking and looked at me. You'd think I had two heads or something. Was it that much of a surprise that I was here? Or was it because of my mom dying?

Rachel looked over her shoulder and said, "Don't worry about anything. You're fine with me."

I smiled because I wasn't sure how to respond. Was something going to happen that I needed to be afraid of? Rachel found two chairs on the other side of the pool and we sat down.

"Having fun yet?" Rachel asked.

I shrugged my shoulders. "We just got here." I pasted on a smile.

"It'll liven up as more people show up. Kyle's parties are never a disappointment. It'll get wilder as the night goes on."

More people? I wanted to question but only smiled because I wasn't sure how to respond to that. I didn't really think I'd been missing much not coming or being invited to these parties. Maybe it had to do with my mom dying the way she did. That alcohol killed her. I looked down at the cup in my hand. The foamy light brown beer stared back at me. It wouldn't hurt to have just one sip. I raised the cup to my mouth and took a small drink. It tasted disgusting.

"The more you drink the better it'll taste," Rachel said. "I didn't like it at first either."

So, to her suggestion, I took another drink and then another until the cup was empty. "It still tastes gross," I replied.

"You weren't supposed to drink it all in one gulp," Rachel laughed. Then she drank down her entire cup. "Want another?"

I shook my head. "No thanks, I'll pass."

"Okay, I'll be right back."

I nodded as she stood and walked away. I sat there gazing around the backyard and that's when I spotted him. Travis Evans was in the backyard putting logs in a circle for a bonfire. I watched his biceps bulge against his thin t-shirt as he lifted a log and leaned it against another one. He looked so hot out there, and I wondered if he was here with anyone. I hadn't seen him at school with a girlfriend, but that didn't mean he didn't have one from another school, right?

"What are you looking at?" Rachel asked as she plopped back down in the chair beside me.

"Nothing," I replied as I turned my eyes away from Travis.

"Well, it looked like you were staring at something or should I say, someone?" Rachel smiled and wiggled her eyebrows up and down. "He's hot looking. You should go say hi."

"No," I quickly replied. "I can't talk to him."

Rachel's eye grew wide. "You like him?"

"Quiet, not so loud," I growled at her.

Rachel smiled. "So, Travis, huh?"

I tried to hide my expression from her, but I couldn't hide my feelings for him. "Please don't tell anyone, especially Scarlet."

"Don't tell me what?" Scarlet asked from behind me.

Shit, I fumed inside.

"Just that she's never had alcohol before," Rachel said, changing the subject.

God, I loved her for that. If Scarlet found out who I liked, she'd make it known and humiliate me in front of everyone at this party. I couldn't let that happen. Travis was my secret crush, and I didn't want anyone, well, except Rachel to know because I trusted her as my friend. I hoped I wasn't too trusting and that she wouldn't betray me or my secrets.

Twenty-Seven

Rachel

I led Laura away from Scarlet and made our way back inside the house and found the food. There was an assortment of chips and dip on the kitchen counter along with pizza, wings, sandwiches, and pasta; Kyle went all out on the food this time. I wondered why we even bothered eating before we came here.

I grabbed a plate and placed a handful of chips on it along with some wings and pasta. "Trust me," I said to Laura. "Even though we ate already, never drink on an empty stomach. You need something to absorb the alcohol, so you don't puke." I flinched after I said the words, looking wide-eyed at Laura. "I'm sorry, I didn't mean to say that. Shit, shit, shit, I'm such an ass."

"It's okay, really. You're only human and I can't expect you not to speak what's on your mind."

"I know but shit! I should think first before speaking."

"No worries," Laura replied.

After we filled our plates, we walked back toward the same chairs we were sitting in before going for food, but other kids had taken the chairs. I looked around but saw no empty seats.

"Let's go sit by the fire," I suggested to Laura. I could tell she was hesitant but went, anyway.

Around the bonfire were Adirondack chairs for people to sit in. It surprised me to find most of them empty. The fire felt warm against my skin as I had worn the flower dress that Laura didn't wear. I didn't think about the weather cooling down once it got dark and now, I was freezing.

"Hey, can I join you girls?"

I looked up and saw James Larose known to everyone as JJ, standing above us. "I guess so," I replied. I had forgotten to tell Laura that Scarlet was setting them up. With her mom dying and everything, my mind had been elsewhere. If he did anything, I'd jump in and stop it from happening. I wouldn't let her get hurt by him. I knew JJ to be a player, and I didn't want Laura to get sucked in.

"Hi, I'm JJ," he said, holding his hand out to Laura. "I haven't seen you around here before."

Laura turned to face him, the fire lighting up her face. I could see recognition come across his face or he was playing dumb.

"Laura Stevenson?" he asked.

She nodded. "Yeah, what can I help you with?"

"Nice," I whispered.

He frowned at my words. "You look nice tonight," he said, showing off his gorgeous smile. At least he had that going for him.

"Thank you, but I'm not interested in sleeping with you," Laura shot back.

I laughed, almost choking on my food.

"What makes you think I want to sleep with you?" he replied with hurt in his voice.

Oh, snap.

"Because it's who you are and again, I'm not interested in being your girl toy for the night, so please find someone else."

"Bitch," JJ mumbled before walking away.

I laughed.

Minutes later, Scarlet walked over and stood in front of Laura. "Why did you do that? JJ wanted to hook up with you."

"I didn't want to hook up with him," Laura replied.

"All right, fine, then who do you want to hook up with?" Scarlet asked as she sat down beside Laura.

"No one." Laura popped a chip in her mouth. "I didn't come to the party to sleep with someone; I just want to have fun and hang out. Isn't that what you do at a party?"

"Not exactly. You should have fun having sex," Scarlet said a little too loud.

"Are you wasted already?" I asked. "Laura doesn't have to do anything she doesn't want to. Her mom just died, give her a break."

"Okay, sorry, I didn't mean to spoil your fun," Scarlet said, making quotes in the air.

"Yeah, you did," Travis said, sitting a few seats down from us. "Everyone knows that Scarlet has a reason for everything."

"Oh, shit," someone mumbled on the other side of the fire.

"Just last week you started hanging around Laura; everyone knows you have hated her since Jr. High. So, the question is what do you have planned, Scarlet?" Travis asked.

"What?" Scarlet screeched as if she'd seen a snake. "Laura's my friend. Sure, I may have hated her a long time ago, but I've gotten to know her, and I like her," she said, then turned to face Laura. "You don't believe him, do you? You're my friend, Laura, right?"

Laura looked over at Travis and then glanced at all the people sitting around the bonfire who were listening. When Laura and I locked eyes, she had tears in her eyes. I shook my head to say to her without words, "don't cry".

Laura sat up straight. "Scarlet, I know you mean well, but I'm just not interested in dating anyone."

"Okay, sorry for trying," Scarlet said as she stood and left.

I watched as Travis stood and then sat down next to Laura. "You're smart not to let her get to you," he said.

"Thanks," Laura said in almost a whisper.

Laura fought back the tears she almost let slip out in front of Scarlet. I could tell she was sweating bullets inside right now. Her crush was sitting beside her, and she was afraid to move. To speak. If it were light out, I'm more than positive that you would have been able to see that her face was flushed from being nervous.

"I'm sorry to hear what happened to your mom. My dad died when I was three. I know it's not the same. I didn't even get to know my dad," Travis said, looking straight ahead into the fire.

I didn't know that his real dad wasn't around. His mom must have remarried because I'd seen her with a man at all the football games.

"I'm sorry," Laura whispered.

"It's cool. Not too many people know about what happened to him. I mean I was only a baby when he died, so…" Travis trailed off. "I'm glad you came to the party," he said, changing the subject before standing and poking the wood into the fire to keep it lit.

"Oh my God!" I whispered in Laura's ear. "He's incredible."

Laura nodded. "Yeah, he is," she smiled. Her face looking soft and at ease as she stared in Travis's direction.

Twenty-Eight

Scarlet

"You said you could get her to like you?" I asked.

"How did I know she'd shoot me down? Maybe she's not into guys. Did you ever think of that?" JJ replied.

I looked toward the bonfire where Laura was sitting with Rachel. It bothered me that Rachel was hanging out with Laura instead of me. We always hung out together at these parties.

"What's your plan now?" Kyle asked before chugging down the rest of his beer.

"The night's still young, and we have plenty of alcohol left to get her drunk. She'll see things my way. Let's get her dancing and then JJ here can make his move."

"Look, she shot me down already. What makes you think she'll want to dance with me?"

"Why are you being such a wuss, JJ? I didn't know you'd give up so easily. Do you want Kyle to do it for you?"

"Me? Why me? Aren't we together?" Kyle questioned.

I cozied up to Kyle. "We are, baby, but," I nudged my head toward JJ. "He doesn't want to play."

"Oh, I'll get her to dance with me," JJ said as he walked away.

I smiled as I watched from the other side of the pool. JJ walked back to where Laura was sitting, sat down next to her, and lathered her with his charm. It must have worked because Laura stood and followed JJ. "Let's go get our bogey on," I said, pulling Kyle to the dance floor. Seconds later, Rachel joined in along with several more people.

I brought over a few cups of beer, handing one to Laura and Rachel. I added a little spice to Laura's drink to help relax her. Many minutes later, I could see that Laura was chilling and having fun, which made it easier for JJ to rub up against her while dancing. After several more songs, JJ took Laura's hand, and they walked into the house.

"I told you it'd work," I said to Kyle.

"What will work?" Rachel asked.

"That I would get Laura to unclench her reins and relax. You know have some fun."

"I hope that's all you're doing. She doesn't need JJ to push himself on her."

"Why don't you let her decide for herself instead of babying her. She's old enough to take care of herself," I replied.

"I just care, that's all. Her mom just died."

"And that's all the more reason that she should let loose and have fun. Besides, you can't keep using the death card, Rachel. Let Laura decide what she wants to do and stop deciding for her."

Rachel didn't say another word to me. She walked away and went back to the fire and sat down next to Travis. I could tell they were talking, but of course I had no idea what it was about. I really didn't care. I got what I wanted. Laura and JJ were hopefully having sex and then on Monday, he'd finish what I started. Laura would run away, humiliated. She'd never cross my path again. I wanted to wait until homecoming but what was the point in waiting when I can ruin her life now.

Some time had passed since Laura and JJ disappeared. I made my way into the house to use the bathroom. The door to the bathroom was locked, so I stood to the side waiting for whoever was inside to come out. Ten minutes went by and no one came out.

I knocked on the door. "Hey, is anyone in there? I have to use the bathroom," I yelled, knowing the music was too loud for them to hear. No one answered, so I left and climbed the stairs to use his parent's bathroom because their room was off-limits to everyone.

After using the bathroom, I stood out in the hall. I was curious where JJ and Laura had gone. There were two other rooms upstairs, and both doors were closed. I strolled over to the first one and knocked.

"Occupied," someone yelled.

It didn't sound like JJ, so I went to the last door. The bedroom that belonged to Kyle. I knocked, but no one answered. I turned the knob, but it was locked. I knocked again, heard noises but no voice.

"Everything okay in there?" I asked. Nothing. I shrugged and walked back down the stairs to find Kyle.

Out on the deck, I searched around but didn't see him anywhere. Rachel was still sitting by the fire with a blanket wrapped around her. I joined her before Laura came back and weaseled her way beside her.

"Hey," I said, sitting next to my best friend in the entire world.

"Hi," Rachel replied. "Have you seen Laura?"

I shook my head. "Want to share?" I asked, hinting at the blanket around her.

Rachel opened the large blue blanket and strung it across both chairs.

"Have you seen Laura?" JJ said, appearing in front of me.

"No, isn't she with you?"

"No, we went inside, and she said she had to use the bathroom. I left to get more beer and when I came back, she wasn't there."

Rachel shot up and hurried to the house.

"Rachel wait," I hollered, but she must not have heard me. I followed her into the house and to the downstairs bathroom where I was earlier. The door was shut. Rachel turned the knob, and it opened. Laura wasn't inside.

"Help me check the rest of the house!" Rachel demanded.

"Why? She's probably somewhere having sex with some random guy," I said, but Rachel must not have heard me.

"I will check out front; maybe she needed some air," Rachel said, walking away.

I stood there wondering why it was so important for her to find Laura. We went out the front door. There were people everywhere. I hadn't noticed how many people had shown up for the party from the backyard. There had to be hundreds of them here.

"Laura," Rachel yelled. "Are you out here?" People we didn't know were looking at her, but she kept calling Laura's name.

"I don't think she's here," I said.

"Maybe you're right. You don't think she left, do you?" Rachel asked.

Twenty-Nine

Laura

I told JJ that I had to use the bathroom and locked myself inside. Then someone was yelling and pounding on the door, but I still didn't leave the bathroom. I waited until no one was outside in the hall before slipping out and heading up the stairs to find somewhere to lie down.

If this was what my mom felt like every time she drank, I couldn't understand why she did it. My body seemed to move in slow motion like in a dream where you're running, but you don't feel like you're going anywhere.

I held onto the banister and climbed up the stairs which seemed to never end. I tried all the doors, and they all seemed to be locked except for the last room at the end of the hall. I closed the door. As far as I could tell, the room was empty. I walked over to the bed and laid down on top of the blankets and closed my heavy-lidded eyes. I don't know how much time had passed after I closed my eyes; yet, I still knew of my surroundings when the door opened.

I tried opening my eyes, but they felt heavy as lead. I couldn't tell if it was dark around me or my eyes were still closed. I willed them open and blinked, but my mind was fuzzy, and I couldn't see who had come into the room. I didn't like this feeling that I was experiencing. I didn't have control of myself. I couldn't think and it was hard to move my body, which felt beyond heavy.

The door clicked shut and then the mattress moved. Something or someone was getting on the bed. Then my arms were being pulled above my head and a large, sweaty hand on my mouth, pressing my head into the mattress. I tried to move, but I was too weak from all the alcohol in my system. Whoever this person was, reached under my dress and yanked down my panties, pushing his way inside me. Pain like I'd never felt before shot through my abdominal area with each penetration, but I couldn't scream. There was a burning sensation as he slammed himself inside me until the weight of his body released, and then he let go of my arms and the hand covering my mouth.

Tears streamed down the side of my face as I lay there on the bed, feeling not only ashamed but disgusted as I had allowed this to happen. I was stupid to come to this party and drink to the point I couldn't protect myself.

I smelled the scent of beer and hot breath against my ear. I flinched. "Say one fucking word to anyone, and I will destroy you. Do you understand?" he hissed.

I whimpered. "Yes." A river of tears cascaded down my face. I didn't move a muscle, waiting for whoever had raped me to leave the room. I wished I could see his face, but it was too dark inside the room as I'd kept my eyes closed to force the pain away. There were so many people at the party it could've been any guy here. With all the noise from the music, I couldn't recognize his voice either.

The bed shifted as he stood. I could see flashes behind my eyelids, but I remained still, holding my breath. The door opened and closed. The person had left.

I waited a couple more seconds before I slowly rolled over and slinked to the floor on the other side of the bed. I wanted to hide from anyone that came into the room. I didn't want anyone to see me like this. I lay in the fetal position, hugging my knees to my chest. I was in so much pain.

Minutes later, the door to the room opened. I hugged my knees in closer to my chest, afraid to let go. Afraid that he was back to do it again. To take whatever I had left of myself away from me.

"Laura," a voice called into the room. "Are you in here?"

I was sure it was Rachel.

I started crying harder when I recognized her voice. The light flicked on and Rachel was on the floor next to me within seconds.

"Laura are you okay?" she asked. "I came looking for you. You had me worried that you'd left. I came upstairs to check the rooms. Kyle was leaving this room."

Kyle? "It was Kyle that was in here?" I cried out. My mind raced back to the attack just minutes ago. The smell of his cologne. How had I not known it was him? His locker was next to mine at school. I'd smelled that same cologne every day since school started.

"Yes, why?" Rachel asked, sounding confused.

"He… he held me down. I couldn't move. God, it hurts so bad."

"Oh my God!" Rachel shrieked, slapping a hand over her mouth. "What did he do to you? Did he rape you?"

"Please, don't tell anyone. Don't tell Scarlet. She'll say I provoked him," I pleaded with her.

"We should tell the police. He raped you, Laura."

"No! Please don't tell them. He said he'd hurt me if anyone found out. If I told anyone," I whimpered. "He can't know, you know."

"That bastard. He was always a dick, but rape?"

"I couldn't stop him. I couldn't move. He pinned me down and, oh my God, I think I'm going to puke," I muttered as I scrambled to my knees and then to my feet. I stumbled toward the bathroom, dropping in front of the toilet and retched.

Rachel gathered my hair hanging down around my face and pulled it back. "God, I'm so sorry I let this happen to you. Jesus, you'd think after your mom dying, I'd have more sense than to let you drink."

I lifted my head, wiping my mouth with the back of my hand.

"Here, let me get you a washcloth to wipe your face," Rachel said, as she searched the cabinet for a washcloth, then turned on the faucet.

I wiped my face as I sat on the floor with my back against the wall. "I'm sorry," I said.

"What? Are you kidding me? I'm the one that gave you the beer."

"Yeah, but you didn't make me drink it."

"Scarlet shouldn't have made you drink the last two beers," Rachel hissed. "Your body hasn't had alcohol before, so you were bound to get drunk quicker."

"Still, not her fault," I replied. "I did it, and I'm paying for it now. God, how did my mother do this every day?"

Rachel gave me a look that said she felt bad. "It still doesn't give that asshole, Kyle, the right to take advantage of you when you're incoherent and can't defend yourself."

Just thinking about what he'd done to me made me feel sick again and hugged the porcelain toilet until there was nothing left but dry heaves.

"I will go find Scarlet and tell her we're leaving. I'll call my mom to come get us if you don't want to stay at Scarlet's house," Rachel said as if asking me if I wanted to still spend the night at Scarlet's house.

I shook my head. "I want to go home, but will your mom be mad at us? I don't want you getting into trouble because of me."

Rachel stared at me then said, "No, she'll be happy that I called her instead of driving drunk. Are you okay to walk downstairs?"

"Yeah, I think the worst is over." I stood and looked down at my dress that had blood on it. "Shit, I can't go out there looking like this."

Rachel walked out of the bathroom and started rummaging through the dresser drawers. "Here put this on," she said, handing me an oversized t-shirt.

My stomach rolled as I put on one of Kyle's t-shirts after what he'd just done. I didn't want his scent on me, but I had no choice unless I wanted everyone to see the blood on my dress. Rachel helped me as I stuck my head through the opening, my body swaying side to side.

My panties were missing—the same ones that he had ripped off me— Rachel must have noticed too because she looked up and into my eyes.

"I think they're on the bed," I choked back a cry.

Rachel left the bathroom to look but came back empty-handed. "I looked under the bed and on it; I didn't see them," she said. "Do you think he kept them?"

Disgust washed over me. "I don't… I can't believe he'd do that." Then I wondered if maybe he had done this before to some other poor drunk and helpless girl. Keeping their panties as a souvenir like murderers do with their victims.

"Let's go," Rachel said, pulling out her phone. "My mom will be here in ten minutes."

She wanted to get out of this room as much as I did. "Okay, but what if Scarlet sees us? Shouldn't we tell her we're leaving?"

"I'll explain to her you don't feel good and that it's best we go back to my house."

"What about our things?"

"We'll stop by and pick them up tomorrow," Rachel replied.

Rachel opened the door and looked out to see if anyone was in the hall. She wrapped her arm around me. We slipped out the bedroom door and down the stairs. The party seemed to be larger than I recalled from earlier.

As we made our way down the stairs, I looked for him. For Kyle, praying he wasn't watching me. I didn't see him anywhere, but my vision was still a little hazy. We headed out the front door and walked down the driveway, making our way to the main road to meet Rachel's mom.

Twenty minutes later, we were in Rachel's house and heading toward her bedroom.

"Is everything all right?" Rachel's mom asked as she stood in the doorway of the master bedroom.

"Yeah, we're fine. I just wanted to come home," Rachel replied. "Thanks for picking us up."

"Okay, just glad you're home safe. Goodnight, girls," her mom said before closing the bedroom door. I was glad that it was dark in the hall, and she couldn't see how messed up I was.

Rachel flicked on the bedroom light and closed the door. It was the first time I had felt safe and secure since we'd left the party.

Although I'd read that you should preserve evidence when you have been a victim of rape because it was a way for the police to catch the person who did the horrific act, I wasn't planning on telling the police what happened. I climbed into the shower and washed away all the filth of Kyle's body that he had left on me. How had I let this happen to me? Did I do or say something that made him think I wanted this?

I replayed the night over in my head and came up with nothing. I hadn't even been alone with Kyle, nor had he made advances toward me or me toward him. Well, except at the mall last week. I was drunk and was sure I didn't recall everything that happened at the party.

But why? Why did he rape me? I didn't know the answers to those questions and would probably never know because I would not ask him. I would stay as far away as I could from Kyle. After tonight, I would never have another drink again. I would never be my mother.

That night I slept beside Rachel instead of in the guestroom. I didn't want to be alone. I was afraid to be alone. I was afraid of the darkness.

Thirty

Scarlet

I woke the next morning in Kyle's room, wasted from the night before. I had looked all over the yard and through the entire house for Laura and Rachel, but I couldn't find them anywhere. Kyle had dragged me back outside with him, telling me to forget about them. We danced and drank until I passed out.

I grabbed my pounding head in between my hands before scrambling out of bed and running into the bathroom to throw up. The headache I had was disappearing, making me feel eighty percent better than I had just a few minutes ago.

I closed the door and undressed. A hot shower was exactly what I needed. When I finished, I wrapped a towel around my body and went in search of some clean clothes that I kept here for when I spent the night. I dressed and went to find Kyle.

As I descended the stairs, I looked at the mess left behind from the party. God, my father would kill me if I had a party and left the place looking like this. It was a good thing Kyle's parents weren't returning until Monday.

I opened the slider door and walked onto the back patio. Scattered everywhere were beer cans and garbage even the pool had crap in it. This would be an all-day job to clean up.

I scanned the yard, looking for Kyle but didn't see him anywhere. No one was by the bonfire, so I headed back inside and searched the main floor. Random people were sleeping on the floors and on the two sofas in the family room. I opened doors to all the bedrooms until I found him in the downstairs furnished basement next to some naked broad, I had never seen before.

"What the hell?!" I yelled, kicking him in the side.

He opened his eyes and saw me standing above him, then looked beside him. "I can explain," Kyle pleaded.

"Well, this ought to be good because the evidence is lying next to you. Naked! We're finished! I'm done with you! Give me my cell phone back," I snapped.

He fumbled in the clothes next to him and held it out to me.

"Thanks, asshole," I said and walked away. "Sleep with whoever you want to now. You're not my concern anymore."

I climbed the stairs, making my way to his bedroom. I gathered up all my things and left. "Screw him," I muttered, fighting back the tears as my heart was breaking in two.

How could he do this to me? He said he loved me. He said I was his only girl, but I was more upset because he didn't come chasing after me, saying he was sorry.

I went out the front door and got into my car. Tears ran down my face. Feeling humiliated and hurt. I loved him, but I'd be a fool if I stayed with him.

I pulled into my driveway, still wondering what had happened to Laura and Rachel last night. I hoped that they weren't still at Kyle's house. Had they come back here? I doubted that they would have.

I climbed out of my car and saw a man from across the street waving at me. I wasn't really sure why he was waving at me and turned away, ignoring him as I went inside.

"Well, it's nice to see that you came home?" Lianne said. "Where were you last night?"

"I stayed at Kyle's house," I said, then scolded myself for saying it.

"Kyle's?" she questioned. "Don't you think spending the night at your boyfriend's house is against the rules? Where are your friends?"

"I'm not sure where they're at, but so you know, nothing happened at his place." Why did I feel I needed to confide in her about my sex life?

Lianne laughed at my words. "Okay, yeah, sure, I believe you. I know you're a slut, so don't play dumb with me."

I wasn't in the mood to fight with her today and headed up the stairs to my room.

"I'm telling your father about this," Lianne hollered up at me. "I'm telling him everything."

"Whatever," I mumbled under my breath. I hated her more than anyone, even more than Laura. I shut and locked my bedroom door, throwing myself onto my bed. How had I gone from being the most popular girl in school to someone who's boyfriend slept around on her? I was Scarlet Fitzgerald, but I guess that meant nothing to anyone anymore.

I slid my phone from my back pocket. I would text Rachel and find out where they are. When I opened my phone, it went straight to my photos. I flipped through the pictures I had taken last night at the party. I laughed at a few of them until I came across some that were of a naked girl. She was lying on a bed, possibly passed out because they pushed her clothes up and you could see everything. Then, it hit me. I recognized the dress. It was the same one Laura had worn last night.

"What the hell!" I shouted, feeling sick again. "Who the hell took these pictures?" I sucked in a breath as I recalled the events of last night when I remembered loaning my phone to Kyle.

Thirty-One

Laura

The following morning, I was in the bathroom doubled over in pain. I hadn't realized sex would hurt this much, but he wasn't particularly gentle either. Sex was to be consensual. Between two people who loved each other. Not forced or rough.

"Laura, are you okay?" Rachel asked as she tapped on the bathroom door, bringing me out of my thoughts. "Can I come in?"

I didn't want her to see me like this, but I didn't know what else to do. I held onto the counter, stood, and unlocked the door.

Rachel opened the door and slipped inside. "Are you okay?" she whispered. "You've been in here for over a half an hour," she sounded worried about me.

"I'm just having some pain, and I'm bleeding down there."

Rachel's face drained of color. "Oh, my God. Should I get my mom?"

"No," I said defensively. "I don't want her to know what happened. She can't know. No one can. You promised me," I cried out. I could see the concern on her face, but she couldn't tell anyone about this. "It'll pass. I just need to lie down in your room."

"How bad are you bleeding?"

"I think it's because of the torn skin down there," I said. Rachel's face was looking more concerned. "I got it covered. Don't worry about me." It didn't occur to me that Rachel may have never had sex before because she seemed new to the whole thing, but I also haven't either but have read about things online.

"Okay," she said. "Let me at least help you to my room."

She opened the door, scanning the hall before we made our way back to her room. It hurt to walk, and I shuffled slowly to her room. I crawled under the covers and laid on my side. Whenever I didn't feel good, I laid with my knees to my chest.

"What do I tell my mom? She will ask what's wrong. She'll come in here," Rachel asked frantically.

"Tell her I have the flu or something. That'll keep me from having dinner with your family tonight."

Rachel nodded.

"Rachel," I whispered.

"Yes?"

"I think I remember him taking pictures of me last night. You know after he finished."

"Oh my God! Are you serious?" she shrieked. "What an asshole." She stared up at the ceiling and then said. "We need to get ahold of his phone. If I know Kyle, he might show his buddies."

"What if Scarlet sees them? She'll think it was my plan all along. That I got him to have sex with me."

Rachel didn't say a word for several minutes. "You're right. We need to go to his place and erase those pictures."

"You can't," I said. "You're not supposed to know what he did. He'll kill me if he knew I told you."

We both laid there silently, neither saying a word. She was trying to think of a plan, but there would be no way without Kyle finding out, for us to get his phone away from him.

"When he's at practice on Monday after school, we'll go into the boy's locker room and get his phone."

"Great idea, but unless you know his locker combination, how will we get into his locker?" I asked.

"Don't you volunteer in the office? You can go onto the school's computer. They should have all the students' lockers and information on there. It'll be easy," Rachel said. "You can text it to me as I'm waiting in the gym, and I can go delete the photos."

"Sounds easy, but I don't know. What if I get caught? Or what if you get caught? What will you tell the coach or whoever catches you why you're inside Kyle's locker?" We needed to think this through.

"Okay," Rachel continued, "how about you get the combination and meet me at the gym. Then you can keep an eye out while I delete the photos."

"But why is it you who deletes the pictures?" I asked, suddenly concerned, I didn't want anyone to see them, especially Rachel.

"Because I didn't think you'd want to see them," she said.

She was right. Those photos weren't of me posing for him. I was drunk and unaware of what he was doing. He violated me. I shuddered at the thought of what he'd done, and my mind flicked back to last night and what I went through.

Again, I wondered if I had done something that made him think I wanted this? Did I flirt with him? No, I didn't think so. Kyle wasn't my type at all, besides JJ was always with me until I snuck away from him.

"Laura," Rachel whispered my name. "Are you all right?"

She was only asking because I had tears running down my face. The floodgates had opened again, and I couldn't stop myself from crying. Too much had happened in only a few days. I hadn't mourned over the loss of my mother; not like I did when my dad and brother died. Then Kyle doing what he did. It was all too much to bear, and I couldn't stop as my body convulsed.

Rachel wrapped her arms around me, hugging me in close. I hadn't known how much I needed to cry.

"I'm so sorry," Rachel whispered in my ear. "I'm here for you."

This made me cry harder.

There was a knock on the door. "Rachel? Is everything all right in there?" Mrs. Sawyer asked.

"Yeah, Mom. We're fine."

"I just heard someone crying," she said. She must have realized it was me. "If Laura needs anything, please let me know."

There was kindness in her voice which made me go into another crying fit, but Mrs. Sawyer didn't stay because the floorboards creaked under her weight as she walked away. A few minutes later, like turning off a faucet, I stopped. There wasn't even a sniffle. I was good at the sudden turn of emotions; it's what I've had to learn to do.

Rachel pulled away and grabbed a few tissues from the box beside the bed so I could blow my nose.

"Thanks," I replied.

"I will get you some Advil for the pain," Rachel said as she slid off the bed and out the door. That's when my phone dinged and I slowly rolled onto my other side, trying not to cause myself more pain. I grabbed my phone from the nightstand, horrified at the photo staring back at me.

Thirty-Two

Rachel

I should have known that Scarlet would eventually find out about what Kyle did to Laura, but I had no idea it would be this soon. I went into the bathroom to get Laura some Advil, and my cell phone chimed from the back pocket of my jeans. Scarlet had sent me a picture of Laura from last night. I shuddered from the image and ran back to my bedroom.

"Laura, did you see this?" I asked but knew my answer before she said anything. She was sitting up in bed with her phone in her hand.

She looked at me panic-stricken. "Scarlet knows." Was all Laura could muster up. Then a text came through.

Scarlet: **Did you know about this?**

I wasn't sure if I should answer her, but I was certain she knew I'd seen the photo already. I hit the (i) with a circle around it at the top by Scarlet's name and turned off my send/read receipts. It's a feature on my iPhone that lets the other person know if you've read their text.

Scarlet: **Did she have sex with him?**

Laura's phone dinged with a message. "What does it say?" I asked.

"She thinks I had sex with him," Laura replied. "How did she get my number? I never gave it to her."

I swallowed. "I gave it to her."

"Why?"

"She was being nice to you. She said she wanted to text you. I didn't think she'd do this."

"Was she the one who took the pictures?" Laura asked. "Was she in the room too?"

"No!" I answered quickly. "No, of course not. I remember her sitting with me by the fire and then JJ came asking about you. That's when I went looking for you and saw Kyle coming out of that room. Scarlet was with me the whole time."

"Yeah, but that doesn't mean she didn't tell him to take the pictures of me."

"I really don't think she'd tell him to rape you," I said, horrified at the thought.

Scarlet wouldn't do that, would she? God, the thought of her telling Kyle to do something like that made me feel sick. No, she wouldn't. I was second-guessing myself. I wasn't so sure anymore. Scarlet was doing a lot of things lately that I had no idea she'd be capable of. Rape? No, God, no!

"Not to rape me, but to take pictures of me passed out," Laura said. "Naked pictures. Rachel, what if she sends these pictures to everyone? What if she planned this?" Laura began to freak out. "I can't show my face at school. I can't go back."

"No, Scarlet wouldn't do that! He raped you. You didn't consent to it," I replied and started texting Scarlet back.

Me: **Did you plan this? Did you have Kyle take these pictures of Laura passed out?**

Scarlet: **WTF! No, why would I have him take naked pictures of her?**

Me: **That's what I'm asking. You've been wanting to humiliate Laura since we started hanging out with her, but I didn't think you'd stoop to this level.**

Scarlet: **What? Kyle borrowed my phone last night because he said his phone had died. I didn't know he would do this. Besides, why would Laura let him take these?"**

Me: **She didn't. Can't you tell she's passed out? Can't you tell that he did this to her? He raped her!** I hit send before I had the chance to change my mind.

Scarlet: **Kyle wouldn't rape her! What kind of monster do you think he is? She did this. She planned to get him in bed with her. I will take her down. That bitch will die for this. He's my boyfriend and now she thinks she can just walk right in and take my man away from me?**

I wanted to text back that Laura wasn't like that, but knowing Scarlet, she wouldn't believe me, anyway. I didn't reply to her text. Laura didn't make him do this. No human being would ask for someone to do this to them. Scarlet was trying to blame Laura, but Laura was innocent.

Without thinking of the consequences, I powered down my phone. I would not let Scarlet bully me into thinking Laura made this happen. That she lured Kyle into that room to have sex with him and then take pictures of her.

"What do you think she will do?" Laura questioned.

I didn't know how to answer that question. It was hard to tell what Scarlet might do. I was sure she would not let it go, but Kyle needed to pay for this. Even though I didn't want him to get away with what he did, it wasn't my call to make; it was Laura's. I didn't know how to talk her into going to the police or telling my mom who could help her.

"I'm not sure. I know Scarlet to get her way, but I'm here to support you. I know you did nothing wrong," I replied, hoping that my words found comfort with Laura, but I had my doubts. Scarlet could be deceitful. If she wanted to, she could ruin people's lives. I didn't want to see that happen to Laura, who was harmless. We had to stick together and figure out what we would do if Scarlet posted these pictures on the web.

If it were someone I liked and was dating, I wouldn't want people to know what he did, but then again, he wasn't in any of the pictures. No one would know who took them. I wondered if it was Kyle's plan from the beginning. My mind flashed back to when we were at the mall. "Kyle touched my leg," Laura had confessed.

I believed that Scarlet and Kyle were in on this together. Now I just needed to get proof for Laura's sake.

Thirty-Three
Scarlet

Could Rachel be telling the truth? Did Kyle rape Laura? I didn't want to believe he'd do something like that, but I caught him downstairs naked with another girl. I couldn't let Laura tell people what she thought Kyle did to her. They would believe I had something to do with it. I needed to talk to Kyle and find out the truth. I needed to know if he did what Rachel was accusing him of.

I texted Kyle to see if he could meet me at the small park by my house. I wanted to talk about what happened when I left this morning. It wasn't like I could just come right out and ask him if he did it.

Several minutes passed with no reply, which could mean his phone was still dead. I guess the only way I would get answers was to go to his house and get them.

I headed downstairs to leave but heard my father talking to Lianne. They weren't talking in calm and rational voices; they were yelling at one another. I ran down the stairs and slipped into the family room, so I could hear what they were fighting about.

"I'm not sending her to a boarding school when she only has eight months left of school here," my father said.

"But she'll ruin your chances to get reelected," Lianne replied.

"What are you talking about? She has done nothing to jeopardize my political stance."

"That boy Kyle. She's been seeing him behind your back. Sneaking out at night to be with him."

"What are you talking about? When has she been doing this?"

"I caught her coming in late at night."

"That doesn't prove she was with him. With Kyle."

Silence filled the air.

"I'll talk to her for you. See if I can get her to be civil with you. She'll be leaving for college next fall. Then it'll just be us," my father said.

My heart sank. All I wanted was to feel loved, but with her here that would not happen. I needed to get rid of her and soon. I was about to leave and walk out the front door when I heard my mother's name. I stayed put with my back pressed against the wall.

Waiting.

Listening.

"What did you tell Scarlet about her mother?" Lianne asked.

"What are you talking about?"

"How she really died."

"Scarlet needs not to know the specifics on how she died. It's not important and besides, it happened a year ago. Why would you bring this up now?"

"Because she's friends with the daughter of the two people she killed," Lianne said.

"What?" I mumbled under my breath. My stomach flipped, feeling nauseous suddenly. My father had told me she died of a brain aneurysm when I was on my way to school. I dug deep into my memory of that day so long ago. She wasn't home that morning. My father had a car take me to school and drop me off. It wasn't until I had gotten home that afternoon that I found out my mom had died. I had assumed that it happened here. I never asked questions and all he had said was that it happened quick. That it was an aneurysm that killed her. But was he telling me the truth back then? Was that how she really died? I needed to know and before I could stop myself from staying hidden, I burst into his office.

"What is she talking about?" I asked. "What friend of mine? And how did Mom really die?" My body trembled all over. I had never felt this scared before. Why was I so afraid? All I needed were answers. Answers people close to me were hiding from me.

Thirty-Four

Laura

I wasn't sure if I was doing the right thing, but Rachel and I talked and decided that we would go along with our plan. We would need to delete the photos from Scarlet's phone. This would be harder to do because Scarlet was never without her phone. I was just praying that Kyle wasn't smart enough to send them to himself. But there'd be no way of knowing unless we checked his cell phone too.

All this talking and thinking about last night was making me feel nauseous all over again. I didn't know what to do. I was afraid to go to school on Monday and have everyone look at me differently. I liked it when no one looked at me at all.

Rachel's mom believed that I had some kind of bug, and I could lie in bed all of Saturday and Sunday. By Monday morning, it didn't hurt for me to walk or go to the bathroom.

Once we got to school, I gazed around at all the faces of my so-called classmates. No one looked in my direction, so I was sure that Scarlet hadn't spread the pictures around. In fact, we hadn't heard from her for the rest of the weekend.

Our plan was to stay after school and do what we talked about to Kyle's phone. We hadn't come up with a plan to get into Scarlet's.

At lunch, it was just me and Rachel sitting at a table. In fact, Scarlet hadn't showed at all. She wasn't at school. I saw Kyle, but I don't think he saw me. The only bad thing was that my locker was next to his, so Rachel took all my things from my locker and put them into hers, which was down a different hallway.

When the final bell of the day rang, I went into the office to make copies and use the computer. Rachel sat out in the hall waiting for me. Twenty minutes later, I came out of the office and we headed toward the gym.

"Okay, so I'll go in first and do a walk-through; when I come out, then you'll delete those pictures if there are any," Rachel said.

I nodded.

It didn't take her long to walk into the boy's locker room and check it. When she came out, I found Kyle's locker. Sweat surfaced on the back of my neck and rolled down my spine. The temperature seemed to be hotter in here than in the gymnasium. And smelly too.

I went through all the numbers, but the locker didn't unlock. I scrambled the numbers and tried again; this time it worked. I opened the locker door. Musty, dirty sock odor came out, filling my nostrils. I started to gag at the smell but regained my composure. I had a job to do and had to do it quickly.

I rummaged through his things and found his phone. I held it in my hand and the images of Friday night resurfaced. My hand began to shake, so I had to take in a deep breath to help calm myself. It didn't work. "Crap," I muttered. "Get ahold of yourself."

I held down the home button and swiped to the right. I wasn't sure what I would do if he had a passcode on his phone. I scanned through the apps and found the photo app. My stomach clenched as I scrolled down to the most recent pictures. There weren't any of me, but there were pictures of other girls that looked like I did on Friday night. They didn't appear to know what was happening. Their heads turned to the side and their skirts pulled up showing everything. What kind of person does this?

I tapped on his albums and found one titled "girls" and opened it. "Oh my God!" I shrieked and looked around to see if anyone heard me. I quickly sent the file to my phone and then erased my phone number from iMessage. Before placing his phone back under his clothes, I emptied his trash in the photo app. I closed the locker door and scrambled the numbers, then ran to the door to get out of the boy's locker room.

I reached for the handle when voices emerged. "Shit," I whispered. Someone was coming, and I needed to find a place to hide. I didn't know if Rachel was still outside the door and would stall them, but unless she got the person far away from the door, I would not get out without them seeing me.

I looked around the room and saw a door to my left. I ran in that direction and went inside. It looked like the equipment room. I huddled down behind a rack of basketballs and took my phone from my back pocket. I needed to text Rachel and let her know that I was hiding.

Seconds later, she texted back all clear. I stood and quickly ran out the door, meeting her in the gym.

"Did you do it?" Rachel asked.

"I'll tell you once we're away from the school," I replied.

"Is everything okay?"

It hadn't occurred to me until now that I should have looked through his messages. Praying he hadn't sent them to anyone or if Scarlet had texted him. There was nothing I could do about it now.

"Laura, is everything okay?" Rachel asked again.

I nodded. "Yes, I think I got what we need, but... but I have to show you what else I found."

We walked to her car and drove back to the house. We went straight to Rachel's bedroom and closed the door.

"I need you to see this," I said.

"Are you sure? I don't want you to feel you have to."

I opened my messages and there sat the file from Kyle's phone. "I wasn't his only victim," I said as I motioned for her to sit down beside me.

"What?" Rachel questioned.

We both sat there and slowly went through each photo. There were girls I didn't know, but a couple I recognized from our school. Though they had graduated last year, and I had no idea where they were now.

"Oh, my God! I can't believe he would do this," Rachel said.

"Me either," I replied.

Thirty-Five

Scarlet

I stayed home from school on Monday because I couldn't face seeing Laura. Not because of what Kyle did, but because of what I now knew had happened not only to my mother but to Laura's dad and brother.

My father sat me down in his office and told me the truth. The truth he had helped cover-up in this town. My mom didn't die from an aneurysm as he told me she did but from being high on cocaine. She went out the night before and never returned home. She had been out driving from wherever she had come from and crossed into the path of Laura's dad's car, killing all three of them instantly.

All this time I hated my mother for leaving me, but it's different now that I know my mom also took two other people with her. I was sure that Laura didn't know the truth, and if she found out, I don't know what she would do. This was a secret she couldn't find out.

I was lying on my bed when I got a text.

Laura: **We need to talk.**

Me: **About what?**

Laura: **I'll tell you when we meet.**

Me: **Is this about the pictures?**

I believed her because of the photos, and I could tell she was oblivious to what was happening to her. It made me sick to know that Kyle did this. He took advantage of Laura when she was unconscious and then took pictures of her, for what? To look at when he was alone, by himself? Was this some kind of a turn on for him? My stomach tightened from the thought.

Laura: **Yes.**

Me: **Where and when?**

Laura: **Meet me at the park by Rachel's house alone.**

Me: **Who else would I bring?**

I shouldn't be responding with my usual bitchiness, but I just couldn't help myself.

Laura: **10 minutes.**

I gathered my things and went out the door, heading towards the park. After parking, I walked over to where the swings were and sat down. Two minutes later, Laura showed up. Just seeing her made my stomach flip. I remembered when her dad and brother died and how depressed and distant, she had become at school. Then I realized that my mother had died, and I became an angry person, turning into the bitch I was today.

Laura sat down beside me and handed me her phone. "Rachel and I went into Kyle's phone to delete any pictures he may have had of me and I found these."

I took her phone and skimmed through the photos. "Oh, my God. Did he take all these? He…" I was speechless and couldn't believe what I was seeing. A guy I loved and had sex with for two years took pictures of naked girls after he slept with them or raped them? I ran to the nearest tree, heaving up the breakfast I had this morning. Laura came and stood by me, helping me with my hair. I leaned against the tree, wiping my mouth with the back of my hand, wishing I had some water to rinse out my mouth.

"There's more that you haven't seen yet," Laura said.

I held the phone up and scrolled through the rest of the photos. "Oh, God. How many?"

"On this phone? Nine."

I wanted to believe that this was all a dream, and I was about to wake up from the hellish nightmare, but it wasn't. Nine girls? He raped nine girls. My mind was spinning. First, my father told me about what happened to my mom and now this with Kyle.

"At first, I didn't want to, but now I think we should tell the police. We need to stop him from hurting anyone else," Laura said.

"No, he'll lose his football scholarship to Notre Dame," I muttered.

"Really? Do you care about that? Look what he did to all these girls. There are at least eight different girls in these pictures besides me," Laura emphasized.

I rested my head against the tree and looked up at the sky. There wasn't a single cloud, just a beautiful shade of blue. I started to think about how I had gotten to the place I was at right now. Everything that had happened since high school began. My mom dying and becoming friends with Rachel and being popular. What changed? What am I supposed to do?

"I know he's your boyfriend."

"Was my boyfriend," I said. I could tell that my statement confused Laura.

"Okay, was your boyfriend. He can't get away with this. These girls have a right to know what he did to them. What if he posted these pictures around the school? This would humiliate them. Unless that's what you want since you're good at chastising other girls."

I shook my head. "Wouldn't he have done that already? We don't know that he raped them."

"Really, Scarlet. Do you want to take another look at the photos again? We can't let this go. We have to do something."

"What if the police received an anonymous call that he had these on his phone?"

Laura's face lit up. "Before he deletes them?"

I nodded.

"I'm listening," Laura said.

"I'll phone the police and tell them that there are some naked pictures on his phone and that the girls looked unconscious," I said.

"I don't know. It will not prove that he raped them unless we all come forward," Laura indicated. "How do you think I feel, Scarlet? He did this to me. He held me down with his hand over my mouth, so I couldn't scream. He forced himself inside of me and I couldn't defend myself. I couldn't stop him. I want him to pay for this!"

Hugging my knees to my chest. Everything Laura was saying was true. These girls were taken advantage of, and he took pictures of them afterward.

"If you don't say something, I will," Laura said.

She wasn't bluffing. Laura had nothing to lose. She had no one else. I was hiding the only secret that would destroy her.

Thirty-Six

Laura

After parting ways with Scarlet, I walked around the block to clear my head. Twenty minutes later, I walked up the sidewalk that led to Rachel's front door and went inside. There was no one in the kitchen, although I could smell dinner cooking. I walked down the hall and stopped outside Rachel's bedroom. I took in a deep breath and opened it. "Hey," I said as I entered. "What are you working on?"

Rachel looked up from her book. "History."

I nodded and joined her on the bed. Rachel, I came to realize was a nerd. She was always studying something we're working on in school, where I hadn't even finished Friday's homework.

"Have you decided what you want to do?" Rachel asked. "Since you don't want to go to the police or let me tell my mom. What is it you have planned?"

That was the thing. I had nothing planned. No clue what I would do about this after talking with Scarlet. But I wanted to find out who the other girls were in the pictures. Maybe Rachel was right, and we should go to the police or tell her mom. The more girls we have to back us up, the better chance we had at getting Kyle put in jail. My brain was in overdrive.

"Okay," I said. "Let's come up with a plan to find out who these other girls are first, and then we'll talk to your mom and then go to the police together."

"Really?" Rachel questioned.

"Yeah, I think you're right. If we don't stop him now, then he will never stop."

✦ ✦ ✦

I spent my free time going through yearbooks that Rachel had. My mom had never gone to the extreme of buying me a yearbook each year, but I also didn't care that much to have my own. There was no reason for me to own one because I had no friends that would sign it or any reason to look through them. I couldn't wait for school to be out, and I'd never look back once I left this place behind. Except now that Rachel and I were friends again.

At school, I tried to look at all the girls' faces to see if I recognized them from the photos. So far, no luck, but there were a lot of girls at our school, there'd be no way to see them all. I also had no idea when these pictures had been taken. Had they been recent or possibly months or years ago? I didn't want to believe Kyle would have been raping or taking naked pics of girls for years.

There was also a chance they didn't go to our school. It was possible that Kyle went to other parties and met up with girls and did the unthinkable to them. It was also possible that other teenagers came from other towns to his parties. Either way, I wasn't getting anywhere.

Rachel ran up beside me on our way to lunch. "Are you going to Homecoming?" Rachel asked.

"Where did this come from?" I questioned. After everything, Homecoming was the last thing on my mind. To be honest, I hadn't thought about going at all. It really wasn't my thing.

"The cheerleaders are hanging up some banners. We usually make a big thing out of it. You know me and Scarlet."

Oh, I thought. "I wasn't going to," I replied. A part of me wondered how she could want to go to some stupid dance after everything we'd just found out.

"Oh, why not?" Rachel asked.

"I don't have a date for one," I said. But if Travis asked me, I definitely wouldn't hesitate, but he was popular and wouldn't go out with someone like me. I wasn't anyone special.

"What about Travis?" Rachel asked. "You like him still, right?"

I smiled, not that I was trying to hide it from her. "Ever since middle school," I replied. "But don't you dare tell anyone? He can't know how I feel."

"Are you serious? How come you've never told me you've liked him all these years?"

"I don't think I need to answer that question because I'm sure you already know the answer."

"Scarlet."

I nodded.

"Any luck on finding the girls?"

I shook my head. "No, I have a feeling they don't go to our school."

"Oh," Rachel mumbled.

If all of this bothered her, she was hiding it well. "I must figure out another way; otherwise it's just our word against his, but at least we have the photos."

"Not if you go to the hospital and get a rape kit done. They'll have actual proof he did it. I read online that even after you have showered the police can still get DNA from the victim a week after it happened."

I was sure this was true, but I didn't think I could do that. "No way am I going to the hospital. Once I do, the word will get out about what happened. No one will believe me over Kyle."

"Not if we tell them not to say anything. Patient/doctor confidentiality," Rachel said.

"True, but it's not just me. He did it to others too," I murmured. After that, neither one of us said another word about Kyle. "Who do you want to go to Homecoming with?" I asked, changing the subject.

"I don't really have anyone I like, but I doubt anyone will ask me. Usually, Scarlet and I go together, so there's that if you want to go with me and not a guy from school," Rachel said.

"Let me think about it. We still have some time before the dance," I replied, knowing that it wasn't a priority on my list right now.

Thirty-Seven

Scarlet

It made me sick to death that Kyle was capable of rape. I only wanted JJ to take pictures of Laura so I could post them online for all of Craven Falls High to see. My stomach churned, wanting to erase the thoughts in my mind.

As for my father, I hadn't spoken to him or Lianne since finding out about what really happened with my mom. All those times I had seen her lying in bed, I had thought she was ill but was high on drugs. My mother was a drug addict. I had paid no attention when she came through the front door when I was getting ready to leave for school every morning. My mom didn't work outside the house, but it was also a year ago, and I had so many other things on my mind like being popular.

✝ ✝ ✝

The days slipped by as I spent them sitting alone at the park instead of going home after school. I hadn't spoken to Kyle since the morning after the party. There were other hallways to take to avoid him and his friends.

I wanted him to tell me the truth and nothing but the truth. I needed to know if he was this guy who took these photos and raped those girls. How did I not know he did this? Two years we'd been seeing each other. There was no way he had done this. I wouldn't allow myself to believe he did it. Just because it was on his phone didn't mean he was a rapist. Yes, one of his friends could have done these horrible things and sent him the pictures of the girls.

But then I recall Laura telling me it was Kyle who had come into the bedroom upstairs and violated her. I laughed. Yes, of course, Laura said it was Kyle, but that didn't mean it was him. She could have told Rachel that because he was my boyfriend and to get back at me.

Day turned into night as I stood and dashed to my car and jumped inside. I left the parking lot and drove toward Kyle's house. I would find out the truth. I would get him to tell me everything.

It took me less than fifteen minutes to get to Kyle's from the park. I drove up the long-wooded driveway. When his house came into view, it looked deserted, but Kyle's Jeep was sitting in the driveway which told me he was home. He went nowhere without his Jeep. If he was hanging with the guys, they were in his Jeep.

I parked the car and walked up the brick walk to the front door. Once on the porch, I noticed that the front door was ajar. I turned and looked around the scenery. Woods surrounded the property at every angle. If there were anyone hiding in those woods, you wouldn't see them. Turning back toward the door, I swallowed and pushed the door open with my shoe. I prayed everything was okay, and that someone had just forgotten to close the door on their way out. But that didn't explain the house being dark.

I stepped inside, closing the door behind me. There were no lights on in the house and in these woods, it made the place look dark.

"Hello," I called out. The words echoed through the downstairs living room. I made my way into the kitchen and flipped the light switch. Light-filled the room, everything looked as it always did, neat and pristine. The way Kyle's mom Cheryl loved it.

Instead of going upstairs to check Kyle's bedroom, I walked toward the sliders and looked out onto the deck where the pool was. There was something floating in the pool but wasn't sure what it was. Kyle had all kinds of floating rafts for the pool. I slid the slider open and stepped outside, making my way toward the pool. My eyes scanned the woods all around the backyard before focusing on the raft in the pool. As I walked closer, I realized it wasn't a raft, but a person.

A scream escaped from my mouth as I stopped, frozen in place. "Help them!" I yelled at myself. When I could finally get my legs to move, I raced to the side of the pool and looked down at the body. It was hard to tell who it was. The body seemed to be larger than Kyle's, but the person was wearing his swim trunks. Could it be him? How long had he been in the water for his body to bloat?

He was too far from the side to reach him with my arm, so I looked around for the pool net to help drag him in, but then it hit me. This was a crime scene, and I needed to call the police. If I touched his body, then I would contaminate evidence.

I pulled my phone out from my back pocket and quickly dial 9-1-1. Tears poured from my eyes as I told the dispatcher the address and what I had found.

"Should I try to get him out of the pool?" I asked.

"Are there any signs of him moving?" the dispatcher asked.

I shook my head. "No, nothing. I don't know how long he's been like this. I just walked in. The front door was already open when I arrived here. Who could have done this?" I asked.

"Ma'am, the local police and paramedics are en route to the house."

Sirens sounded in the distance. I jumped to the sound of someone behind me. I turned toward the voice. "They're here," I said, and the phone fell from my hand to the floor. I tried to remain calm, but my body seemed to sink to the ground, and then everything went black.

✢ ✢ ✢

I woke with a police officer beside me and an oxygen mask on my face.

"She's back," said the man.

I removed the mask from my face and tried to sit up. "What happened?" I started to ask, then everything came rushing back to me. I tried to get to my feet, but dizziness swam through my head. My head turned in the pool's direction where I had seen Kyle's body floating, but he wasn't in there anymore. I looked around, scanning the area. There he was, lying on a stretcher. The paramedics were zipping the black bag up, covering his body. I wanted to run over to him, but I couldn't move my legs, which seemed glued in their spot. Black bag, my mind repeated. Kyle was in a black bag which meant…

"I'm sorry," the officer said. "But your friend didn't make it."

The officer grabbed onto my arm and then wrapped his other arm around me. Had he known I was about to crumble to the ground again? I hadn't known myself to faint before.

"Let's get you to the hospital, Scarlet," he said.

Confused at how he knew my name? I hadn't told the dispatcher on the phone. I looked at the man's face which I hadn't done since I snapped out of my blackout. I had recognized him. He was my neighbor from across the street. I didn't know that he was a cop. Although this was all irrelevant to the situation, it felt good to know someone was helping me. Because let's be honest, I wasn't anyone's favorite person lately.

"I'm fine. I don't need to go to the hospital."

"Are you sure?" Officer Swig asked.

I nodded. "Yes, I'm fine really. I just want to be with Kyle."

"I'm sorry, Scarlet, but I'm afraid he's dead," Officer Swig replied. "You don't want to see him that way. Remember him that way."

He was right; I didn't, but he was still someone I loved very much.

"Shouldn't I confirm the body to make sure it's him?" I asked, but he seemed to ignore me.

"Do you know where his parents are? Can you call them and tell them what happened and that they need to come to the hospital where we're taking him?"

I nodded, although I had no clue where they were. I'd have to look for their phone number on Kyle's phone. It would be on his phone. I got to my feet and looked around the deck then in the pool, thinking it may have been on him. I didn't see it at the bottom, so I made my way around to the chairs.

I didn't see it anywhere. I'd have to go upstairs and search. It had to be somewhere. Kyle never went far without it.

"Ma'am," a different officer said. "Can you answer some questions for us? Can you tell us what happened here?"

The officer motioned me to a chair, and I told her what I had done when I arrived. "The door was open. There was no other vehicle in the driveway. The house was dark. Even the pool lights were off, which Kyle never left off. He loved swimming at night with only the pool lights on. Did that mean the killer turned the lights off?" I stated. "When they left?"

"It's possible, but we'll check out every scenario."

I nodded. Then it occurred to me that the person would have to know where the lights were. If you hadn't been to the house before, you wouldn't know that they were on the wall in the kitchen. The killer could have turned them off on their way out. Or, and this I was sure not the case, "Did Kyle kill himself?"

"If there's anything else, please call me; my name is Officer Crystal Rosmus." She handed me her card.

I nodded again, which seemed to be the only thing I could do at this moment. I followed the officer out of the house, which was now a crime scene. I climbed into my car and drove home in a hypnotic state. When I pulled into my driveway, I turned off my car, but couldn't find the will to go inside. I pulled my cell phone from my back pocket.

I needed my friend.

I needed Rachel.

Thirty-Eight

Laura

As we sat on Rachel's bed, her phone began to buzz with texts one right after the other. I looked at her as she read them.

"Oh my God!" Rachel said. "Kyle's dead!"

"What?" I questioned.

"Scarlet went over to Kyle's house and found him floating face down in his pool."

Thinking back to the last time when I had seen him, which was a couple of days ago. "That's awful," I replied. Although I hated him with everything I had inside me, it was terrible to think about such a thing, but he deserved what happened to him. I wanted to feel remorse for him, but I couldn't.

"I've got to go to her house. She needs me," Rachel said as she jumped off the bed. "This will kill her."

"Why does it have to be you?" I asked.

Rachel turned and glared at me. "Because I'm her friend. Her best friend. And that's what friends do. I know a lot has happened lately, but something terrible has happened and I need to go. Friends are there when bad things happen to them," Rachel said and left the room without saying another word.

Her words stung like a bee sting. Does that mean I wasn't her friend? She had been there for me when my mom died, but that didn't mean she liked me as a friend. That I had replaced Scarlet because apparently, I hadn't.

I wanted to go after her. I wanted to stop her and tell her that Scarlet wasn't worth her time. That Scarlet didn't deserve to have her as a friend. But I didn't move. I couldn't move. I let her leave and drive to that bitch's house to console her. The thought made me feel sick. Kyle raped me, and Rachel ran to comfort Scarlet, who honestly and probably was behind the whole thing. Was Rachel that naïve? Was she forgiving the bitch so quickly?

Scarlet always wiggled her way back inside. God, I hated her so much. I wanted to crush her skull in. I wanted her to regret ever talking to me weeks ago and wanting to humiliate me in front of the school. Well, two can play at this game. Scarlet won't know what hit her when I'm finished with her.

Thirty-Nine

Rachel

I know Laura didn't understand why I had to leave the moment Scarlet texted me. Scarlet was still my friend even after everything. Sounds stupid, but when you've been friends with someone for years, there's just something about them that makes you still care no matter what they've done to you.

I've been mad at Scarlet before, and we have always made up and forgiven each other. We would get past this. I don't expect Laura to understand. She and I weren't the friends that Scarlet and I are. We weren't that close. We didn't tell one another the secrets Scarlet and I had. The secrets that friends take to their graves.

I drove straight to Scarlet's house. I didn't even knock on the door; I just went up the stairs to her room. I found her lying on her bed crying.

"Scarlet, how are you doing?" I could plainly see that she wasn't doing well at all. I walked to the bed, climbed on top beside her, and wrapped my arms around her, pulling her in close. I let her cry until she couldn't any longer.

She rolled over and looked at me with red puffy eyes. "I can't believe it," she whispered. "He was just floating there in the pool." She let out another howl as she gulped for air.

"Did the police say what happened?"

"No," she replied. "I didn't even see him after they pulled him out. I sort of fainted," Scarlet sobbed.

I said nothing. I just looked at her waiting for more. "When was the last time you saw him? I mean alive?"

She shrugged her shoulders. "I've been trying to ignore him after, you know, the photos. What he did to..." Scarlet stopped talking.

To Laura is what she was going to say but couldn't. I needed no explanation.

"What about his parents? Where they there?" I asked, though after I said the words if they had been there, wouldn't they have been the ones to find him in the pool? "Did you get ahold of his parents?"

"Shit," Scarlet swore. "I totally forgot to call them."

"I think the police should do that. It's their job, isn't it?" I questioned.

"Yeah, it is," she whispered. "Thanks for coming. I didn't think you would. What am I going to do?" she sobbed. "I can't live without him. He was everything to me. I need him."

The words Laura had said entered my mind. Why does it have to be you? Although the words hurt, she was right. After everything Scarlet had said and done, why was I here for her? She had been a real bitch to Laura. Disgust swam over me and I rolled off the bed and stood looking down at her. Why am I so stupid sometimes? Why do I always come running the moment Scarlet calls out to me?

"What's wrong?" Scarlet asked.

"I don't know, but I can't be here. I'm sorry." I turned to leave.

"Wait, what?" Scarlet hollered, looking confused. "Someone killed Kyle, and you're leaving when I need you the most?"

Shaking my head, I turned back around. "It's not all about you, Scarlet. You're right, Kyle died and yet you're making it all about you. I'm sorry that he died. I really am. It's a terrible thing that happened."

"No!" Scarlet hollered. "You don't understand, someone killed him, Rachel! He was an excellent swimmer. There's no way he drowned.

There's no way he killed himself, either. I can't believe you would leave me in a time of need."

She was right. Kyle was on the swim team and had won several medals, but what was I supposed to do? I wasn't a detective. "Leave it to the police, Scarlet. That's their job."

"I think it was Laura," she mumbled. "She has the motive for wanting to kill him. He raped her, and she wanted him dead," Scarlet stated.

"Laura?" I questioned. "She isn't capable of killing Kyle, he's twice her size. How could she drown him?" Though it sounded plausible, I just couldn't picture Laura doing such a thing.

"Maybe she drugged him first. Then he wouldn't have been able to fight her."

I stood there, the image of Laura doing this danced in my head. Was she capable of killing someone? She'd been through a lot with her entire family dying, but I couldn't see it. Could Kyle have sent her over the edge? No, she couldn't have done this. I refused to believe what Scarlet was suggesting.

"You're thinking about it, aren't you?" Scarlet asked. "Laura isn't as innocent as you think she is, Rachel. You don't know her as well as you think you do. You haven't been her friend in years. You don't know what she is capable of," Scarlet said.

I needed time to think. This could be all part of Scarlet's plan. To get me to think Laura is a monster. A killer.

I turned, ran out of the room, and down the stairs. I sat inside my car, letting the words roll around in my head. It was all too much. Laura couldn't have killed Kyle; she was always with me. Wasn't she? I had to go somewhere and put the puzzle pieces together.

Before driving away, I looked up. Scarlet was looking down at me through her bedroom window. Then something appeared in the side mirror. I leaned forward so I could see better and saw Lianne standing in the doorway with a hint of a smile on her face. I remembered their fight the night of the party. It would thrill Lianne that I tossed Scarlet aside like some unloved and unwanted rag doll. But there was something else about her. Something I couldn't quite put my finger on.

Forty
Scarlet

I wasn't sure what was going on in Rachel's mind when she ran out of here. But I was positive it was Laura who killed Kyle, who else would have done it? My head began to spin in circles. The images of Kyle floating in the pool made me feel nauseated all over again. I wasn't ever going to get them out of my mind. He had to have been in the pool for a couple of days because otherwise, he would have been at the bottom of the pool, which would also explain the bloating.

Hugging the blankets to my chest as I laid on the bed, letting my mind comb through everything that had happened. Then I remembered Kyle's phone was missing. I couldn't search his house for it. The police told me it was a crime scene, and I had to leave if I weren't going to the hospital. I needed to go back there and hunt for his phone and erase anything that might lead back to me, and I can't take that chance.

I sat up and looked at the clock next to the bed. It was after nine in the evening. I was sure the forensic team wouldn't be there, but that didn't mean his parents weren't home. Though, if it were still a crime scene, the police would have had them stay at a hotel for two nights. I had to go there and look around.

I changed my clothes, dressing in all black and left my bedroom. As I started toward the stairs, I could hear Lianne talking to someone, though I was sure it was my father. She always seemed to be in a heated discussion with him. How did he put up with her always nagging him about things? Probably still trying to get rid of me.

I crept down the stairs made of marble, opened the door, slipped out, and raced to my car. Once inside, I noticed my father's car wasn't in the driveway which meant he wasn't home, so who was she talking to? I decided it had nothing to do with me and got into my car and drove away before Lianne the wicked stepmother spotted me.

It only took me ten minutes to arrive at Kyle's house as he didn't live far from me. I drove up the long driveway, hoping with all hope that the police weren't here. I came to the clearing of the two-story ranch home with its wrap-around porch.

I parked and made my way to the front door. There was caution tape placed across the doorway. Reaching out, I turned the knob; it didn't turn. I stepped back and lifted the flowerpot by the stairs to grab the key, but it wasn't there. Had they moved it? I checked under all the pots and still found no key.

I stood and gazed around; I had to check under everything. It wasn't anywhere, which meant that either his parents had taken it or the person who killed Kyle had the key.

I walked around the entire porch, checking windows, hoping one was unlocked. No such luck. They sealed this place like a prison. Then it hit me. Kyle had once told me that a spare key was in the garage taped under the wooden table along the far wall. Something his father had done when Kyle was younger because he seemed to always lose his key.

I walked to the garage and punched in the code, praying they hadn't changed that too. They hadn't. The place was dark as the door lifted above me. I took my cell phone from my back pocket and turned on my flashlight app. I walked to the table against the far wall and slipped my hand under the table feeling for the key. With the key in hand, I made my way back to the house.

Seconds later, I was inside, and the alarm was off. This must mean Kyle's parents hadn't been here. Using the light from my cell phone, I moved around the house, looking for anything out of the ordinary, foremost Kyle's phone.

After not finding it downstairs, I climbed the staircase to the second floor. The boards creaked, echoing through the vacant house. When I reached Kyle's room, the door was closed. Placing my hand on the metal knob, I turned and opened the door. A cold draft smacked me in my face. It felt like a freezer in here. Using the flashlight app on my cell phone, I shined the light toward the far wall and saw that the window was open and hurried over to close it. Had someone gone out the window? Maybe the killer?

I fanned my phone around looking on the floor, end tables, and even his bed. Still no sign of his phone anywhere. Then it hit me and wondered why I hadn't thought about it before. I dialed his number and listened.

Nothing.

But that didn't mean it wasn't here somewhere in this room. The ringer could be off, or it was dead, as it went straight to voicemail. My eyes scanned the room again before landing on Kyle's computer. They set some phones up to save things right to your computer these days. At least with an iPhone, you could do that.

Pulling the chair out, I sat down and turned on his computer. To my surprise, it wasn't password protected. Not like Kyle to want to secure his privacy, unless. Unless he had nothing to hide. A laugh erupted from my throat. Yes, because my Kyle wouldn't take pictures of naked girls or rape them.

I clicked on his photo app and scanned through the pictures. I didn't see any of the photos he had on his phone of all the girls, but this was also something he wouldn't want anyone to find. So, Kyle wasn't stupid.

I closed out of the app and rooted around on the desktop and saw a file named g-pics. I clicked on it, but instead of seeing photos, a password bar appeared. Smart, I thought. Now, I had to think about what he would use as the password. Knowing Kyle, it would have something to do with me or sports. I typed in football01, for his birth year, but then changed the two numbers to his jersey numbers: football37, I hit enter. A try again appeared. I wondered how many tries I had before the computer locked me out completely.

ScarletF37, nope. I put password after password in until I got a warning that told me I had two more tries.

I looked around the room, thinking how not so smart Kyle was until my eyes stopped on a book sitting on his shelf, which to me was strange. I hadn't known that Kyle read. I typed in the book's title. Bingo, the folder opened.

I clicked on a photo. It was of some girl I didn't know. I clicked on several more. It was of the same girl but in these; she was naked and looked passed out. Oh my God, it was true. Kyle was taking advantage of girls when they were drunk. These weren't the same pictures on his phone. Which meant there were more.

I continued clicking on the photos until I came to one that looked like… "Oh my God! I don't believe it," I shrieked in horror. "That bitch!" I flipped through the next couple of pictures, hoping my eyes were playing tricks on me, but they weren't. There was one with a video camera symbol on it. I clicked on it.

Forty-One

Laura

Scarlet would probably have Rachel spending the night with her and they would become the best of friends once again, leaving me all alone with no one to give a shit about me. Like it had always been.

"Hey," Rachel said as she came walking into her bedroom.

"Hey," I said back. "I figured you weren't coming home."

She did that swallowing thing as she stopped and stood in the middle of the room. She was hiding something, or she had something she needed to tell me. Either way, Scarlet, I was sure, had something to do with the way Rachel was acting.

"What's wrong?" I questioned.

"Scarlet thinks you're the one that killed Kyle, but I told her you were with me every single minute," Rachel said.

"You lied to her?"

Rachel walked over to the bed and sat down, facing me. "I know you didn't do it. You couldn't have," Rachel protested.

Shaking my head. "No!" I shouted. "I hated the guy for raping me, but to kill him. No way." I shook my head again. Rachel exhaled, her shoulders relaxing. She was trying hard to believe I wouldn't do something like that.

Did she honestly think I'd kill someone? "Rachel?" I questioned. "You think I did it?"

Her head was down and flew up, her eyes wide. "No," she shook her head. "You wouldn't, would you?"

And there it was. She thought I could kill someone, and I wondered if she thought I killed my mom too? Did Rachel picture me as this violent person capable of murder? I knew Scarlet caused this. She planted those thoughts into Rachel's head and as naïve as Rachel can sometimes be; she allowed herself to think I would, that I could kill someone.

"I mean you didn't," Rachel reassured me.

Though I believed she said it more to reassure herself, not so much me.

"Look, let's forget what Scarlet said and watch a movie to get our mind off things. The cops will find out who did it. I'm sure Kyle had lots of enemies." Rachel stood, making her way to the bedroom door. "I'll make us some popcorn; you pick the movie."

I didn't get up to follow her. I sat, wondering how we could pretend that everything was okay. A classmate was killed, or it could have been an accident. He could have been drunk and fell into the pool. Maybe hit his head. It has happened before in this world. But that wasn't what my mind thought about. If they had his phone and found all of those pictures on it. Then the police would think I did it. That I killed Kyle.

"Laura, are you coming?" Rachel hollered from down the hall.

I climbed off the bed and walked out of the room. "I'll be there in a sec," I shouted back before slipping through the open door into the guest room. I opened the third drawer of my dresser and reached underneath my t-shirts for the box. A box I kept things I didn't want anyone else to know about inside. Things that were given to me throughout my life and some things I had taken. I opened the lid of the box, and there staring up at me was the key to Kyle's house.

Forty-Two

Scarlet

The sounds echoed through the bedroom of Lianne and Kyle having sex? I flew out of the chair, ran into the bathroom, and heaved into the toilet. The images of them together kept flipping through my mind like a slideshow. The sound of their lovemaking. I clenched my stomach as I vomited violently again.

Leaning back, I rested against the wall. How had I not known? My mind skimmed over all the times Kyle had come to my house when my dad wasn't home. Had they ever been alone together? How long had this been going on between them? I didn't know the answers and couldn't very well ask Lianne, not without proof.

After cleaning myself up, I went back to the computer. I needed to tell my father. He'd throw her out on her ass, and she would have nothing. Which was exactly what she deserved, cheating on my father like that? I didn't like her before and really hated her now.

I wondered if there had been others or was Kyle the only one? It didn't matter, really. My father wouldn't forgive her whether there was one guy or two. What sickened me was that Kyle was only seventeen. A minor in the law's eyes. Dad had already covered up my mom's accident to save his own ass and reputation. What would he do to cover this up too? I couldn't go to the police. This was a family matter. I finally had something to hold over that bitch's head and would make her pay for what she's done.

After emailing myself all the files, I erased them from his computer and left the house. I didn't need Kyle's phone when I had these in my possession. I finally had a way to get rid of Lianne.

By the time I arrived home, my father was there, sitting in his office like always. Was that the reason Lianne had found comfort with someone else? My dad was a workaholic. Had always been since I could remember. He was a powerful man and wouldn't allow anyone to ruin his career in the Mayor's seat.

Then it occurred to me. Had this been the reason my mother did drugs? Because she was lonely, and it made her feel better? Had she too been cheating on my father? This I didn't know and as far as I was concerned, I didn't want to know. I wanted to remember my mother as someone I loved and looked up to.

"Hey, princess," my father said. "Where were you?"

I stopped at the bottom of the stairs, turned, and pasted a smile on my face as I walked toward him. I didn't want him to think something was wrong.

"Hi, Daddy. I'm just coming back from my friend's house."

"Oh, was it Rachel? I like that girl. She's sweet," he replied.

I had never heard my father once ask or talk about my friends, especially Rachel. "Yeah," I lied. I couldn't very well tell him the truth, now could I. Not yet, anyway.

The smile left his face. "You're not still hanging out with that Laura girl, are you? It will only cause trouble if she knows what really happened that day," he said, his eyebrows drawing together.

"No, not really, but she lives at Rachel's house now since her mom died."

"I heard about that."

"I'm not sure what happened," I lied.

"I'm so sorry for her loss. Poor girl." Although he didn't sound sincere.

I nodded and started to turn away. I couldn't stand here having a conversation with my dad knowing it would crush him when the truth came out and for the first time, I didn't want it to be me doing it. He was my father, and I loved him.

"Goodnight, Daddy. I'll see you in the morning," I said as I walked up the stairs toward the only place I wanted to be right now.

Lianne was standing in the kitchen's doorway watching me as I was halfway up the stairs. She had been listening to our conversation. I mouthed the words. "You Fucking Bitch." And smiled at her. She didn't have a clue about what I now knew, but she would soon.

Forty-Three

Laura

I woke in my bed, drenched in sweat. I was having another nightmare but not the same one. Not the one of my dad and brother. This dream was about my mom and Kyle. People that I have been in contact with that were dying.

I grabbed my cell and checked the time. It was four in the morning and I was fully awake. There would be no going back to sleep, not with all that had happened in the past couple of weeks.

The key to Kyle's house plagued my thoughts. I went over to his house to confront him, although my nerves were a mess. The key was in the door's lock. The door was open for anyone to enter. I pulled the key out and placed it in my pocket. Remembering this now, I wasn't sure why I had taken the key. Why hadn't I just left it in the lock and walked away? I had been frozen with fear and hadn't gone inside; mostly because I feared him. What if he attacked me again? Would I be able to stop him if he tried to do what he had already done before? That's when I left his house, forgetting until I arrived back here at Rachel's house that I still had his house key in my pocket.

Forty-Four

Scarlet

The next morning, I went through all the photos and separated them from the rest. I made a single folder with only Lianne and Kyle; plus, the video he had made of their lovemaking. My stomach spasmed with disgust as I looked at the photos and watched the video. I had to make sure I had incriminating evidence on her. That bitch was going down. I wasn't sure what my father saw in her. Maybe it was a rebound when my mother died, and Lianne was the first woman that came along. When I finished, I did what Kyle did and put a lock on the folder. I didn't trust Lianne.

I sketched out how I would talk to my father about Lianne and her sleeping with Kyle. It was Sunday, so he should be home. It wasn't like him to be at work, though it didn't stop him from working in the office downstairs.

After checking the office first, I made my way into the kitchen and then outside on the deck by the pool. He was nowhere, and neither was Lianne. I decided I would see if his vehicle was here before walking around the entire house as it had eight bedrooms and five bathrooms in it, which he wouldn't be in any of them.

I opened the front door when he pulled into the driveway. Lianne wasn't with him. This was my chance to tell him everything. I marched outside and hurried down the steps toward his car.

"Daddy, I need to talk to you," I said as he rolled down the passenger window.

"What is it, Scarlet?"

"Can we go for a drive? I need to talk to you about something."

"Is everything all right? Did something happen?"

Well, besides Kyle being killed and Lianne sleeping with him. I would say something happened. I opened the passenger side door of my father's Cadillac and climbed inside. We drove until we came to the park a mile down the road.

My father shut off the car and turned toward me. "Okay, what is going on that we couldn't talk about this at home?"

"I hate to be the one to tell you this, but I have to."

"Tell me what?"

"Lianne was sleeping with Kyle," I said. I could feel the heat rising in my face. He had to believe me and if he didn't, then I would show him the pictures and the video.

"Are you sure?" he questioned.

It broke my heart to see him hurting like this. I will destroy her for doing this. "I have photos and a video of them having sex."

"What!" he yelled. "I didn't think she'd do something like that to me!"

I did. "I know, Daddy, but she's a horrible person. I've been trying to tell you, but you always take her side."

He had been looking out the windshield and turned to face me. "Let me see the pictures."

"Are you sure?"

"Yes, let me see them now!" he demanded.

I took my cell from my back pocket and tapped on the email that I had sent myself, the one I had forgotten to delete in fear of Lianne finding it. Once I had it opened, I handed it to my father.

He went from being shocked to angry, in seconds. Then Kyle's voice filled the car and knew he was watching the video.

"I'm so sorry," I whispered. But inside I was glowing with happiness.

He handed me back my phone, turned on the car, and backed out of the parking lot.

"You go to your room. I will handle this with her," he said.

"Okay," I replied, smiling inside. Lianne was finally getting what she deserved.

We pulled into the driveway; Lianne's car was sitting by the garage which hadn't been there when we left.

Once we got into the house, I hurried up the stairs, but I didn't go to my bedroom. I wanted to hear what she would say to him. I dared her to deny what she'd done to my father.

"Lianne, are you here?" My father called out. Her name echoed off the walls.

Lianne appeared a minute later, dressed in khaki's and a red blouse. Her hair neatly braided back away from her tan face, from laying out in the sun all day.

"What is it, William?" she questioned. Only she called him William, while other people called him Bill.

"I need for you to pack your things and get the hell out of my house," my father said in a stern voice.

I was beaming with joy. She would finally be out of my life forever.

"Why, what is this about?" she asked.

"I have proof that you have been sleeping with Kyle Tanner. I want you to get the hell out of my house or I will call the police, and have you dragged out of here!"

"William, wait. I can explain. Don't do this to me. To us," she cried. "I love you. I didn't sleep with Kyle."

"Yes, you did. I have proof," my father said. "I just can't deal with this right now. Leave and we'll discuss this matter another time. Get some of your things and get out!" he demanded.

I quickly ran to my room and closed the door. I couldn't let her know that I caused all this, but I was sure she already knew. Who else would have told my father about her and Kyle?

I went over to my computer and deleted the email I had with all the photos on it, but not before sending it to my father. He would need the evidence to prove her affair. The worse thing was, well, actually there were many things, one being that Kyle was a minor. If my father wanted to make her pay, he could.

There was a sound outside my door and was certain Lianne was standing on the other side. I walked over to my bedroom door and opened it. She stood there in front of me with red swollen eyes.

"If I find out you did this, I will make you pay. I swear to it," Lianne hissed.

"What on earth are you talking about?" I asked as I stood up straight and stared at her. Playing dumb was too easy with her. Besides, I'd like to see her try. "Whatever it is you're talking about I'm sure you deserve everything you have coming to you, Lianne."

"Not as much as you do," she said and walked away. "You'll get what's coming to you," she shouted as she walked away, a suitcase in hand.

Forty-Five

Laura

Rachel and I sat at the dinette in her kitchen eating cereal when Rachel's mom brought up Kyle's death.

"I'm sorry to hear what happened to Kyle," Mrs. Sawyer said, shaking her head as she stood at the counter by the stove.

"Did they say how it happened?" I asked.

Rachel's mom straightened. "If I tell you, it doesn't go any further than this room, am I clear?" she said in a stern voice.

Rachel and I both nodded and crossed our hearts like we did when we were kids.

"According to Officer Rosmus, they're saying it was an accident. They're waiting on his toxicology report. They think he may have overdosed and fell into the pool and drowned."

Rachel and I looked at one another. In my mind, it seemed odd that Kyle would have drowned the way he did, but I guess if he was drunk or took too many drugs it could have happened.

"Had you two seen him at school last week? Did he seem different? Depressed?" Mrs. Sawyer asked.

"Actually, I hadn't seen him all week," I stated.

"On Tuesday, or maybe it was Wednesday. I'm not sure, but I don't think he was at school for the last couple of days. Why?" Rachel asked.

"Well," her mom hesitated. "Officer Rosmus said he had been dead for at least three days."

The image of his body floating around in the chlorinated pool for three days made me feel nauseous, and I pushed my bowl away. I couldn't eat another bite if I wanted to.

"Oh my God," Rachel whispered. "Three days? Shit!" she said. "Sorry."

"It's okay. The whole thing is sad since they can't locate his parents," Mrs. Sawyer noted.

"Mr. and Mrs. Tanner don't know?" I questioned.

Her mom shook her head. "No, it's terrible. I couldn't imagine what they will do when they get the news their son is dead."

⚓ ⚓ ⚓

Laughter ricocheted off the wall, as I walked down the hall beside Rachel, watching the cheerleaders hang more banners for the upcoming Homecoming Dance this weekend. Weird how someone in our school had died; yet, we still seemed to move on with our lives as if nothing ever happened. I totally forgot all about the dance. The same one I didn't really want to go to, but Rachel had her heart set on going, so we were going together as friends.

As for Scarlet, she seemed over the top happy for someone who had just lost her boyfriend. I asked Rachel if she knew what was going on; she said she didn't, and I never brought it up again. Life was better without Scarlet causing drama like she always did.

While Rachel went to cheerleading practice, I walked over to the library to work on some homework and to finish my application to North Carolina State University since I would move there after I graduated. It was the same college my father went to, and I wanted nothing more than to walk in his footsteps. Besides, there were beaches close by. Who wouldn't want to live near the beach? I was just looking forward to getting out of this town for good.

As I left the library and walked toward Rachel's car, I saw someone standing behind a huge tree on the edge of the wood line. The person turned and looked in my direction and then back out at the field. She looked familiar. She looked like Scarlet's stepmother, Lianne. I had only met her once and didn't see her as a person who hid in the woods spying on people.

I followed her gaze out to the field where the football team was getting ready for their big game on Friday, the night before the Homecoming Dance. The cheerleading squad was also out on the field practicing their cheers. Was she here watching Scarlet? If so, why wasn't she on the bleachers like all the other parents? Maybe she didn't want Scarlet to know she came to watch her practice. This was possible.

I shook my head at the strangeness of it all, but it wasn't any of my business to know what was going on between the two of them. I stopped at Rachel's car and placed my things inside; then started walking toward the field when the woman from the woods stopped me. It was Lianne. She stood in front of me; neither one of us saying a word. When I tried to go around her, she grabbed my arm, yanking me back toward her. I hadn't pegged her to have a strong grip like she did.

"Watch yourself around Scarlet," she hissed. "She's not who you think she is."

"Then it's a good thing I'm not friends with her," I replied, yanking my arm free.

"How did your father and brother really die?" Lianne asked. "Or better yet, what were you told?"

The words bit at my ear. Did I hear her say something about my father? I stopped in my tracks and turned back around. "What are you talking about?" I stepped closer to her. "They died in a car accident. A semi-truck crashed into them."

"That's what the police want you to believe, but that's not what really happened."

My mind began to reel as the past came rushing back. The police told me that a semi-truck veered off the road and hit my father's car head on, killing them instantly, but then as I started to picture the scene in my head,

I was asking myself why would my dad be on the highway? If he were taking my brother to the doctor's, my dad wouldn't be near the highway. A semi killing them on the streets now seemed surreal, even if it were outside of our town. It couldn't have happened unless the truck was going at a fast speed, fast enough to kill them.

"Why would the police lie about what really happened to them? What really killed them?" I asked. But the question was "who" really killed them? "How do you know what happened?" My body trembled with fear, afraid to know the truth, but I wasn't sure if Lianne was telling me the truth. Why was she even talking to me if she was Scarlet's stepmother? She had to be up to no good.

"All I have to say is, rethink your friendship with Scarlet. She's hiding secrets, and she'll kill to keep them hidden," Lianne said.

"What?" I started to question. I couldn't think. Lianne had come out of nowhere telling me things about my dad and brother that had nothing to do with her, but there had to be a reason, right?

"Call me and we'll talk," Lianne said as she handed me a piece of paper. "I will tell you what really happened that day. But you can't tell anyone what I will tell you."

I looked down at my hand holding the piece of paper with her phone number on it and looked back up. She was gone. I spun around, but I didn't see her anywhere. It was as if she had vanished. I stood there dumbfounded, unsure of what to do.

"Call me and we'll talk." The words repeated in my head. "I will tell you what really happened that day."

Forty-Six

Scarlet

In the distance, I could see Lianne talking to Laura. Why would she be talking to her? I questioned myself. Then it hit me, the accident that killed her dad and brother. Oh, shit! This couldn't be good. If that bitch Lianne was telling Laura the truth about what really happened, it could destroy my father. I needed to stop Lianne, but how? I had already gotten her thrown out of the house. What else could I do to her?

"Hey, Scarlet? Are we going to practice our cheers or what?" Rachel asked.

Snapping out of my thoughts, I turned back toward the other girls in the squad. My eyes scanned over every girl before I answered Rachel. "I think we're done for today unless any of you need a little more practice?" Which they did but I no longer was in the mood to practice. "Just make sure you practice at home and get the routine right."

They all looked at one another then answered in unison. "Okay."

"I think we're good," Rachel replied to the group before looking back at me.

But I had just turned to look back at the area where Laura and Lianne were talking. Laura was now walking toward the field, and Lianne was nowhere in sight. I skimmed the parking lot and the football field. It was as if Lianne hadn't been there at all. I looked back at Laura, who seemed to stare right at me. I couldn't tell if she was angry or just her normal self, but I was about to find out.

"You guys done?" Laura asked Rachel.

"Yeah, I guess we are."

"Oh, okay." Laura looked at the piece of paper in her hand, then at me.

A cold shiver ran through my body. What did Lianne tell her? I looked away from Laura and quickly gathered my things and hurried away. If Lianne told her what really happened, I wasn't staying around to find out. We couldn't have this discussion with everyone watching us.

Once inside the gym, I grabbed the rest of my belongings, wanting nothing more than to leave before Rachel and Laura cornered me. I didn't bother changing out of my cheerleading outfit; instead, I went out the door closest to my car and climbed inside. As I sat behind the wheel waiting to see if Rachel and Laura were coming after me, my eyes caught sight of a note under my wiper. I opened the car door and grabbed the paper, looking around to see who might have left it, then read the note.

You're going down bitch.

I had a notion whose handwriting it was, Lianne's, and she was about to unleash my family's secrets. If Laura found out that my mother was the one who killed her dad and brother, I would pay for her mistake.

The Scarlet Fitzgerald that everyone saw and knew at school wasn't who I really was. If they knew I was afraid, they'd make me pay for all that I have done to them, and I couldn't let that happen. I had to take care of this before my father and I lost everything.

Forty-Seven

Rachel

Laura was acting weird ever since we left the school though I kind of figured it had something to do with Scarlet. Maybe she thought Scarlet, and I were friends again, but we weren't. At least not the friends we once were.

Scarlet had run off like she was afraid of Laura. Had they exchanged words since our last get-together? I didn't think so. Laura had been with me all weekend, plus she lived at my house, so I would know if she had left to meet up with Scarlet. Then again, they could have exchanged words through a text. I wanted to ask, but was it any of my business?

A few minutes later, we pulled into my driveway. I shut off the car and turned toward Laura. "Everything okay with you?"

"Yeah, why?" Laura replied.

She was hiding something from me. "You know you can talk to me about anything, right?"

"Yes."

She was lying to me. Her answers were short, and she didn't even look at me. She was staring down at her hands.

"What's in your hand that you keep looking at?" Laura made a fist, hiding the small piece of paper she didn't think I'd seen.

"Nothing," she quipped, opened the car door, and hurried out.

I grabbed my things and followed. "Laura, wait!" I hollered. She stopped before going inside. "What is going on with you? Did something happen with Scarlet? Did she say or do something to you?"

Laura shook her head.

"Then what is it?" I pleaded.

"It's nothing. I just have some things on my mind that I have to figure out. It has nothing to do with you, I promise."

I nodded. "All right. I'll let you figure things out. I'll be here if you need me."

"Thanks," she said and walked into the house.

I still wasn't convinced that Scarlet had nothing to do with whatever was bothering Laura. Scarlet caused everything going wrong with us. She wasn't a good person, and she would always get even. If she was still planning on getting back at Laura, she would, but when?

Since our little outing, I had no clue what Scarlet had up her sleeve. Was she still planning on humiliating Laura at the Homecoming Dance? Now that Kyle was dead, her sidekick, who did she have to help her? Was she planning on doing it all herself?

Later that evening, Laura said she just wanted to be alone and went to her room. I didn't want to pressure her or try to figure out what was bothering her.

That evening as I lay in bed, the house quiet as a morgue—a squeak pierced my ears and I sat up in bed. Slipping out from under the blankets, I quietly opened my bedroom door and tiptoed out. Once in the hallway, I stood outside Laura's bedroom. A draft came from under the door, along with the scent of pine needles and earthy soil; then it disappeared. I turned the knob and slowly opened the door. The room was dark, but not dark enough that I couldn't see the bed and that Laura wasn't in it. I looked toward the window that was closed, but not all the way, which meant Laura had gone out the window. Where could she be going at this time of night?

I hurried over to the window and peered out. I couldn't see a thing except bushes. I ran back to my room, trying hard not to make any noise. I went to the window which faced the street and looked out. My eyes searched the yard when I saw Laura getting into her car parked on the street. Where the hell was she going at midnight? I needed to follow her.

I quickly changed my clothes and snuck out of the house, praying that my parents wouldn't wake and notice that the cars were gone. There was no way I would follow her by walking as I had no clue where she was going.

I hopped into my car and put it in neutral. The car rolled down the driveway and onto the road. Once I was on the street, I started the engine, but kept the headlights off. Laura had at least a five-minute lead on me.

As I drove down the road, I looked in all directions when crossing intersections. I didn't see any taillights, which meant Laura hadn't gone down them. To my luck, lights appeared up ahead. It had to be her. I stayed far enough back so she wouldn't see my car, not that she would know it was me in the dark. I still had my headlights turned off so I wouldn't be visible. I followed her until we came to a park. The one just before exiting the town of Craven Falls, which seemed to be a popular park these days with us. She pulled in next to another car. One I didn't recognize.

I drove ahead and pulled into a deserted driveway and parked my car. I climbed out and walked through the shallow woods, hoping I could see who she was talking to.

By the time I got close enough, whoever was in the other car was already sitting in Laura's car. I couldn't see who the person was, but I could tell by the size and height that it was a female. Was she meeting with Scarlet? If so, why? Were they planning something behind my back? Were they going to do something to me? I couldn't think of any other person she would meet with. And besides, why am I assuming it had to do with me?

My legs began to cramp as I knelt down in the woods. I stood, letting the blood flow through my legs as I shook them one at a time, the tingles disappearing instantly. A car door shut, and I leaned forward as if that would help me see better. The person turned; it was Lianne, not Scarlet. Why would she be meeting with her? Did they know each other? My mind was reeling, trying to find the answers, but I kept coming up with nothing.

My mind was trying to put the pieces of the puzzle together, forgetting that Laura would know that I followed her if she got home before me. I had to hurry back to my car and head home before she did.

I drove in the opposite direction and cut down State Street, which connected to one of the back roads in Craven Falls. Pressing my foot on the gas, I drove as fast as I could back to my house. I turned off my headlights as I pulled into the driveway and quickly exited the vehicle and went inside.

The door to my bedroom clicked shut as I closed it and undressed, crawling back under the blankets. Sweat burrowed along the hairline of my forehead. I wiped it away and listened to the surrounding sounds. A car door slammed shut outside. Laura was home, and she would climb back through the window, pretending she had never left.

Should I be in her room when she returned? Or wait and ask her questions tomorrow? My mind would not stop searching for answers, so I crept out of bed and stood outside her bedroom door until I heard the window opening.

Forty-Eight

Laura

I had to talk to Lianne and find out what she was talking about earlier. If she knew how my dad and brother really died, I needed to know.

Me: **Can you meet me at midnight?**

Lianne: **Where?**

Me: **Meadow Park, just before you leave town. It's on the right side.**

Lianne: **Yes, I can meet you there at midnight. Come alone.**

Come alone? Why would she tell me to come alone? Who else would I bring? Did she think I'd ask Rachel to come with me?

Me: **Of course, I'll be alone.**

Lianne: **See you then.**

Fifteen minutes before midnight, I climbed out of my bedroom window and into my car. There was no one on the streets at this time of night. The houses were dark, and everyone was asleep and dreaming their happy little dreams. Something I wish I did these days, but sleep wasn't my friend. Too many lightning bugs flashing around in my head, keeping me up at night.

I pulled into the parking lot and parked next to a dark blue Nissan. A pit of terror opened in my stomach, waiting to swallow me whole. This wasn't a good idea. I was mixing with the Fitzgerald's, which meant nothing good would come out of this. But I just had to know what she knew about my dad and brother. What really happened to them.

I hoped it wasn't some game she was playing to get even with Scarlet. Rachel had confessed that Scarlet and Lianne were fighting the other night when we were at their house. The night of Kyle's party. The night that I'd never forget.

The passenger door opened, and Lianne slid into the passenger seat. She was wearing all black with her hair tied back into a ponytail. She looked like a cat burglar.

I swallowed and cut to the chase. "What do you know about my father's death?" I asked.

"I see you're eager to know what Scarlet's hiding from you."

"Just tell me, please. How did they really die?"

"Okay, fine. You want to just jump into the boiling water. Here's the truth. Scarlet's father covered her mother's death by telling everyone she died from a brain aneurysm at their home. It was the same morning your father and brother died."

"I remember that." Something about that day stuck in my head. Why hadn't I realized that her mom died the same day as my dad and brother? I had thought nothing of it because I had heard it was from a brain aneurysm like Lianne had just said.

"Something like that."

"But she didn't die of a brain aneurysm?" I questioned.

Lianne shook her head. "Not exactly."

"Okay, then how did she die?" I asked, wondering what this had to do with me. She needed to get to the point, or I would lose my shit.

"She was in a car accident. The same one that killed your dad and brother."

At first, I was speechless, not sure what she was saying. Then one by one, the scene unfolded in front of my eyes. "What?" I questioned as my brain put all the pieces together. It made more sense than a semi-truck hitting them. "I don't understand. Why would he cover up her death? Why would he lie about how she died?" My mind was spinning in all directions.

"Because William is a powerful man, and he doesn't want people, especially the town, to know his wife was doing drugs. If one word got out that she drove that car and killed two people along with herself, his seat as Mayor would have crumbled to the ground. You know how people get when they find something on a politician. The publicity alone would have ruined the career he worked so hard to build," Lianne said.

"So, you're saying that Scarlet knew her mother killed my father and brother and never said a word?"

"That's exactly what I'm saying," Lianne lied.

I couldn't believe what I was hearing. If this were true and Scarlet knew this whole time, then she was just as much responsible for killing them as her own mother was. It was all starting to make sense to me now. Scarlet caused everything that went wrong in my life.

My insides constricted. Scarlet's mother killed my dad and brother. I couldn't let her get away with it. She had to pay. Anger grew inside me, erasing all signs of nausea and turning into rage.

"Look, just be careful around her. She's nothing but trouble."

"Why are you telling me this all of a sudden? Did she do something to you, and this is your way of getting even?" I pried, according to Rachel they didn't get along.

"You could say that," Lianne said with a smirk. "The bitch needs to pay for this. She can't get away with killing your family."

"What do you want me to do?" I asked.

"The bitch needs to die."

The words echoed through the car. She wanted me to kill Scarlet. Then I remembered finding my mother in her bed and how she had died. The thought sickened me.

There was no way I could go along with Lianne's plan to kill Scarlet. I didn't think I could do something like that. What if I got caught? Then I'd go to prison. Everything was happening way too fast.

"Laura, you can do this. I'll help you destroy her, we'll do this together," Lianne said. "Think about it. I'll text you when we should meet again."

Lianne opened the car door and climbed out, shutting it behind her. Just like that, she ended the conversation. I sat there as she got into her car and drove away. I couldn't kill Scarlet, could I? Murder? I had a whole life ahead of me. But her mother killed my dad and brother and she knew about it. I couldn't let her get away with this. She had to pay for their deaths. *She knew,* was the only thing swirling around inside my head.

Several minutes later, I started the car and drove back toward Rachel's house. I parked beside the curb and sat there in the silence of my car. The car that was once my mother's. The words kept rolling around in my head. *The bitch needs to die. Help me destroy her.* Lianne had said. *Could I do this? Am I capable of killing someone?* Although Scarlet deserved whatever came her way for all the bad things she had done to others, I didn't think I could hurt someone else. Lianne was losing it. She even sounded like an evil villain out to destroy the world.

I got out of my car and walked around the house and pushed up the window. I climbed back inside and closed it behind me. Sleep wasn't happening with everything spinning around in my head, but I undressed and crawled underneath the cold blankets and laid there, staring up at the ceiling. My brain felt like it was in overdrive. Sleep was the last thing I would get tonight.

The knob on the bedroom door turned and light filtered in. I closed my eyes, pretending to be asleep. Knowing it had to be Rachel. I didn't feel like talking to her tonight. I had too much on my mind. I could feel her eyes on me, watching me. Then, in what seemed like forever, she finally closed the door and left.

Forty-Nine
Scarlet

Later that night after spotting Lianne's white BMW parked at a house two roads away, I sat in my car and waited. She would eventually leave the house she was now living in and when she did, I would follow her.

Around 11:45 p.m., Lianne climbed into a dark blue Nissan, which wasn't hers because she owned a white BMW like mine. Where was she going and what was she up to? I had no way of knowing, so I followed her until she turned into the park at the edge of town. There were no other cars in the parking lot.

I drove by with my headlights off and parked across the street in another parking lot. Few people knew about this other lot because it was secluded behind a thick row of trees. It was a place that Kyle and I came to to have sex sometimes.

I walked through the woods until I came to a huge tree and crouched down. I spotted Laura's car next to Lianne's and then Rachel's car drove by. We were all here for the same reason; well, at least two of us were. I just wanted to know if Lianne would tell Laura the truth about what really happened to her dad and brother?

As much as I wanted to run over to Laura's car and drag Lianne's ass out of it, I didn't. I waited until everyone left before heading back to my car and leaving. I had no idea what I would do. I needed to find out what Lianne was up to. I was sure it had to do with Laura's family. It would be her way of getting even with me and my father.

I drove back home thinking of nothing but getting Lianne out of our lives for good. She deserved whatever happened to her for cheating on my dad. Actually, Laura and Lianne needed to both go, but it would look suspicious to everyone.

When I ran into Laura the next day at school, she didn't seem any different from before, which told me Lianne didn't tell her about my mom killing her dad and brother, or Laura was an impressive actress. Either way, I would try to figure out what she knew; I just didn't know how to go about it. By the end of the day, I was nowhere closer to finding out than I had been yesterday.

As the week rushed by, nothing seemed different between Rachel and Laura. I hadn't seen Lianne hanging around the school when I was practicing our cheers for Friday's game which was tomorrow night, then the Homecoming Dance on Saturday. With Kyle dead, I had no date. Not that I couldn't get a guy to go with me, but I didn't want to go with just any guy. I missed Kyle so much and realized I hadn't really mourned over him the way I should have. Of course, I was angry that he had cheated on me, and even more upset that one of them was Lianne. There was so much going on lately; I honestly wasn't myself. Who could be when tragedy overcomes you?

My father wasn't home when I arrived around six that evening. He had been working long hours at the office. More so, since he had kicked Lianne out of the house which made me wonder what he was doing? The house seemed quieter; something I hadn't noticed in all these years. I always had Rachel over or was with Kyle. Now, it was just me. I had no friends, no boyfriend. And for the first time, I felt alone and sad. This was definitely not something I was used to. How did someone live with a life so secluded with no one around?

I climbed the stairs to my bedroom and noticed that my door was open. Maybe the cleaning lady had forgotten to close it when she finished. I walked inside and to my horror my Homecoming dress was shredded to pieces. I screamed, but there was no one here to see what was wrong. No one would know if they had murdered me. No one would save me.

I scanned the room; there were pieces everywhere. On my bed and the floor. There was only one person capable of doing this, Lianne. I screamed again as anger rose through my body. That bitch was going down. I was so finished with her!

I left my bedroom and got into my car. I needed to go shopping for another dress. I wouldn't let that bitch win. She wouldn't ruin my night on Saturday. I would make her regret ever meeting my father and coming into our house.

FIFTY

LAURA

It was all true. Everything that Lianne told me was true. I went to the police station and asked about the case from last year. Although the files were locked in a room, I told the officer what I was looking for. The same officer that had come to my house when my mom had died. She took it upon herself to check it out for me. She said that she had only been working at the station for a few years, but she'd investigate the accident that happened on the dates I had given her.

Officer Rosmus called me two days later and said that there were some discrepancies hidden in the files. There had never been a semi-truck at the scene. The officer read further down the paper and saw the name of Martha Fitzgerald from Craven Falls who was pronounced dead at the scene, along with two other bodies: Michael and Josh Stevenson from Craven Falls, also pronounced dead at the scene. No word about a semi-driver anywhere in the report.

"I had to do some digging, but finally found the original files of the accident," Officer Rosmus said. "Someone didn't want this to get out. Someone made a new file that had different facts about what happened that morning. They must have known some powerful people to get the file sealed from the public."

"Thank you," I said and hung up the phone.

I couldn't believe it. Scarlet's mother had been the one who killed my dad and brother, and her father had lied about it. Scarlet helped cover-up the accident, so her father's reputation wouldn't get ruined because his wife had been under the influence and hit and killed two people along with herself.

I needed to talk to Scarlet and let her know about what really happened. What better night than at the Homecoming Dance. It would be a great opportunity. I'd have other people around, so she couldn't lie about it. I just couldn't believe she knew and said nothing. What kind of person does that? She might as well have been involved. Been the one who killed them.

"Hey, what are you doing out here?" Rachel asked as she stepped onto the deck outside her house.

I wiped at the tears running down my face, but there was no way Rachel wouldn't know that I was crying. I was sure that my eyes were red and swollen. I cleared my throat. "I needed some air, is all," I said without facing her.

She sat down on the stairs. "Want to talk?" she asked.

I wasn't sure if I should tell her the truth about what had happened that day. It wouldn't bring them back even if I wished it would. But it could help me find closure. I had always felt there was something else about the day they died that haunted me.

"Laura, what's going on? You know you can always talk to me," Rachel whispered beside me as if she didn't want anyone to hear her. "I feel you're ignoring me."

I shook my head and faced her. "No, of course not. I just have some things on my mind," I lied.

"Things that are making you cry?"

Rachel would not stop asking me what was wrong. "I was just thinking about my dad and brother and how they died."

Rachel nodded. "Yeah, I'm sorry I wasn't there for you when it happened. I was a terrible friend."

Actually, you weren't my friend at all. I wanted to say but couldn't. She was here now, and that should count for something, right? I wasn't sure. I needed her more now than ever, and I promised Lianne that I wouldn't tell anyone. I had always kept my promises even if I should tell someone. But I decided not to. I'd wait until I had my talk with Scarlet, which I decided would be alone, away from everyone.

Rachel put her arm around me. "Well, if you don't want to talk about it now, I'm here when you do," she said and squeezed me into her.

✢ ✢ ✢

The next day, Rachel had to stay over to practice her cheers with the rest of the cheerleaders, so I drove myself to school. On the way home, I stopped at the police station. I had asked Officer Rosmus if I could have a copy of the police report. She couldn't give me everything, but I could get what I wanted. The names of the people involved in the accident.

I went back to Rachel's house and shut myself in my room. I needed to be alone. I read the papers over and over until it was embedded into my brain. Then I took it upon myself to find out everything I could about Scarlet's parents. Tomorrow I wanted to confront Scarlet and end this jealousy war we've had between us once and for all.

Fifty-One

Rachel

When I arrived home from practice, Laura was in her room. I tapped on the door, but instead of waiting for Laura to tell me to come in, I just opened the door. She was sitting on the bed and there were papers scattered everywhere.

"What is all this?" I questioned.

Laura scooped the papers into a pile. "Nothing. They're nothing," she said.

"Then why are trying to hide them from me?"

"Look, it's none of your business, so just leave!" Laura snapped.

I recoiled, stepping back until the door frame touched my back. "I'm sorry." My heart was beating fast beneath my sweatshirt as I closed the door and hurried down the hall back to my bedroom. Not only did I feel scared by her reaction but also hurt as I fought back the tears that blurred my vision. By the time I was in my room with the door closed, the tears flowed down my cheeks.

Something wasn't right, and I needed to be careful about what I did around her. It had to do with Lianne; I was sure of it. I needed to find out what she told Laura because she hasn't been the same since the other night.

⚉ ⚉ ⚉

An hour later, I left the house and drove back toward the school. The game started at six-thirty and I had to meet up with the other cheerleaders before the game. I parked my car in the school lot and turned off the engine. Leaning my head back against the seat, I took in deep breaths, closing my eyes as dizziness swam through my head. I just had to get through tonight.

Boom-Boom-Boom.

My eyes flew open as I jumped in my seat. Someone was pounding on the driver's side window. It was Travis. I turned the key enough to power down the window. "What the hell!" I shouted at him. "Were you trying to give me a heart attack?"

"Sorry, I tried your door first, but it was locked."

"Oh, well, I'm fine, no thanks to you," I replied, opening the car door and climbing out. Travis was at least a foot taller than me. His muscular build towering over me. "Was there something you wanted besides to scare the shit out of me?" I wasn't sure why I was getting so angry over this, though I was sure it had to do with Laura and her yelling at me earlier.

He shook his head, then said. "I was wondering if you think Laura would like to be my date tomorrow," he paused, clearing his throat. "To go to Homecoming with me?"

A smile appeared on my lips. I couldn't believe it. He liked Laura and wanted to go out with her. "Yes, oh my God, she'd be thrilled to go with you."

He smiled. "She would?"

"I would bet my life on it."

He smiled. "Okay, good, then I'll ask her tonight. Is she coming to the game?"

"I'll make sure she's there," I said, leaning back into the car and grabbing my cell phone from the console and texting Laura.

He leaned down and kissed my forehead. "You're such a good friend Rachel," he said and walked away.

But was I a good friend? I didn't think so. I hadn't been there for Laura in years and felt shitty about tossing her to the side for Scarlet, who didn't deserve my friendship. Lately, all I've felt like was the monkey in the middle between the two of them. Laura needed me, but I needed her more.

FIFTY-TWO
SCARLET

The sun was setting behind the bleachers when I spotted Travis and Rachel in the distance talking, and then he leaned in and kissed her. Granted, it wasn't on the lips, but he still kissed her. I'd never seen Travis with any girl before, at least not from our school. Rachel, well, she wouldn't be my first choice as a girlfriend if that's what he was looking for.

Stretching down one leg and then the other as I watched them from afar. Travis was a good guy. He had always kept to himself, though I'd never seen him outside of school with anyone except maybe Kyle. Although Rachel and Travis were not any of my business, but with everything going on at home, I needed something to distract me.

I stood and dabbed the sweat from my face, then grabbed the bottle of ice water and drank some down. Seeing them together made me miss Kyle even more. I didn't have a date to the dance and felt sad by the realization that I'd be going alone for the first time since high school.

I didn't even have any girlfriends to hang out with. Since Rachel had traded me in for Laura, the other girls who hung out with us occasionally had walked away from me. Not that I cared but Rachel; she was the only one I trusted to talk to. Even though I didn't always tell her everything.

Everyone had secrets that they kept from people. Secrets that they'd take to their own grave if they had to.

Rachel appeared next to me with a huge smile on her face. "What are you so happy about?"

"Oh, nothing," she said.

"Bullshit," I spat. "No one is that happy. What did Travis say to you?"

"Nothing, and even if it was something, I wouldn't be telling you," Rachel said.

Bitch. "You know I'll find out what's going on."

"Maybe, maybe not, but it's still none of your business. You don't have to know everything, Scarlet Fitzgerald."

I hated it when she used my last name when she was stating something. I tossed my towel over my shoulder and walked to the tree near the shed. It was too hot to be standing out in the sun, and I didn't feel like arguing with her.

I sat down under the tree and looked through the slats of the metal bleachers onto the field. I had never noticed how secluded it was back here. No one could see if someone was behind them if it were dark out. Not that I'd be out here at night.

My mind recalled the moments Kyle, and I had snuck out of class and had sex under this very tree. Then wondered if he had brought other girls back here to do the same thing. I shook my head. I didn't want to know if he did or didn't, that part of my life was over whether I wanted it to be. Kyle was dead, and I couldn't change what happened to him.

Music sounded, and I looked down at the cell phone in my hand. A number I didn't recognize appeared. Normally, I wouldn't answer calls from unknown callers, but something told me to answer this one. "Hello."

"Scarlet Fitzgerald?" a male voice questioned.

"Yes, this is she," I said, trying to figure out if I'd heard the voice on the other end before. "Who is this?"

"Oh, sorry. It's Allen, your neighbor from across the street. Was just calling to see how you're doing since you fainted a couple weeks ago."

"Oh, right? I forgot about that. I mean not what happened to Kyle, but ah…" My words were scattered and not coming out right. This had never happened to me before. I could talk to anyone.

"Scarlet, you there?" Allen asked.

"Yeah, I'm here. Sorry about that. I'm not sure what's wrong with me."

"Are you all right? Do you need me to come check on you?"

My breath caught in my throat. Was he hitting on me? "I'm fine, really. I think it's the heat." I couldn't understand why he was even calling me to begin with. Did police officers often call people they had helped? I didn't think so.

"Well, make sure you drink a lot of water. Stay hydrated in this heat wave we're having, especially at the game tonight."

"Yes, I will. I have my water right here." What the heck was that, my head screamed at me. All I wanted was to get off the phone because he was creeping me out.

"Okay, well, you have my number now if you need to call me," Allen said. "Call me whenever you want."

"Okay, thank you for checking on me." I hung up. The call made me feel uneasy. Since when had my neighbor cared if I was okay? Trying to remember if I'd ever talked to Allen. Had we waved to one another? Yes, a few weeks ago. A shiver ran through me.

I guzzled down more water as the rest of the cheerleading squad walked onto the field. The game would start in an hour. People would show, taking their seats on the bleachers.

"Scarlet, are you heading in with us? The coach wants to talk to us before the game," one girl asked.

I nodded and stood. Normally, I'd lead us into the building, but I didn't feel like being in the front today. My balance was off somehow, and I didn't have time to figure out what was wrong with me. Maybe the heat was getting to me. We were having cooler weather and then an Indian summer came flying around the corner, smacking us all in the face with its hot and sticky heat.

"Okay ladies," Coach Lutz said. "Let me remind you it is hot out there today. Let's make sure we keep hydrated. Don't need anyone going to the hospital tonight with dehydration."

Yeah, don't need Allen showing up to save my ass again.

"One more thing, ladies."

We all seemed to lean in as if the coach was whispering. Waiting for her to finish the sentence.

"Let's cheer like hell tonight. Let's make those Beehives find a new nest to live in and win this game."

We all cheered at her words, which seemed to liven me up. In ten minutes, the game would start so I led the girls out to the field as people were filling the stands. As I came around the building where the field began, for one split second, I saw Kyle everywhere. But he was dead, wasn't he? Was I losing it completely? I closed my eyes and when I opened them; I realized it wasn't Kyle, but his jersey #37. The whole team was wearing his number.

"Are you okay?" Rachel asked as she came up beside me.

I slowly nodded as I wiped a single tear away. This wasn't the place to cry.

Rachel put her arm around me and walked out to the field. "You'll be okay. They wanted to wear his number because he couldn't be here to play."

"I know. He would have liked that the team did this for him. Remembering him on this day."

"Yeah, he would have. He also would have made some kind of snide remark that they can't win this game without him," Rachel said, laughing.

I laughed along with her as we made our way onto the field. We took our place on the sideline and looked up at the stand. There at the very top of the bleachers was Lianne, and she was staring at me with eyes that could burn through to my soul. What the fuck was she doing here? She had never since I've known her had come to any of my school festivities, so why now?

FIFTY-THREE

LAURA

I wasn't sure about going to the game, but since Rachel texted me to come, I agreed, besides I didn't want to sit in this house alone with all my demons. I had done enough of that when I locked myself in my own home because of my alcoholic, abusive mother. I didn't have to worry about her anymore, and this was my senior year. My last year of high school and needed to enjoy it because I was leaving this town behind once I graduated next year.

There was no parking spot at the school, so I had to park down the road and walk. Cheering sounded all around me, which told me that one team must have scored a touchdown or something.

The closer I got; I could see that the bleachers were packed like sardines. It was way too hot to be crammed together like that. I gazed around the open grass near the bleachers away from everyone and sat against the wall of the shed. It was far away from the field, but I could still see and hear what was going on. Besides, I wasn't really into sports. I just didn't want to sit at Rachel's alone.

My phone chirped, and I slid it from my back pocket. I recognized the number as Lianne's. What did she want now? I've been staying away from her since she mentioned killing Scarlet. I wasn't into hurting her in that way. Not that she didn't deserve to die, but it was my life on the line. Prison wasn't where I wanted to spend the rest of my life just because Lianne didn't like Scarlet. Their shit was their own to sort out, not mine. I planned on confronting Scarlet about knowing the truth, that was all!

End of story.

No one needed to die.

Lianne: **You can come sit with us.**

Us? I questioned myself. Who was she referring to? I scanned what I could see of the bleachers looking for her but couldn't see her anywhere. There were too many people here, and all the faces seemed to blend as the sun started to fall behind the bleachers. But she could apparently see me.

Me: **Who's us?**

Lianne: **Just my younger brother, Allen.**

I wasn't aware Lianne had a brother, but I also had only met her twice. So, I knew nothing about her or where she came from.

Me: **Oh, okay. I'm fine where I'm at but thank you.**

Lianne: **Suit yourself. Maybe we can get together after the game?**

Did she think we were best buddies now because she'd told me about the car accident? How was I going to get rid of this woman? I appreciated her telling me, but she was taking things a little too far.

Me: **Ah, thanks, but I got other plans with my friend.**

Lianne: **Sure, no problem.**

Her reply didn't sound very heartwarming. Besides, why would she want to hang around with someone at least ten years younger than her? I wasn't sure and really didn't care.

When the game ended, Rachel walked toward me. Everyone was cheering and knew there was sure to be a party somewhere tonight. For a split second, Kyle's house popped into my head and what happened there that night. I wouldn't be going even if he would not be there. Or I could go and not drink this time. That was also a possibility.

"Hey, Laura," Rachel greeted. "What a game, right?"

"Yeah, we really stung the Beehives asses tonight," I laughed.

Rachel laughed at my joke and plopped down beside me. "There's a party at Rob's tonight." She looked away out toward the football field. "Do you want to go? We can drop your car off at the house and ride together."

I said nothing.

"Nothing will happen this time, I promise. I'll be there the whole time."

"You were there last time, and it still happened," I said without looking at her.

"Yeah, but…"

"I know Kyle won't be there. And yet, someone's still having a party even though he's dead."

"It's because we won the game."

I turned toward her, looking into her eyes, then away again out at the almost empty football field. "Okay, but I'm not drinking at all!" I emphasized.

"No problem. I'll only have a few and if I'm too drunk, then you can drive us home."

I laughed. "Okay, deal." I knew one of us needed to watch out for the other after what had happened to me. I'm surprised that Rachel wanted to drink at all.

✝ ✝ ✝

We arrived at the party an hour later. We had gone home to not only drop off my car but also because Rachel wanted to change her clothes. Everyone from school seemed to be here, and I wondered if Rob's parents were home. There were underage teenagers dancing and drinking. I think I had my answer.

"Let's go sit outside by the bonfire," Rachel suggested.

I looked outside and saw that Travis was out there and felt ill suddenly. I wasn't sure why I was so nervous around him. He was a nice guy and never seemed to say anything bad to anyone. In fact, if I remembered correctly, he was the one who defended me against Scarlet at Kyle's party.

I nodded and followed Rachel out to the fire. We sat down in the lawn chairs positioned around the fire. This must be Travis's favorite thing to do. Even at Kyle's party he was keeping the fire going.

"Hi, Travis," Rachel said, sitting down beside me.

"Hey, glad you could make it," he replied.

Then he looked at me and smiled his gorgeous smile. I was about to lose the contents in my stomach. He was so hot. Calm down, you'll be fine. I smiled back at him and nodded.

Travis walked over and grabbed another chair and sat down beside me. "So, you going to the dance tomorrow?" he asked.

What? the voice in my head screamed. It's not like he's asking you to go with him. He only asked if you were going. Right?

I nodded. "Um, ya'," I tittered. "Me and Rachel are going together." You sound like a dork.

"Oh, okay."

Oh, okay? Why did he sound hurt?

Rachel elbowed me and tilted her head toward Travis. "I think he's asking you to go with him," she whispered.

"Oh," I mouthed back, then suddenly the words she had said sunk in, and my eyes grew wide.

"Are you serious," I mouthed to her.

Rachel nodded and smiled.

I turned to face Travis. "So, who's your lucky date to Homecoming?" I asked, swallowing the lump in my throat but still looking at him. Whoever his date was will be so lucky.

"Well, I was hoping you'd go with me. That you'd be my date," he said as he gazed into my eyes.

"M… Me?" I stuttered.

"No, Rachel. Of course, you," he laughed.

"Oh, uh," I looked from Travis to Rachel. She gave me a smile and a wink. "Yes. Yes, I'd like that," I replied.

I had never felt my stomach flutter the way it did at that moment. It felt remarkable. I, Laura Stevenson, was going to the Homecoming Dance with the hottest guy at CFH. I couldn't stop beaming as his words kept replaying over and over in my head. Tomorrow would be the best night of my entire life.

Fifty-Four

Rachel

She looked so happy sitting here talking with Travis, so I left them by the fire and went inside. Maybe a drink and something to eat would distract me enough to not think about going to the dance, once again—solo. Well, it wasn't as if I had tried to find a date.

I entered through the slider off the main deck that led me into the kitchen. I couldn't believe that there were so many kids here from school. Everyone was here after all that had happened lately. Kyle was a popular guy at the school. But no one seemed to be missing him. Though this shouldn't be a shocker—Kyle was a dick to everyone, even to his own guy friends. Sort of like Scarlet was a bitch to her friends.

I grabbed a can of coke from the cooler, then grabbed a plate and filled it with some chips and dip. Resting my back against the wall, I looked at all the people dancing and drinking in the living room. This place would be trashed when it was all over. If it were my house, which I'd never throw a party. My parents would ground me for life if they found out. But that's the difference between me and a quarter of Craven Falls High. I had parents that cared about me and were home, and not in some other country working or traveling.

The place was wall-to-wall with kids from school. Their shoulders touched as they jumped in place with whatever song was playing. Along the far side was a ping-pong table set up, and people were playing beer pong. I used to be the first to play the game and the first to be outside puking my guts out. Not my thing now, it was more of a dare that Scarlet made me do. Besides, I wasn't planning on drinking tonight. I wanted to keep a clear head. After the last party, I would not take any chances of something bad happening to my friend Laura.

"Hey," Scarlet said as she weaved through the crowd toward me. "Fancy seeing you here."

Actually, I was thinking the same about her. "Hi," I replied, then ate a chip.

"Are you here alone?"

I chewed, drank, and answered her annoying question. "No, Laura's out by the fire talking with Travis." Damn it. I didn't want to tell her, but the chances of her finding out on her own was slim to none.

"Travis?"

It was almost like she was asking me if it was the Travis Evans from school. Who else would I be talking about? "Yes, Travis from school. He asked her to the Homecoming Dance."

"You're kidding me, right? Didn't he ask you?"

"Me?" I laughed. "What gave you that idea?"

"Well, before the game tonight, you were talking to Travis, and you had a huge smile on your face. You were so happy."

I laughed again. "That's because he asked me if she were going with anyone."

She nodded as clarity came to her. "So, are you just hanging out in here?"

"Yeah, for now. I wanted Laura and Travis to have some time to talk."

"Gotcha. So, are you excited about the dance tomorrow?"

"No, why would I be excited? It's just a dance."

"Why don't we go together, like old times?" Scarlet suggested.

So much had happened over the past month. I wasn't sure we were the same people we were four weeks ago. Two best friends hanging out all the time, telling each other our secrets and fears. They exchanged words. Hateful words that I wasn't sure I could forget. We couldn't be the same friends we had been for all these years. There was no way I could accept her proposal.

"I don't know, Scarlet. Do you think it's a good idea to go together?" Disappointment spread over her face. She really believed we could kiss and make up.

"Well," Scarlet said. "I'm willing to let what happened between us go and start over again."

"Can we start over again? Is it that simple?" I immediately lost my appetite. I handed her my plate and walked away as if she was a stranger bribing me with candy and luring me into her van. I wasn't sure I had made the right choice by turning away from her, but for once I had to stand up for myself and not let Scarlet order me around like she always did.

FIFTY-FIVE

SCARLET

She left me standing there by myself, holding her stupid ass plate in my hand. Who did she think she was, walking away from me? I was getting sick and tired of Rachel treating me this way. I had enough shit to deal with. Lianne and this Allen guy; whoever the hell he was. If Rachel really didn't want to be my friend than all she had to do was say so.

Her words stuck in my head. Can we start over? Is it that simple? The words replayed over and over until I understood what she was saying. We had both said terrible and hurtful words to one another. Words that couldn't be forgotten, but I was willing to forgive her for the things she'd said. In all reality, Rachel should apologize to me, not the other way around.

I threw the paper plate in the trash and walked outside onto the deck, which gave me a straight view of Laura and Travis. They were laughing and having a good time. Something snapped in me. Why was she allowed to be happy when I had lost the man I loved? I would let her have her night of bliss. Tomorrow night, she would pay for killing my boyfriend. I know she did it. She had the motive to kill him after what he did to her and those other girls.

Part of me wanted to waltz out there and demand her to tell me and everyone else the truth. That she is a killer. But I couldn't move from where I stood. I needed to keep my cool and finish this tomorrow.

Alone.

Behind the bleachers where no one would see us.

FIFTY-SIX

LAURA

We stayed at the party until 1 a.m., then drove back to Rachel's house. I couldn't stop smiling the whole night and on the drive home. Travis and I were going to Homecoming in less than twenty-four hours. Eighteen, to be exact. This would be the best night of my life. I had dreamed of him and now it was all coming true. What a way to start my senior year!

I looked out the passenger window; it was darker than it had been in a long time. It was as if there were no moon in the sky, not even stars. I didn't know what that meant. I wasn't into astronomy or anything like that. Maybe there was a storm coming. Like something terrible was about to happen here in Craven Falls.

When we arrived home, we both went our separate ways. Both heading to our own rooms. I stopped and looked at Rachel. Something wasn't right with her, and I wondered if I'd upset her. Wow, how the tables had turned. She had said the same thing to me the other day.

I started to open my mouth and ask, but she slipped into her room and closed the bedroom door. Maybe she needed some space. Besides, I was exhausted. I couldn't wait to dream about my night I just had with Travis Evans. And the night I was about to have with him.

I slept until ten the following day, feeling refreshed and excited all at the same time. Tonight, I would dance with Travis and hoping he would kiss me. I've imagined the kiss a thousand times. Never wanting the dream to end. I couldn't believe it took all of high school to get him to ask me out. Was it because of me being friends with Rachel? Now that I was semi-popular, he noticed me. I shook my head. It didn't matter why. Travis asked me out, and that's all that mattered.

I slipped out from under the blankets to use the bathroom, then walked into the kitchen thinking Rachel would be in there since I didn't see her in her room. Her bedroom door had been open, and I peeked inside to find her bed empty and made as if she hadn't slept in it.

I looked out the front window and didn't see her car in the drive or her parents' vehicle. I was alone in the house. Sad that Rachel didn't wake me and ask if I wanted to go with her wherever she had gone.

I grabbed a bowl from the cabinet and poured myself some cereal. No one had arrived home in the time it took me to eat. I rinsed out my bowl and decided I would lie back down. I would not go back to sleep, but I didn't want to shower too early and then mess up my hair for tonight.

The house was too quiet, and I began to get antsy. I dressed and pulled my hair up into a messy bun. I needed to finish the rest of my mom's house, so I could sell it. Although Rachel had brought over some of my stuff, I still had a few boxes left at the house.

Minutes later, I pulled along the curb, looking at my house from across the street before backing into the driveway. I needed to just sit and look at the place I had grown up in. It had been my home since I was born and now it wasn't. So much had happened behind those walls. I let the memories of my dad dance in my head. Him playing catch with me outside in the yard. Him tickling me on the living room floor until I had tears running down my face. My stomach aching because he made me laugh so hard. Hearing my laughter fill the house.

I hadn't noticed before that my mom looked upset; almost angry at me for being so happy playing with my dad. Had she been jealous of me? It made perfect sense. Why had she taken things out on me after he died? My brother Teddy was the apple of her eye. Had I been jealous of them? I didn't think so because I had my dad.

Flashes of my brother and I came into view. I could see now how my mom favored my little brother over me. He was her baby, and I was no one to her. I scanned through the memory I had of my brother, and I could see now that I was my father's favorite and my mother hated that. I had always thought I'd done something wrong to upset her. I caused her to hate me. But I hadn't. It was her all along. She had a problem, and I was the solution.

I wiped away the single tear that slid down my face. I didn't want to think about her on a day like today. Not when I had so much to look forward to tonight.

FIFTY-SEVEN

SCARLET

Last night after Rachel walked away from me, I ran into JJ. We got to talking, and I found out he didn't have a date to the dance either, so we went together. Although he wouldn't have been my first choice in men, I didn't want to go alone. Feeling lost without Kyle beside me. We were going together to honor Kyle, who was JJ's best friend and my boyfriend.

At four that afternoon, I had an appointment to have my hair and make-up done. Normally, it was something Rachel, and I did together, but she had chosen who she wanted as her friend. She wanted nothing to do with me. I wasn't happy about her decision and would eventually make her pay for leaving me in the dust, but tonight wasn't about her. Laura, well screw her. She would get what was coming to her. I have something in store for her tonight. She will not get away with ruining my life. I will have the entire school laughing at her, and there's nothing she can do about it. I was done being nicey-nice to her. She deserved whatever happened to her and ten times more. I don't give a shit that my mom accidentally killed her father and brother. They probably deserved to die, anyway.

I wasn't sure where all my anger was coming from, but it felt good. Rejuvenated.

The limo arrived at exactly 7:00 p.m. with JJ inside. I had the driver pick him up first and then come to my house. My father wasn't home, not that this surprised me, but more hurt that he wasn't here to see me off to the dance. My last Homecoming Dance of high school.

He seemed to live at the office more now that Lianne didn't live here. It was as if I wasn't enough for him. Although he wasn't one to take pictures; that was something my mother had done before she died.

I had the driver take us the longest way to the school. I wanted an entrance where everyone could see me in my dress that I had bought at Saks Fifth Avenue. It looked gorgeous on me, but everything usually did. It was a Marchesa Notte Ombre Gown that had a haltered neckline, leaving my shoulders and back bare. It tightened at the waist, puffed out a little at the hips, and flowed to the ground. I loved the way the dark blue started at the top and lightened as it reached the floor. They elevated the dress with velvet trim and a stunning sheer overlay.

Everyone's eyes were on me when I entered through the doors of the gymnasium, whispers filling the surrounding air. I smiled and linked my arm through JJ's and walked toward the line to have our pictures taken.

He was sweet and kind, nothing I had ever seen in him before. JJ seemed to be a different guy tonight. Not his normal jackass self. I was just hoping he stayed this way the rest of the night, even though I smelled the alcohol on his breath and leaking from his pores. Was he already buzzed?

After we had our pictures taken, we found our table in the middle of the room, practically in front of the dance floor, and sat down. I wasn't looking forward to dancing with JJ, but what harm could it do? He was, in fact, my date.

I looked around the room to see if Rachel the traitor and Laura the bitch and her date Travis had arrived. I didn't see them which meant they'd be here soon. As my eyes scanned the rest of the room, I spotted Lianne in the far corner. "What was she doing here?" I said to myself. Heat rose through my body. This was my night, and she was here to ruin it, just like she ruined everything.

Without hesitating, I stood and stormed toward her. She looked in my direction as she stood next to Principal Harding. She tilted her head back a little and laughed. I've seen her do that with my father. She was chatting about God knows what with the principal. My principal. It disgusted me to imagine her slithering her way into his bed, just like she did with Kyle.

"Scarlet, it's so nice to see you," Lianne said in a pleasant voice.

She had to know that I was furious with her being here tonight. This was my night to have fun with the people I went to school with, so why was she here? To ruin my night.

"How do you know each other?" Principal Harding asked.

"I'm her stepmother," Lianne answered before I could.

Not anymore, you're not. I pasted on a smile. "Yes, so nice to see you here, Mother," I said as a metallic bitter taste entered my mouth. I had bitten the inside of my lip, tasting blood. I wanted to reach out and claw her throat out. I hated the witch with everything I had in me. I hated her more than I hated Laura. "You didn't tell me you would be here tonight."

"Sorry, yes, I'm chaperoning the dance tonight. Principal Harding sent out an email asking for chaperones. One lady on the committee told me when I was at the grocery store and thought since I wasn't doing anything tonight, why not?" Lianne said with a smile so wide it almost touched her ears.

"I'm so glad she did, few volunteered," Principal Harding replied.

Since when did Lianne shop at the grocery store? "Yes, so glad she did," I said. "Wouldn't be a dance without her here." This bitch was out to ruin my night. There was no other reason for her to be here. "Well, I should get back to my date."

"Yes, of course, say hello to James for me," Lianne sang.

How did she know his name? I swear if she does one single thing with him tonight, I will kill her. I mean there wasn't anything going on between JJ and me, but he was my date and that meant she needed to keep her fucking hands off him.

I walked back to the table and saw JJ sitting there nursing a drink which I was sure had alcohol in it. Kyle once told me that JJ always carried a flask with him filled with vodka, which was odorless.

As I approached, he raised his glass toward me. "Hey, you look like you need one of these."

I did. "Yes, please." Sitting down beside him.

JJ looked around and poured some of his special drink from his flask into my cup with no one seeing.

"Here's to us," JJ said as we clinked our glasses together. "And to Kyle who loved a good party. We will miss you, bro."

I was speechless by his words and hadn't thought what Kyle's death was doing to JJ and the rest of the football team. I, as usual, only thought of myself. Just like Rachel had said to me.

JJ drank down a few more drinks in the next passing hour. Pouring more vodka into his glass with nothing else in the cup. He was drunk. It shouldn't surprise me; it's what he always did at parties. He spoke more freely the drunker he became. The words he said next baffled me.

FIFTY-EIGHT

RACHEL

Laura, Travis, and I arrived shortly after seven. The photographer, a client of my mom's, let Laura and I take some pictures together and then Travis and Laura, and then all three of us. This was a night I'd never forget. I wanted Laura to have an amazing night too, so I vowed to not hang out with the two of them as much. Laura needed this. Laura deserved this.

Scarlet was sitting with JJ. I had heard whispers that they were each other's dates. Scarlet wouldn't do anything with him. He wasn't her type. Who knew what was going on in her mind after the death of Kyle? His bizarre drowning still had me stumped. Since I wasn't hanging out with Scarlet any longer, I had no idea if they had got a hold of his parents. I hadn't asked my mom about the case, knowing she couldn't really talk about it with me, anyway.

I felt so alone tonight. I had always been with Scarlet. Never once had a date. Tonight, I wanted that. I wanted to dance with someone I liked or even loved, but there was no one here at Craven Falls that I crushed over.

I grabbed a cup of punch from the refreshment stand and stood to the side, scanning the room. The DJ played the latest tunes like, In My Feelings by Drake, Girls Like You by Maroon 5, and Perfect by Ed Sheeran. Songs that were popular and had almost everyone out on the dance floor, dancing to the beat. My mind again started wondering what it would be like to be out there just enjoying myself like everyone else. Someone to dance with. Someone that mattered to me, and I mattered to them.

I spotted Travis and Laura on the dance floor. They made a good-looking couple, and I hoped that they stayed together after tonight. I wondered if she thought he would kiss her. Although, what happened between the two of them should be the last thing on my mind.

Something was going down tonight. I could feel it on my skin and in my bones. Scarlet had a plan from the beginning unless she'd changed the original scheme from before. The plan to humiliate Laura wouldn't ruin her, but it would make everyone at school laugh at her and probably keep them talking for weeks, maybe even months. The lies of Laura sleeping around town with any guy that would have her. Scarlet said she was going to photoshop Laura's face in as many pictures she could and pass them around the school or on the projector screen mounted on the stage behind the DJ. Would she use the same photos that Kyle had taken? God, I hoped not. I also hoped that Travis wouldn't believe the lies and not want anything to do with Laura.

My stomach tightened as the images popped into my mind of what Kyle did to her. Scarlet probably thought I'd stop it from happening, which I would, and so she probably changed her plan. Laura's my friend and Scarlet needed to stop being a bully and a bitch to everyone in this school. I just didn't know when she would play her prank.

I looked back at the table. Scarlet was still sitting there with JJ. They looked to be in a serious conversation. I looked away and scanned the dance floor. The song The End of Love by Florence and the Machine was playing. I didn't see Laura and Travis dancing. I looked at our table and only saw Travis sitting there nursing a drink, keeping to himself and talking to no one. I needed to find Laura and quick before Scarlet got her hands on her.

Before I could go look for her, a guy I hadn't seen before stopped me.

"It's Rachel, right?" the guy asked.

"Yes," I replied. "Do I know you?"

"Doubtful. I haven't gone to this school in years. You wouldn't remember me."

Then why was he here? And why was he talking to me? "So, who are you then?"

"Allen."

I scanned my brain, thinking if I had ever heard of his name, but nothing came to me. He said he hadn't gone to his school in years. By the look of him, I would say he was five or more years older than me. "Allen what?" I asked.

"Allen Swig. I'm Scarlet's neighbor. I live across the street from her."

I nodded. He still didn't ring a bell to me.

"I'm a cop here in Craven Falls. I was the one who came to the scene when Scarlet found Kyle dead in the pool."

Scarlet had never mentioned him. She was too panic-stricken about finding Kyle. I nodded as if I recalled him. I just wanted to get away and find Laura.

"So, why are you here then if you don't go to this school? If you're not a student?" I asked.

"Oh, I'm here for my sister, Lianne. You know her."

He wasn't asking me; he already knew I did. If he lived across the street in the house, I think he lived in, then he most likely saw me every time I came to Scarlet's house. But I honestly didn't care who he was. I needed to get away from him and find Laura.

"Sorry, but I need to find my friend," I said and looked away, scanning the room.

"Sure," he said. "I hope you find her in time."

His words registered in my brain, I turned back around to look at him, but he was gone. I scanned the crowd of people, but he was nowhere in sight as if he'd vanished into thin air. I needed to find Laura now because I believed her life was in danger.

FIFTY-NINE

LAURA

I couldn't stop smiling ever since Travis arrived at Rachel's house to pick us up. He wore a black suit with a red tie to match my dress. He was so sweet and held the door for both me and Rachel. I couldn't wait to see our Homecoming pictures together. This was the best night of my life.

I was beyond nervous thinking about our first kiss that hadn't happened yet. Imagining his lips on mine made my stomach flip inside and prayed I wouldn't get sick on him when we were on the dance floor.

After we left the dance floor, I excused myself to use the restroom. Still feeling woozy from him being so close to me. I stepped outside and stood around the corner of the building so no one would see me if I got sick. The fresh evening air felt calming as I breathed it in, though I could smell a hint of rain in the air.

Looking up at the sky, I noticed the fast-moving clouds as if they were racing to get out of here. A breeze came out of nowhere, making my hair whip and untangle from the braid Rachel put in before we left for the dance. I needed to get back inside before I looked like I was in a tornado. I had worked hard to look my best tonight and didn't want to have the evening ruined by coming outside for fresh air.

I was about to leave and head back inside when an all too familiar voice filled the night air around me. Scarlet was outside, and she was talking to someone. I wasn't sure who, and I didn't want to peek around the wall. I didn't want to ruin my night fighting with that bitch.

"You need to leave!" Scarlet shouted. "I don't know why you're following me everywhere. You were at the football game and cheer practice before that. And now you're here? What do you want from me? Why are you following me?"

"Because you told your father about me, you bitch. You got me kicked out of the house," Lianne screamed back at Scarlet.

So that's why Lianne told me what really happened in the accident. She was getting even with Scarlet. I still wanted to confront Scarlet about what she knew but now wasn't the time. I didn't want to get involved in their little pow-wow.

"Actually, you did that yourself by sleeping with my boyfriend, you fucking bitch!"

Oh, snap! This was too good to be true. Lianne slept with Kyle and Scarlet found out, and then most likely she told her father about the whole thing and now her ass was out of the house. Wow! So, Scarlet's life wasn't so perfect. She presented herself as having the perfect life and family, but she didn't have a loving family.

"I also know how Kyle died," Scarlet said.

"What? How does Kyle dying have anything to do with me?"

I could hear the faint hesitation in Lianne's voice, but I don't think Scarlet heard it.

"Oh, don't you dare try to deny what you did to him," Scarlet said.

"I don't know what you think you know, but you better get your facts straight," Lianne replied.

"My facts are straight. You're the one who went over to Kyle's house to persuade him not to tell anyone about the two of you and you killed him," Scarlet growled.

Oh my God, I couldn't believe what I was hearing. The small, not-so-perfect family that everyone admired had a closet full of secrets. Lianne killed Kyle? I couldn't picture her small petite frame overtaking Kyle. He had muscular arms because of all the sports he played. My mind went back to the other day when Lianne had grabbed my arm and how she was stronger than I had imagined her to be. Could she be capable of killing Kyle?

"Prove it!" Lianne screamed. "If you can prove that I had anything to do with Kyle's death, then show me or else piss off and get out of my face!"

Crap, I wished I had thought to record this on my phone, but it was in my purse at the table with Travis. Travis, shit! He was probably wondering what happened to me and would come looking for me. I had to figure out a way to get back inside but with Scarlet and Lianne fighting by the door I came out of; I had no way to get back inside. At least not through that door. I would have to walk across the football field to get to the front of the school.

"Oh, I have my proof, Lianne. And tomorrow, I'm going to the police. So, you better enjoy the rest of your night. Because it's the last bit of freedom, you will have."

"You fucking worthless bitch!" Lianne yelled. "I should have gotten rid of you a long time ago!"

There was a slap.

"Ouch, you bitch," Lianne cried out.

Then another slap. Those two were going at it like feral cats trying to claim their home. Something tickled my nose, and I sneezed. Shit! The second it happened; silence filled the surrounding air. They heard and knew someone was out here who had overheard everything. I had to get out of here before they found me.

I turned and started running across the football field, hoping that they wouldn't see me. I stopped and slipped the high heel shoes off my feet for better traction in the grass. Out of nowhere, the wind picked up, and the clouds opened. A rumble and then rain spilled from the sky, hitting me with such force, I almost fell. I didn't want to look to see if they were behind me, but I needed to know if I were being chased. I glanced over my shoulder, but I didn't see them anywhere.

I spun around in circles, but they weren't behind me or around me. Maybe once the rain came, they changed their minds and went back inside.

I was being soaked to the core. The rain ruining my dress and hair. There was no way I was going back inside looking like this. How would I explain the way I looked? I guess I could tell someone that I had overheard Scarlet and Lianne fighting and then them chasing me, which they weren't.

Then it came to me. I'd go to the shed and wait for the rain to stop. No one would come looking for me in there. I unlocked the lock with the combination I got off the computer in the front office. The perks of helping the ladies out in my free time. Besides, I had needed a place to go when my mom was too drunk and was hitting me. It was the only place to go. To get out of the rain until it stopped.

Once inside, I closed the door and turned on a small camping lamp I had stashed in a box. Thankful the shed didn't have a window in it. No one would know that I was in here unless they saw me come in.

I grabbed a towel and started drying myself. I also had a small kit I had brought from home to clean myself up when my mother beat me. I wiped away my make-up, which smeared from the rain. So much for being waterproof.

I wrapped the towel around my shoulders as I began to shiver from the wetness of my clothes, hoping I wouldn't have to stay in here all night. I finally got to be with Travis and now the evening was ruined. He probably thought I ditched him. Then, a thought hit me. My purse was still at the table which hopefully would tell him something was wrong, and he'd come looking for me.

There was a sound outside, but I wasn't sure if it was the raindrops pelleting against the metal roof of the shed which occurred to me was a stupid place to hide in a thunderstorm, or if they were cries of terror piercing through the booms of thunder.

SIXTY

SCARLET

Everything seemed to happen fast. The second we heard someone sneeze, Lianne turned away from me. I was too busy scanning the scenery to pay attention to what she was doing. When I looked back at her, she was holding something long in her hand.

My first thought was to get out of there, so I took off running as fast as I could, but my high heel shoes were slowing me down as they sunk into the mud. I bent down, slipped off my high heel shoes, and peered over my shoulder, scanning over the football field. Darkness loomed all around me in a haunted cemetery kind of way, as if waiting for the dead to rise. I couldn't see a damn thing in front of me or behind me; then the sound of water splattering.

Lianne was coming for me.

I turned back around too quickly and stumbled forward. My foot had caught the fabric of my Marchesa Notte Ombre Gown, causing me to trip, but caught myself before falling to the ground. Once I righted myself, I took off running again.

The light posts that stood along the edges of the field cast a faint glow but not enough for me to see where the hell I was going. Then a lightning bolt shot across the sky, lighting my way. Up ahead were the bleachers. The same bleachers I performed in front of as fans watched from their seats as I cheered and shook my pom-poms in the air. It was where we played all our football games in our small, quaint town. It was also my only place to hide from the bitch chasing me.

"I'm coming for you, bitch," hollered Lianne from behind me.

I didn't stop; I just kept running until the connection of something hard sent shock waves of pain through my skull and down my spine. I squeezed my eyes shut, an instant reaction to the pain coursing through my cranium. The automatic reflex of my hand went to my head, feeling something warm and wet. I was sure it was blood and not the rain but didn't have time to look at my hand to confirm. How had she caught up to me so fast?

I had to run.

I had to hide.

If I'd known I would be running in the rain, I wouldn't have worn such an expensive dress. My father would kill me if Lianne didn't get to me first.

By the time I made it to the bleachers, hoping to find shelter, something hard struck me on the back of my leg. My high heel shoes and clutch purse flew out of my hand as I fell to the ground like a hundred and twelve-pound bag of potatoes.

I tried to scream, but the sound was knocked out of me when my body smacked the wet, hard ground. This was a nightmare. A bad dream. I couldn't be living this, but I was, and it was more real than anything I had ever experienced before in my life.

I grabbed my right leg as the pain shot through my body. Shattered in several places. I crawled, dragging my right leg across the wet, freshly cut grass, gritting my teeth. I slinked along, fighting the sharp, throbbing pain coursing up my leg and into my back. I would die if I didn't find safety, but the bleachers wouldn't save me, only camouflage me behind the monstrous metal seats, still, I moved toward them.

Once under the bleachers, I collapsed onto my side. I couldn't go any further; not only from the pain but because I was losing blood from the large gash, I now had on my head. Lianne wasn't trying to hurt me; she wanted me dead for ruining her life with my father.

Water slid between the metal slats of the bleachers and fell onto my face. The rain changed from a light drizzle to pouring down in an instant, dropping onto my bloody split-open head. My vision was hazy as I looked out the corner of my eye, blinking away the water as it fell harder from the sky.

My head pulsated from the blow I'd received just minutes ago; a headache wasn't surfacing; it was already there, shouting out obscenities. My reflexes took over when a movement to my left appeared. I curled myself into a fetal position to shield myself from what looked like a wooden bat about to slam into my body. The same wooden bat I had seen before at Laura's house, but I couldn't be sure.

The bat came down shattering the bones of my ribs. "Please, stop!" I cried out as a sharp pain coursed through me, feeling the snap of each bone breaking. It became harder to breathe as I sucked in an agonizing breath and cried out again. "I'm begging you. Please stop!"

She didn't stop. She would not stop until she finished what she'd started. I would not leave here alive. She would finish the job, and I would die here. No one would ever know the truth of what happened. The school was closed on Monday. By Tuesday, who knew what I'd look like after lying in the wet, soaked grass for two days?

The blows came down hard one after another, hitting every part of my body. There was anger in each hit. She hated me with everything she had inside of her. I would not survive. She'd make sure I didn't because I now know the truth about her killing Kyle.

She had made it look like he had overdosed by adding Percocet's to his drinks and then she led him to the pool and held him under the water. With all the drugs found in his system, there was no way for him to fight back. She stood there in the shallow end of his pool as Kyle went under one last time. She held his head just below the water, waiting for him to stop breathing. Then she climbed out of the pool and cleaned everything with her prints on it and left the house, leaving no trace of her ever being there.

The one witness to the crime that she hadn't known was watching her the entire time. This witness had been upstairs in Kyle's bedroom when they heard splashing in the pool. The witness went to the balcony overlooking the pool. They had seen everything. After Lianne left, the witness fled the scene because they had been on probation from a DUI and couldn't risk getting caught in the house with all the drugs and alcohol lying around. This was something I had found out tonight before my encounter with Lianne.

I guess I will take the truth to my grave of what happened to Kyle. My only thought was, "we would soon be together again."

"That's enough, Lianne," said a voice I knew all too well. But I wasn't sure with the cracks of thunder if it was really him.

She stopped hitting me. I lay motionless as the rain continued to drip onto my head and run down my face.

I couldn't move.

I was afraid to move. You wouldn't have known I was crying from all the rain running down my face. I forced in a haggard breath that smelled of cologne. The same smell that lingered in our house. The man I shadowed my entire life knelt in front of me. I held the breath I had just taken. My lungs were screaming for me to exhale as a piercing pain sliced through my shattered chest, my legs, and my head. I couldn't believe with my own eyes who I was seeing in front of me. My chest tightened as fear washed over me.

"I'm sorry but this needed to be done. You ruin everything good in people's lives. You set out to destroy without a care in the world, only thinking of yourself. You took all that they cherished and ripped it apart. You are so much like your mother was. And to think, I once loved you both," my father said.

"Yeah, you should've known better than to fuck with us, bitch!" Lianne said from above me. She looked taller in that small frame of hers. Stronger too, but who wouldn't be with my father's power to guide them?

"I'm sorry, but I'm tired of your charades, Scarlet Marie. You lied about the photos of Lianne and Kyle sleeping together. You made a video with false images of Lianne. And Laura. Why would you tell her about what your mother did?" my father said as anger rose in his voice. "Did you think I wouldn't find out? Are you trying to destroy me? Why do you want to take away the one thing that means so much to me since your mother died? I love Lianne and we will be together. I won't let you destroy my entire life. You would have eventually ruined everything I worked so hard to accomplish," he said and stood. "Make sure you get her phone. I don't want any evidence left that she may have on it. Do as we planned and make sure Laura takes the fall for this."

Lianne patted me down and felt around me, but she wouldn't find the phone as I threw my small clutch purse near the shed, hearing it hit the building as I fell and crawled under the bleachers. They wouldn't find it in the rain, but someone would when my body was discovered. I just hoped that my phone wouldn't be ruined by the rain.

I blinked several more times; I didn't want to believe what I had seen. My father had someone kill me. Not just someone, Lianne. The one person I hated with my whole life. No one would know the truth about her killing Kyle and now me. She somehow made my father believe I had made everything up, but I hadn't. Her performance this past year had been immaculate. All along, they had come up with a scheme to get rid of me forever. I wondered what took them so long. Why did they wait?

The rain and the darkness surrounding me distorted my vision. Maybe I had imagined it all, but I hadn't. The pain coursing through my body was real. Through the pelting raindrops hitting the bleachers, faint sounds of laughter filled the rainy night air as my father walked away, Lianne in tow. I wanted to scream out she was the one lying, not me, but I couldn't. It was too hard to breathe, more or less try to scream.

"Daddy, please," I whispered through parted lips, but knew he couldn't hear me. No one could.

Another drop fell from the black sky above and landed on my clammy, cold skin. Pain surged through me, like a burning fury of fire, and I couldn't move. I was afraid to move. They shattered my body. Broken into pieces and left me to die here under the bleachers.

No one would come looking for me, not on a night like tonight. Not in the pouring rain. I blinked as I drew in one last and final breath, staring out at the football field.

Sixty-One

Rachel

"Have you seen Laura?" I asked Travis.

"Not since she had to go to the restroom." He looked at his watch on his left wrist. "But that was an hour ago."

"You didn't think something was wrong when she didn't return?" I questioned with a snip in my voice.

He shrugged his shoulders. "Sorry, don't girls take a long time in the bathroom. You know, doing their make-up and hair."

I nodded. "I will go look for her."

The words Allen said were still fresh in my mind. I had to find Laura and soon. Before leaving the table, I looked down and saw her purse hanging over the back of the chair. She went to the restroom but didn't take her purse? I grabbed her purse and opened it. Her phone was still inside. Shit! I scanned the room looking for Scarlet. She was planning something, but I wasn't sure what and when it was going down.

"What's wrong?" Travis asked.

"I'm not sure but, damn it!" I growled between my teeth. "We need to find her. I think something may have happened to her."

Travis now stood in front of me. His tall, stocky build beaming down at me. "What is it?" he asked, sounding concerned.

I took in a breath and exhaled. "Scarlet is planning on doing something to Laura tonight in front of the entire school. Laura's missing, and I don't see Scarlet anywhere. And this Allen guy said that he hoped I found her in time," I shouted over the music.

"I'll help you look for her."

"I'll check the restroom and you look outside. Maybe they are outside talking or something," I said but knew they wouldn't be talking. Scarlet wasn't one you could just have a casual conversation with if she was pissed and wanted to get even with you.

Travis headed in one direction and I, in the other. I checked all the stalls. No, Laura anywhere. Would she be in another restroom? Usually, for dances, they had all the other doors locked so students wouldn't go walking around the halls and finding rooms to have sex in. Or whatever it is some of them do at these dances.

After leaving the restroom, I walked around the gym, looking at all the faces. I didn't see Laura anywhere. Scarlet was also missing in action. I hoped Travis had better luck.

I made my way toward the front of the school and out the doors. Rain poured from the sky as I stood under the roof that covered the doorway and steps in front of me. It surprised me I hadn't heard it thundering out here, but I guess with the music playing loud, there would have been no way to hear it.

"Rachel," Travis called out as he waved for me to come to him.

I was glad that the roof went around the front part of the building. "Did you find her?"

He shook his head.

"Where could she be?" Had she gotten caught out in the rain and needed to find shelter? Yes, that had to be what she did. Laura wouldn't leave without telling me, would she? She had been quiet and kept to herself lately. I prayed that Scarlet didn't do something to her. But I wouldn't know until the rain stopped so I could go looking for her. Or had I gotten it all wrong and Laura did something to Scarlet? No matter what, I still needed to find her.

I pulled on Travis's arm and had him follow me to the other end of the school. I wanted to look at the parking lot. Once there, I scanned the vehicles parked in the lot. In the far corner under the dim light hanging from the light post, someone was holding an umbrella and getting into what looked like a Cadillac. The only person with a car like that was Scarlet's father. Why would he be here? I questioned myself. Then I remembered seeing Lianne at the dance tonight. If Mr. Fitzgerald was picking Lianne up, then why wouldn't he have just driven up to the front of the school to get her? Why park out by the football field parking lot? And why would they be out there by the field anyway in the pouring rain?

"Laura," I mumbled.

"What did you say?" Travis asked.

"I think Laura's out there somewhere and she needs our help."

"Why do you think that?" Travis asked.

"I just have a feeling something happened out there." Pointing a finger out at the football field. "We need to see if she's out there."

"Are you nuts? I'm not going out there when it's lightening out." Travis said. "Haven't you heard the phrase, not to play out in the rain when there's lightning?"

"Fine," I moaned. "We'll wait until it slows down and then we'll go searching for her."

We headed back inside, scanning the gym again hoping to see her, but she wasn't in here. I had a terrible feeling that something had happened to her and she needed my help. But I had no idea where to look.

Sixty-Two

Laura

I couldn't believe my eyes. Lianne was beating Scarlet with a bat while Scarlet's father watched. He allowed that bitch to hit his own daughter. What kind of father does that? I couldn't hear what he was saying with the noise from the rain, but he left her there. He left his daughter to die, and I was Scarlet's only witness. Someone they hadn't known was hiding out in the shed with all the sports equipment.

Would I be the next to die? He had the files changed about his wife killing my dad and brother because he was the Mayor. What would stop him from getting rid of me? The last person still alive. I had hopes and dreams. I was leaving next year. If I said anything. If I told anyone. Everything I wanted would be gone. But hadn't I lost everything already? I had no family left. None that I knew of. No one ever came to visit us. I was alone with a choice to make that could change every aspect of my life.

My mind whirled, looking for answers I didn't have. I couldn't change what had happened in the past or tonight. I couldn't worry about anything but to save Scarlet. Scarlet needed to tell the police what happened tonight. I needed to go to her and help her before it was too late.

I cracked open the door again, making sure the coast was clear. That Lianne and Mr. Fitzgerald had left. Oh, how I wanted to say something to him about my father and brother's deaths. How he had covered up the truth of what happened. To protect his own family. He would cover this up and wondered who he would try to blame for his daughter's death? There were other kids at the school who hated Scarlet as much as I did, but to kill her. I didn't think so and besides; I knew who did. I knew the truth.

I poked my head out and saw through the haze of the rain pouring down that they were no longer here. Craning my neck around the door I saw them in the far distance, making their way to the parking lot. I slipped out of the shed and ran to where Scarlet was lying. She looked lifeless as I looked down at her. I scanned the scenery for the bat but didn't see it. Which meant, Lianne took it with her. Which also meant they would get rid of the evidence.

I bent down and gently nudged her. She was hurt. Badly hurt. Blood was running down her face. She didn't move. Was she dead? I swallowed, the bile rising; my throat tightened to prevent the liquids from exiting. I was more than sure she was dead, but I had to check. I placed two fingers on the side of her neck. I couldn't feel a pulse. I stared into her face, into her eyes, but saw nothing but a blank stare.

Then her eyes twitched.

She was looking at me.

She saw me.

"Scarlet, oh my God you're alive. You're alive."

She coughed. Blood spewed and appeared between her lips, then ran down her chin, falling onto the wet grass beneath her face.

Then she was gone.

Dead.

I was too late to save her.

Feeling ashamed for wanting to kill her myself now that I'm beside her lifeless body. Not that she didn't deserve to die for all the things she did to people. She did, but not in the way Lianne had killed her. Killed is such a strong word, and I don't believe I hated her that much to want her dead.

I began to shiver from the rain soaking me to the bones. I needed to get help. Even though she was dead, I couldn't leave her out here. I would want someone to help me if it were the other way around.

"I'm sorry, Scarlet," I said to her before standing and walking toward the school.

Rain pelted the ground in such force that it felt like I was walking through small lakes. The mud squishing between my toes. I smelled the wet grass and tasted the rainwater, slipping in between my lips. I prayed I wouldn't be found out here on the field dead like Scarlet.

By the time I had climbed the last few steps of the school and sat against the brick wall drained of energy, the rain had stopped. I was cold and shivering, exhausted from all that had happened. Someone would eventually come out of those doors beside me and see me sitting here. The towel I had wrapped around my shoulders no longer kept me warm after being soaked by the rain too, but I didn't want to take it off as it comforted me like a blanket swaddling a newborn.

"Laura." Someone called my name.

I turned, it was Rachel, and she had Travis with her. Shit! I didn't want him to see me like this.

"Laura, are you all right? What happened to you?" Rachel asked.

But the only words that slipped out of my mouth before I passed out from the initial shock of all that had happened tonight were, "Help Scarlet."

Sixty-Three

Rachel

When I went back outside to see if it had stopped raining, Laura was sitting against the building under the roof. She was soaked and shivering like a scared dog. I knelt beside her, Travis standing behind me.

"Laura, are you all right? What happened to you?" I asked.

"Help Scarlet," Laura whispered, and then she fell sideways to the floor.

"What's wrong with her?" Travis asked.

"I think she passed out or something," I replied, keeping my focus on Laura. Something bad had happened to her, but I didn't see any blood on her. She didn't look hurt. When she finally came to, I sat her up. "What happened to you?"

She looked from me to Travis. "We have to save… No. We have to call the police," Laura mumbled.

Her words scattered. I wasn't sure what she was trying to tell me.

"Scarlet. Is. Dead."

"What!" I shrieked in horror. "Scarlet is dead? How? Who? You?" I threw out questions after questions. I wasn't sure if I wanted to know if she had killed her. Killed Scarlet.

"I... I don't know who did it. Just call the police and get them out here. We can't leave her out there under the bleachers."

"Travis, call the police," I insisted. He pulled his cell phone out and dialed for help. "Laura, do you know what happened to her?"

"No," Laura answered, looking away.

She was lying. I was good at watching people and knowing when they were telling the truth. She was not. But I would not pressure her into telling me. I'd wait until we were alone.

"Can you tell me what happened tonight? The police will want to know what happened."

"I was outside walking around to get some fresh air and then the rain came down. I found her lying there dead under the bleachers. It looks like someone beat her with a baseball bat or something. I didn't see anyone around. So, I made my way back here to get help," Laura said.

"You didn't see anyone else out there?"

Laura shook her head.

"Okay, I will call my mom and have her come here. She'll know what to do."

Laura nodded.

Ten minutes passed before I finally heard the blare of sirens and the flashing lights cutting through the haze of raindrops.

When the police arrived, Travis waved the officer over to where Laura and I were sitting.

"What seems to be the problem? Is she drunk?" the officer asked.

"No!" I shouted. "She hasn't been drinking." I was hoping she hadn't been but wasn't sure. There was no smell of alcohol on her breath.

"We called you because there's a dead girl under the bleachers." Pointing toward the football field. "Laura said it's our friend's body. She's dead."

"Dead?" the officer questioned. "Can you show me?"

Laura looked at me, then at the officer. "No, I don't want to go back out there. She's dead. I'm not going back out there," Laura pleaded. "You can't make me."

"Officer, she said Scarlet Fitzgerald is under the bleachers. Go to the bleachers on the football field and you'll find her." He looked pissed until recognition set in.

"Are you talking about Scarlet Fitzgerald? The Mayor's daughter?"

"Yes, that's her." I wanted to ask if he knew of another Scarlet Fitzgerald, but I didn't.

"Oh, shit," he gasped. "Shit will hit the fan when he finds out someone killed his daughter," the officer mumbled.

The officer stood and walked away. He paced back and forth, then pulled out his cell phone and dialed a number. I couldn't hear what he was saying or who he was talking to.

"Rachel."

I turned to the sound of my name. It was my mom. I stood and went to her. She took me into her arms. They felt so comforting around me. They always have.

"Are you okay? What's going on here?" my mom asked.

"I'm fine. It's Scarlet. She's dead," I answered in a few short sentences.

"And Laura?" my mom asked, looking over my shoulder. "Is she all right?"

I swallowed. "She's the one who found Scarlet."

"Oh, no. That poor girl has been through enough lately. Dear God, what will happen next?"

My mom left my side and went to Laura. She pulled her up and into her arms. I smiled at the gesture because my mom was such a caring person. Blessed to have her as my mother.

"Laura, what happened tonight? Did you see or hear anything?" my mom asked.

Laura shook her head. "No, nothing," she said.

Laura's eyes looked at me then at the ground. She needed to get better at lying to people if she would have people believe her. I get that she doesn't want to talk to my mom or the police about what happened, but she needed to tell someone.

"Excuse me, Officer? Are you done questioning Laura? I'd like to take her home now if that's okay," my mom asked.

"Yes, but we may send an officer to your house to get a statement or she can come down to the station in the morning to give us a written statement about what happened here tonight."

"No problem. Just let me know," my mom said.

"Travis, thank you for everything tonight. You're such a great friend," I said to him.

"No problem," he said and gave me a hug. Then he walked over to Laura. "Sorry about tonight. I hope you'll be okay." He hugged her and kissed her on the cheek.

She melted into his arms. At least one good thing came out of tonight's events.

Sixty-Four

Laura

I couldn't wait to get back to Rachel's house. I didn't want to be at the school any longer than I had to, especially around all those police officers. They made me nervous. Someone was working with Mr. Fitzgerald. Someone helped cover-up his wife's accident and would do the same with Scarlet. They would find someone to blame.

Once at the house, I stood under the hot steamy shower, washing away the night. The images of Lianne smashing the bat down on Scarlet's body and head. That woman had more hate inside her than the devil himself. So much that she killed a human being. Part of me wondered if she did it before. Killing someone.

I remembered the words exchanged about Scarlet having Lianne kicked out of the house and then Mr. Fitzgerald standing there allowing Lianne to kill his own daughter. Confused about what was going on. Lianne and the Mayor must have been in cahoots the whole time. It's the only thing that made sense. If Scarlet found photos of Lianne and Kyle sleeping together and then told her father, which would have gotten Lianne kicked out of the house, then why was Mr. Fitzgerald in on killing his daughter? Did he not care what Lianne did? Was this all part of their plan? To get rid of Scarlet. I wished I would have heard what he had said to Scarlet before they walked away and left her there.

⚓ ⚓ ⚓

The following morning, I gave my statement leaving out the part about Lianne and Mayor Fitzgerald being the killers. Even though Mr. Fitzgerald didn't lay a hand on her, he still played a part in his daughter's death, but I didn't have proof yet to turn them in.

When we arrived back home, I told Rachel I needed to lie down for a while, but what I wanted to do was to watch the video of Lianne and the Mayor killing Scarlet. Last night when something hit the shed, I opened the door and found a purse lying outside. I grabbed it and opened it. I found Scarlet's phone inside. I only knew it was hers because the wallpaper on the lock screen had a picture of her and Kyle on it. There were screams, and I looked outside and saw them standing over her. That was when I turned on the video recorder and filmed Lianne beating Scarlet with a bat.

As I sat on my bed, I put on my headphones and played the video. As much as I hated watching Scarlet's death repeatedly, I needed to make sure the police saw who did it. I enhanced the image and got rid of the darkness in the video. Now, all I needed to do was to make sure this video got in the right hands, and both Lianne and Mayor Fitzgerald paid for what they'd done.

I went through the rest of her phone and found the pictures of Kyle and the girls. There was no sense on keeping them on the phone because he was dead. I also came across the photos of Kyle and Lianne and a video.

"Oh, shit! That's what they were fighting about. Scarlet had these and showed her father, but apparently the Mayor didn't give a shit what his wife was doing behind his back or he thought they were fake," I mumbled into the room. But I could tell they weren't fake. The images were real.

Kyle must have hidden his phone or maybe even a recorder in his room and videotaped them having sex, then all he had to do was save certain clips of the recording into photos. Lianne most likely didn't have a clue he was filming them; otherwise, she wouldn't have allowed him. At least, I think she wouldn't have. That woman was hard to figure out.

I emailed myself the file and moved it back into Scarlet's Inbox where the police would find it. Not that they wouldn't check the trash. Sometimes the police weren't as smart as they wanted you to believe they were.

Once done, I turned off the phone and hid it under the mattress. Tomorrow I would send the phone to Officer Rosmus because I trusted her. She helped me find out the truth about my father and brother and also sent a copy to the news station anonymously. They wouldn't get away with what they did to Scarlet. Then it hit me. Did Lianne and Mayor Fitzgerald also kill Kyle?

Sixty-Five

Laura

On Tuesday morning, Rachel drove us to school. There were whispers as we walked down the hall about the dead girl under the bleachers. I wasn't sure what story they had heard, but they were all looking at me. Did they think I killed her? No, the police would have arrested me if they thought I did it. After school, I would send out the evidence that will put the real murderers in jail. I just needed to make it through the rest of the day.

I was sitting in American History when two police officers knocked on the door and asked for me to come with them. A chill ran through my body as I collected my things and walked toward the door. Everyone was staring at me as whispers buzzed like a swarm of bees.

"Did she kill Scarlet?"

"Oh my God, it was Laura."

"It's always the quiet ones who are evil." My classmates whispered.

"Do you want me to call my mom?" Rachel shouted from across the room.

I wasn't sure what they needed to talk to me about, so I shook my head. They weren't here to arrest me, or they would have handcuffed me, right? I had done nothing wrong.

They escorted me out into the hall.

"Please put your hands behind your back. You are under arrest for the brutal murder of Scarlet Fitzgerald," the male police officer stated.

"I didn't do it," I pleaded. "I have proof that I didn't do it."

"We have proof you did," replied the male officer that looked familiar to me, but I couldn't think where I had seen him before.

"Laura!" Rachel shrieked in horror as she stood in the doorway. "I'm calling my mom. Say nothing to them. Wait for my mom to get there."

I nodded before the same officer by the last name of Swig pushed me forward and down the hall toward the entrance where the police cruiser was waiting for me. Everyone came out of their classrooms, including the teachers, to see what was going on.

One month ago, I was an outcast keeping to myself. Then Scarlet had to play her dirty little games and pretended to want to be my friend. Now, I'm being arrested for her murder which I didn't commit.

When we arrived at the police station, they escorted me into an interrogation room. They left the handcuffs on me as I sat in a metal chair in front of a puke-green table. Several minutes later, Sheriff White came into the room and sat down across from me. He started placing photos of Scarlet's body on the table in front of me. I had to turn my head away from some of them because of what she looked like.

"Can't stand looking at what you did?" Sheriff White asked. "For a killer, this shouldn't bother you."

"Then maybe I didn't do it," I replied. "I was there, but I didn't kill her."

"Then who did?"

"How do I know I can trust you?"

"I'm the sheriff."

"That means nothing. There's always one asshole in the group."

"Watch your mouth," Sheriff White snapped.

"I only want to speak to Officer Rosmus. Is she here?"

"And why will you only talk to her?"

"Because she's the only one I trust that works in this shit hole. I talk to her or I say nothing until my lawyer gets here." Which I didn't have but knew Mrs. Sawyer would probably represent me.

He gathered the photos into a pile and left the room. I looked around and saw the video recorder on the ceiling by the door. The light was red, which meant they were recording me. It didn't matter. I didn't kill Scarlet. Whatever evidence they had on me wasn't anything like I had on the real killers.

I sat in the small, plain, dark gray-colored room with its two-way mirror facing me, waiting for Officer Rosmus to appear. I was sure someone was standing behind the mirror watching me, but I had nothing to hide from the police. Some people by the names of Lianne and Mr. Fitzgerald were framing me for what they did. I was sure of it.

Then it hit me. The bat. What did they do with it? Had they planted the bat somewhere the cops would find it? Yes, of course, but I had looked for the bat when I was out there, although the rain had been pelting the ground in such volumes that I couldn't see very far in front of me. There would have been no way of seeing it if Lianne had thrown the bat out into the field. They had walked in the opposite direction than I had when I went back to the school to get help.

It explained me being arrested. But wouldn't they have figured out the time Scarlet had died and when I was found outside? I wouldn't have had time to hide the bat anywhere but at the school. I needed to know where they hid the bat.

SIXTY-SIX

Rachel

Several minutes after the officers led Laura out of the school, I texted my mom, letting her know what had just happened. She texted me back in fifteen minutes. "I know, I just saw them bring her in."

"Okay, let me know what you find out," I replied.

"You know I will," my mom said.

I had two more classes before school was over, and then I could go to the station and find out what was going on. I wasn't the person who left school in the middle of the day. No matter how much I wanted to.

I had wanted to talk to Laura for the last two nights, but she had clammed up and said she was tired and wanted to rest. I didn't want to pressure her, so I left her alone. Now I wished I had forced her to talk to me about what had happened out on that field. I believed that she didn't kill Scarlet, but she made it hard sometimes to trust her.

I drove as fast as I could to the police station without going too much over the speed limit. Although I wasn't worried about getting pulled over, as I was sure that all the police officers, we had in Craven Falls were all at the station. When I arrived, my mom was talking to Sheriff White. I walked up to her and tapped her shoulder.

"Rachel, what are you doing here?"

"I need to know why Laura is here. Why did they bring her here?"

My mom pulled me aside, away from everyone. "They have some incriminating evidence on her."

"What?" I muttered.

"They found the bat used on Scarlet at her house. It has Scarlet's blood all over it."

"That can't be. There was no way she could have killed her, driven to her old house, hid the bat, and then come back to the school," I said.

Travis had said that Laura had left the table for more than an hour. It would have given her plenty of time to kill Scarlet, drive to her house, hide the bat, and then come back to the school to make it look like we had caught her out in the storm. But how would she have gotten there? Travis had driven us to the dance. And why would she hide it at her house of all places? Wouldn't she have thrown it in a lake or something?

"Mom, that makes little sense."

"I'm just telling you what the police are saying. Laura's talking to Officer Rosmus right now."

"Without you?"

"I tried telling her I should be in there with her, but she said she has nothing to hide. Hold on to her backpack for me until I can get her released to come home with us."

"Okay," I said, taking the bag. "I will go sit outside. I can't be in here right now."

Mom nodded. "I'll find you if I hear anything more."

I gave her a quick hug and went outside. There was a small park on the left side of the building, so I walked down the steps and sat under a maple tree. I wanted to see if Laura had anything in her backpack, so I unzipped the top and rummaged through her things. Feeling a little guilty, but I needed to know if she was hiding something. There was nothing inside the large zippered area but schoolbooks. I turned the backpack around. There under a flap was another zipper hidden from the naked eye. I opened it and removed a manila envelope. Written on the outside was the name, Attn:

Officer Rosmus. Wait? Didn't my mom say she was talking to an Officer Rosmus?

I looked around and then carefully opened the sealed flap. Inside was a phone. Scarlet's phone. I only knew this because of the phone case on it. Why did she have Scarlet's phone? My mind started thinking the worst. Had she really killed her and then took her phone? No, of course not! I didn't want to believe she'd do that. Laura didn't seem the type to kill someone, especially the way Scarlet had been murdered.

I needed to search the phone. I swiped right and entered the passcode Scarlet had on the phone. The phone opened. "Okay, once I find out why Laura had Scarlet's phone; then I can give it to this Officer Rosmus." I mumbled; thankful no one was around to hear me.

I slid my hand into the envelope and pulled out a piece of paper. On it was written: Watch the video. Don't trust anyone. I went into the photo app and scrolled to the very last video. I hit play.

I couldn't believe what I was seeing. Lianne was hitting Scarlet with a bat. How did she have this video on her phone if she was being murdered? She wouldn't have known that this would set it up to record. Nothing was making sense to me. I needed to show my mom the video. She would know what to do.

I dropped the phone back inside the envelope and ran up the stairs and into the police station. I didn't see my mom anywhere. I hurried up to the officer behind the counter and asked where my mom was.

"I'm not sure," he said.

"What about Officer Rosmus? I need to speak to her immediately!" I demanded.

"Well, she's in with someone right now. Can I help you with something?"

Don't trust anyone. Laura had written on the piece of paper. "No, I need to only speak to Officer Rosmus, now!" I yelled.

"Settle down or you'll have to leave."

"What's going on here?" my mom asked as she walked toward me. "I can hear you all the way down the hall."

"Mom," I said as I took her by the arm and guided her to the far wall away from earshot. "You need to watch this," I said, handing her the envelope.

"What?"

"In the envelope is Scarlet's phone, and it has the real killer or, I should say killers on it," I whispered.

My mom looked at me like I had two heads. "What are you talking about, Rachel? You're not making any sense."

I stuck my hand in the envelope and pulled out the phone. Once I had the video, I hit play and turned it to face my mom.

"Oh my God!" my mom gasped. "How did you get something like this? Did someone give this to you?"

"Laura had it in her backpack, and I found it. I don't know where she got it from. It's Scarlet's phone, Mom."

"Laura had this in her bag?"

"Yes," I replied. I had no more answers for her. I knew as much as she did at this point.

My mom left me standing alone as she headed back through a set of security doors. I had a feeling she was going into the interrogation room where Laura was to show Officer Rosmus the video.

I paced the hall waiting to hear something back from my mom. Minutes seemed to tick by slower than a snail on speed. Then Laura and my mom came walking toward me.

"Laura," I squealed, hugging her tight against me.

"They dropped all the charges against her and are heading over to arrest both Lianne and Mayor Fitzgerald. I will stay here for a while. Why don't you go pick up the boys and I'll meet you at home later," my mom said in a hushed voice. "Don't breathe a word to anyone until they're arrested. It seems you may be right about there being a bad cop on the force Laura," my mom said. "I'll be home as soon as I can."

"Okay," I replied.

⚡ ⚡ ⚡

It was dark outside by the time my mom arrived home. She said to turn on the television to channel five news.

Female reporter: **The murder of Scarlet Fitzgerald has been the talk of the town since her tragic, brutal death on Saturday night. New evidence has come to our attention, as a videotape was released to the police with the killers, yes killers, beating the victim with a bat under the bleachers at Craven Falls High School on Saturday, September 29th, approximately around 9:35 p.m. the night of the Homecoming Dance.**

They arrested Lianne Fitzgerald and Mayor William Fitzgerald for the brutal murder of their daughter, Scarlet Fitzgerald. They released no comment to us on why they killed their daughter. They will hold a hearing on Thursday. No bail has been set.

A second eyewitness has also come forward; no name is being released yet, on the death of Kyle Tanner. The eyewitness said they saw Lianne Fitzgerald drown the victim in the pool at the Tanner residence after drugging Kyle with a large quantity of pain killers mixed in his drink. The police have yet to hear from the victim's parents about their son's death. If anyone has any further evidence or know where Kyle Tanner's parents are, please notify the Craven Falls Sheriff's office at 330-555-2222.

I had no idea who the eyewitness was. I looked over at Laura who was sitting there also with a look of shock on her face.

"This is wonderful news," I said. "Not that Scarlet's dead, but that they arrested Lianne and Mayor Fitzgerald on her murder and Kyle's too."

Laura nodded. "Who do you think saw Lianne kill Kyle?"

"I'm not sure," I whispered. Though my thoughts are that it was JJ who was out at the house that night, but I kept it to myself.

Laura sat there, not saying a word.

"What's wrong? This is good news."

"I know, it's just... I'll never get the images of Scarlet out of my head. Seeing her father allow Lianne to do what she did. I feel bad for Scarlet. The life she had to live outside of school. None of us knew what it was like in that house. It's no wonder she was a bitch to everyone. Not to speak badly of the dead or anything," Laura said.

"She wasn't always a bitch," I replied. "Now I can see why she was so angry all the time."

Laura nodded.

"If you think about it, you two had things in common," I stated.

"Don't go there," Laura replied. "You saw what my mom did to me. Scarlet wasn't abused."

"Not physically, but definitely mentally. That's why she bossed and bullied people around. She was filled with so much hatred inside. They didn't show her any love in that house."

"I wasn't shown love either nor did I bully the kids at school." Laura's voice began to rise.

I knew she was right. "I'm sorry, I guess everyone shows it in different ways. I didn't mean to compare the two of you, just the situations."

Laura nodded. "Sorry, I didn't mean to snap at you. What happened to Scarlet shouldn't have happened? I'm just glad the police have arrested them."

"Well, it was you that saved the day. If you weren't out there when it happened, then the police wouldn't have had the video of them killing her," I said. "Why were you out there, anyway?" Laura had never told me what had happened that night, and I was eager to know her side of the story.

"I went outside to get some air. I was nervous being around Travis," Laura said.

I nodded.

"I was hiding on the side of the building when Scarlet and Lianne came outside. They started yelling and fighting. All I wanted to do was to get back inside the school, but they were by the door. I didn't want Scarlet to see me," Laura expressed. "The only other way inside was across the football field to the front of the school, but before I could leave, I sneezed and knew I had to get the hell out of there before they found me. The rain came down, as I was running across the field, so I hid in the shed. It's where I always went after my mom hit me," Laura explained. "Then something hit the shed. It was Scarlet's purse with her cell phone in it. So, I filmed them. You know the rest."

"Oh my God, Laura. I'm so sorry. And you left your phone in your purse, which was inside the school, so you had no way of letting me know."

"Yep," Laura answered. "With everything that had happened with Scarlet, it didn't dawn on me to use her phone to call you. Besides, I didn't want Travis to see me like that. I was drenched, and my make-up was ruined. It was supposed to be the best night of my life."

"I wish you didn't have to see what they did to her, Laura. I'm so sorry."

Laura nodded. "Me too."

Epilogue

Laura

Three Weeks Later

I catch myself looking out at the football field directly at the bleachers. Certain I would never get the images of that night out of my head. Mrs. Sawyer has taken it upon herself to send me to therapy, something I have needed since my dad and brother died. It seems to help me heal and move past what my mother did to me and also what Kyle did. It's nice to talk to someone who doesn't know me all that well. Who won't judge me in the decisions I made?

Some secrets I can't share with Rachel. At least not yet. She's a great friend, but I'm not ready to let her know the real me since we stopped being friends in the seventh grade. I had gotten used to not having anyone to talk to.

After everything that had happened since the start of our senior year, I had no idea my life would turn out the way it did. But it was nice of the Sawyer family to take me in and give me a home after my mom died. I can tell they care about me, and that's something I haven't felt in a really long time.

I may have hated my mother, but deep down inside she was my mom, and I loved her no matter what. I hoped that she found peace now because without my father and brother she was suffering tremendously.

I believe in my heart that Scarlet was the way she was because of how she was treated in her own home. After her mother died last year, her father practically ignored her, then he married a younger woman who despised Scarlet and wanted nothing more than to get rid of her. They tossed Scarlet to the side and CFH was her sanctuary, sort of like my bedroom was at my old home. She needed everyone at school to make her feel alive and wanted. The people at CFH worshipped her, maybe not the way they should have. It made her feel in control. Loved. I now knew that she only ridiculed and tormented her so-called classmates for the attention she wasn't getting at home. I will always remember Scarlet as "the dead girl under the bleachers" at Craven Falls High for years to come.

I looked back out at the football field; the bleachers staring back at me. Haunting me. I'll never forget what happened there on that dark, stormy night. Lianne and Mayor Fitzgerald, they both will get prison time, according to the news. Since the Mayor hadn't been identified in the video killing Scarlet, they arrested him for being an accomplice and he was waiting to be sentenced.

Allen Swig, a cop in Craven Falls, and also Lianne's brother, had been the one who placed the bat in my house and forgot to wear gloves. They later ran prints on the bat after my release, which came back as being both Allen's and Lianne's. Allen's fingerprints were found not only on the bat but in the house I used to live in. You'd think being a cop he'd know what to do.

The police issued a warrant and searched Allen's house, where they found Kyle's cell phone. My thoughts are that Lianne had asked her brother to destroy Kyle's phone and get rid of any evidence of her and Kyle sleeping together not knowing there was another copy on Kyle's computer which Scarlet had found, but Allen kept it. Allen was hauled in for questioning and later arrested for being an accomplice in the murder of both Kyle Tanner and Scarlet Fitzgerald and withholding evidence. He also was waiting to be sentenced.

They charged Lianne with two counts of voluntary manslaughter for killing both Kyle and Scarlet. They transferred her to Dwight Correctional Center for Women, awaiting trial. Unfortunately, she was stabbed and killed her first night inside the prison. As they say, karma's a bitch.

As for Kyle's parents, I, along with everyone else in this town, have no clues or leads to their whereabouts. It's been over three weeks and no one has heard or seen either of them. Their disappearance remains a mystery to all of us.

About the Author

Donna M. Zadunajsky started out writing children's books before she wrote and published her first novel, *Broken Promises,* in June 2012. She then has written several more novels and her first novella, *HELP ME!*, which is a subject about suicide and bullying.

She is currently working on her next book.

Note from the Author

Word-of-mouth is crucial for any author to succeed. If you enjoyed the book, please leave a review online—anywhere you are able. Even if it's just a sentence or two. It would make all the difference and would be very much appreciated.

Thanks!
Donna

Thank you so much for reading one of our **Teen Mystery** novels. If you enjoyed the experience, please check out our recommended title for your next great read!

Until Proven Innocent by Laura Stewart Schmidt

"A deftly-written, all-American teen mystery deserving of a broad audience." *–Best Thrillers*

CPSIA information can be obtained
at www.ICGtesting.com
Printed in the USA
BVHW031617160220
572477BV00001B/3